LESTRADE
AND THE
SIGN OF NINE

M J Trow

IAN HENRY PUBLICATIONS

First published by Constable & Co., Ltd., 1992
This edition, 2001

ISBN 0 86025 295 7

Published by
Ian Henry Publications, Ltd
20 Park Drive, Romford, Essex RM1 4LH
and printed by
ColourBooks Ltd.
Dublin, 13, Ireland

1

The gentleman with the mournful face and obsolete Dundrearies wandered through his own foundations for the last time. He kicked, in the melancholy way that architects do, the footings of the drains, that would have led, in another, less practical world, from those urinals where the illustrious of the world of opera would have relieved themselves. Don Giovanni peeing hand in hand with Die Fledermaus.

Feet below him, where Ancient Britons had thrown all manner of things into the London clay, two workmen hacked at the grey, unyielding slime with pick and shovel. Sweat ran from their leather caps and soaked the scarves tied roughly around their necks.

''Ow did you get on wiv' Egel, then, Clarence?' the older man asked, rolling up his drooping sleeves.

'All right, Arfur,' his mate said, grunting as the pick bounced on a particularly recalcitrant boulder. The sparks flew upward. 'I particularly liked his concept of Being.'

'Go on.'

'Well,' Clarence paused, inverting the pick and resting on its head as generations of construction workers had done since Time Immemorial, 'Being and the idea are identical. The idea, y'see, contains of itself the capacity for developin' into all the determinin' attributes of being, into all that makes Being Being.'

'Wiv you so far,' Arfur thrust home a shovel.

'O' course,' Clarence wiped the sweat from his mouth, 'Being is at first indeterminate, wivout properties or qualities. It passes out o' this condition and into uvverness, its negation, you might say, its opposite.'

'So,' Arfur took up the man's drive, 'then, this negation, as 'Egel rightly calls it, becomes the principle of a continuous series of 'igher and successive affirmations. Am I right or am I right?'

'You ain't 'wrong, squire,' Clarence assured him, easing himself down on an upturned bucket. 'Vus, pure light is the same as darkness 'and is at first invisible, but after it 'as passed into darkness, it returns to itself, takes on colour and vus becomes visible. I'm not bein' too didactic 'ere, am I?'

'Not in the slightest, Clarence,' Arfur perched himself on a protruding rock. 'After all, when all's said and done, everythin' must 'ave an opposite or contradictory - were it not so, nuffink could come into existence.'

'Quite. But on the' uvver 'and, take panfeism...'

A whistle shattered the morning.

Arfur scanned the skyline of the Strand in search of a clock.

'Not tea break yet, is it, Clarence?'

'It is not, Arfur. 'Ello - that mournful bloke wiv the obsolete Dundrearies looks as though 'e wants a word.'

'We should always listen to the bourgeoisie, Clarence. At least for the time being.'

'In what sense are you usin' the term being there, then, Arfur?'

'Gather round, you men!' the mournful bloke took a central position on a pile of bricks. 'Good morning, men.'

There were a few grumbles in return. A handful of the brown, sweat-soaked veterans took off their caps under the sun. Arfur and Clarence did likewise.

'I am Norman Shaw,' the mournful bloke told them, 'the Architect of this magnificent edifice on the foundations of which you are now actively engaged.'

'Got a good articulacy, ain't 'e, Arfur?' Clarence observed from the corner of his mouth.

'Brilliant, Clarence.'

'I'm afraid I have some bad news, men,' Shaw went on.

The tapping of a hammer from near the river stopped.

'There, I said 'e looked mournful,' Clarence whispered.

'Just as well,' Arfur observed, 'I was beginnin' to fink 'e always looked like that.'

'I received confirmation this morning that this building is not to be used as an Opera House after all.'

There were boos and cries of 'Shame!'

'Oh dear,' muttered Arfur, 'there goes Rigoletto out the winder.'

'Bleedin' disgustin',' Clarence nodded.

'But fear not,' Shaw continued, 'your jobs are not in jeopardy. This building. . .'and he turned away from them for a moment to compose himself. 'This building is to be handed over to the Metropolitan Police as their new Headquarters.'

There was a stunned silence.

'Stone me,' breathed Arfur, 'the unfinkin' lackeys of a bourgeois, Imperialist State.'

'As I live and breave,' Clarence agreed.

'Well, that's all chaps,' Shaw fought back the tears. 'I just thought you ought to know.'

Another silence.

Arfur broke it in the time-honoured way. 'Never mind, sir. Free cheers for Mr Shaw, lads. 'Ip-'ip!'

''Ooray,' the workforce chorused.

''Ip-'ip!'

''Ooray.'

''Ip-'ip!'

''Ooray.'

'Men, men,' Shaw held up a carefully manicured architect's hand, 'I am more touched than I can say. You are white men all.'

'There is that as consolation,' Clarence took up his pick again.

'What's that, ol' son?'

'We are white men. 'Uddled masses, yes. Downtrodden minions of the lumpenproletariat, but at least we ain't black.'

'That's fair enough,' Arfur observed.

''Ere, did you know?' Clarence's pick bounced off the outcrop again, 'did you know that them there stones for the foundations 'ave come from Dartmoor? Where some poor wronged individual what 'as 'ad the misfortune to be born among the People of the Abyss is, even as we speak, spendin' 'is daylight hours crackin' rocks for 'Er Majesty the Queen?'

'Well, there you 'ave it, Clarence.'

'I do?'

'You do. You do realize that your namesake, the Duke of Clarence and Avondale, will, when 'e comes of age, inherit the biggest and most corrupt Empire the world 'as ever known, don't you?'

'It 'ad occurred to me, Arfur. Let's not be small minded. That's the politics of envy, that is. Besides, this is Gladstone's England, you know.'

'Sadly, Clarence, I am well aware whose England it is. 'Owever, the time is coming.'

'Ah yes, the Millennium of the People. When's the Revolution planned for again?'

'February the sixth of next year. Can you make it?'

'I'll 'ave to consult my calendar ... oh, bleedin' 'ell!' Clarence froze in mid swing.

Thinking that some new point of the dialectic had occurred to his young friend, Arfur waited, his shovel loaded with the greasy grey of London's river. Then he saw what Clarence had seen and dropped the lot. The younger man's pick had hacked into what once was a woman. Now it was a torso, a headless, legless, armless thing lying in the London clay. The acidity of the ground had preserved it perfectly and the breasts still had something of the pertness of life.

'Lends a 'ole new meanin' to the body politic, don't it, Arfur?' Clarence whispered.

'It bleedin' well does, son. Get that architect bloke over 'ere, will you? Should be an hour or two's rest in this.'

There was not, on the face of it, a lot happening that February. Policemen all over the Metropolis faced the rather daunting task of executing the Act of the 49th Victoria, viz and to wit that all dogs wandering in the region of the capital should be muzzled. That probably had something to do with the fact that a fox had been killed in Marylebone High Street. Mr Terriss was wowing them at the Adelphi and our brave boys in Burma were complaining, with some justification, that their bayonets were bending on contact with Burmese bandits rather than going straight through the little yellow bastards. There were red faces at Enfield where they made the things. Then the snow came

They crept out from between the black buildings crowned with white, the half starving People of the Abyss. But there were no women in this crowd, no children. Just ragged lines of ragged men, their faces blue and pinched above their knotted scarves, their eyes dark hollows under their beaver hats. Their hobnails crunched on the unbroken snow and their breath snaked out on the crisp air.

No one saw them at first, certainly not the occupants of the hansom parked in Hanover Square. The cabby leaned against his hack, drawing on the roll of darkest shag he had spent the last half an hour creating. In the relative snug of the vehicle two men sat swathed in plaid blankets, one of them sipping now and then from a flask.

'Deuc'd nippy this afternoon, Holmes,' the ruddier of the two noted, tapping on the frosted window.

'February the eighth, Watson', his companion had no need of a calendar to tell him. 'Minus two.'

'I shouldn't wonder. Cocoa?'

The taller man rejected the offer with a quiver of his aquiline nostrils.

'Do you think he'll be much longer?'

'Patience, Watson,' Holmes smiled with the serenity of an

anaconda, 'is a virtue known only to a select few - like myself, for instance.'

'I'm not cut out for surveillance,' the good doctor observed. 'Haven't the bottom for it.'

'Nor the top, I fear, Watson,' Holmes tapped his cranium without taking his eyes off the house in the far corner of the square.

'As you say, Holmes, as you say. What do you think he's doing?'

'The Count?' Holmes allowed himself a hollow chuckle. It was a rare moment in their relationship. 'Mark my words, Watson, in...' he fished out his silver hunter from the folds of his Ulster, '... a little under three minutes, a gnarled old woman will emerge from that house. She will have a severely pronounced limp, of the left leg, I fancy; a spinal curvature which would put my Meerschaum to shame and at least two molars will be missing, presumed lost.'

'Good heavens, Holmes, you never cease to astound me.'

'I know, Watson.'

'Who will she be, Holmes, this vile harpy of the night?'

'This "vile harpy of the night", Watson,' Holmes sighed, 'will be - and indeed is - Count Ortega y Gomez himself.'

'The swine!' Watson bounced the flask on his blanketed thigh so that the cocoa drenched them both. 'Oh, sorry, Holmes! The swine! So that's what he's doing in there - changing.'

'Not uniquely, old fellow,' Holmes mechanically sponged himself down. 'He'll be forging the government papers we spoke of.'

'Ah, he has the testimonials.' All was becoming clear to Watson now.

'Of course. You only have to look at him to know that.'

There was a tap on the window and a grimy cabby thrust his head in, wreathing Watson momentarily in smoke, 'Er ... gents, the meter's runnin' you know.'

Watson batted aside the smog. 'You're being handsomely paid, fellow,' he reminded him.

'Not well enough for them, I ain't.'

Watson followed the driver's jerking thumb. Dark-coated, dark-eyed men were crossing the square, like a ragged battalion on the march, dressing from right to left, cudgels at the slope.

'Er ... Holmes,' the doctor muttered.

'Shut the window, there's a good fellow.' Holmes was intent on the house in the opposite direction.

'Well. that's just it, Holmes, there seems to be rather an absence of good fellows at the moment. Look!'

The World's Greatest Detective turned to Watson's window. 'Hmm,' he nodded, 'they are a little late for the January Sales.'

'Right,' they heard the cabby growl, 'I'm orff,' and he hopped up onto his perch.

'Stay where you are, driver!' Holmes roared. 'I shall report you to the Hackney Carriage Drivers' Association for conduct unbecoming.'

'You do what you bloody well like, mate. This 'ere vehicle is my bread and butter. Up, Bucephalus!' and he lashed the weary animal with his whip.

The crack of the leather seemed to galvanize the horde of black-coated men. The centre made a grab for the horse-collar and bridle, clinging on to the harness until the confused beast was slowed by the sheer press of men. The cabby laid about him with his whip, then someone dragged him off his perch and he disappeared among the shoulders and flying fists.

'Right,' a voice bellowed, 'Let's 'ave them bastards out!' And they wrenched the door off its hinges.

'Shall I use my army service revolver, Holmes?' Watson had dropped his cocoa again.

'Waste of lead, my dear fellow,' Holmes observed. 'They're only the sweepings of the gaols. Hit them with your Gladstone.'

'It's Gladstone!' one of the roughs shouted. 'It's old Glad Eye.'

'Blimey! The Prime Minister. The GOM. 'isself!' and the impressed crowd stood back.

Watson looked frantically at Holmes. 'They think one of us is Gladstone, Holmes,' he hissed out of the corner of his mouth.

'What'll we do?'

'Elementary, old fellow. We do what the real Gladstone would do - make empty promises we can't possibly keep.'

'We, Holmes?'

The Great Detective sighed anew. 'Shrewd of you to spot the plurality of the situation, Watson. Clearly, I cannot possibly pass as a man of seventy-six with a father who grew sugar and owned workshops in Liverpool. You on the other hand have no patrician features to disguise. Things would be different of course were I carrying my Leichner waxes. Well, get on with it, man. Pretend this is the Midlothian campaign all over again and make a speech. And don't forget to wave your arms about.'

Watson hauled the plaid off his knees and in a moment of inspiration wrapped it over his shoulders. He dashed nervous fingers through his hair to give it that Gladstonian mania, pinged his Eton collar up round his ears and balanced gingerly on the step of the cab.

'My mission', he said to the murmuring, jostling crowd, '... er ... is to pacify Ireland.'

There was a silence.

'Never mind about Ireland, your honour,' a voice called back.

'Wot abaht the workers?'

The cry was taken up.

'Er...' Watson held up his hand, 'I can offer you ... um ... nothing but blood, sweat and tears,' he said.

'Who killed Gordon?' another voice bawled.

'Er ... we will fight them on the beaches,' Watson countered, without conviction, but the crowd surged forward, chanting 'M.O.G.! M.O.G.! and rocking the hansom backwards and forwards, holding the head of the whinnying horse.

'Promise me, old fellow', Holmes gripped the upholstery, 'that you'll never try a career in politics.'

'I thought those bits were quite good, Holmes,' Watson bridled along with the hack, 'the blood, sweat and tears bit and that thing about fighting them on the beaches.'

'Didn't do much good, did it, old fellow?' Holmes hissed through clenched teeth. 'I've changed my mind about your service revolver. Shoot a few of the working class bastards.'

A shot shattered the noise. The crowd pulled back, letting the hansom rock quietly to stillness. The dazed cabby hauled himself upright and clung desperately around the neck of his horse, his head pouring with blood.

Watson checked his pocket. No, the Webley hadn't gone off by accident. There was no smell of powder and no gaping hole where his testicles used to be. It did give him pause for thought however about carrying a pistol with no safety catch so near his staff of life. He poked a crimson head out of the gap where the door had hung.

A small knot of uniformed policemen, no more than six men strong, stood, truncheons at the slope, behind a yellow-faced ferret of a man in a bowler hat and ageless Donegal who twirled with a certain dexterity a twelve-bore shotgun, still smoking in the crisp morning air.

'Gentlemen,' he said, 'I am Inspector Lestrade of Scotland Yard. You are all under arrest.'

'What for?' a rough yelled.

'Disturbing Her Majesty's Peace,' Lestrade told him. 'Damaging a hansom cab, thereby rendering it less than handsome; frightening a Hackney horse - no doubt the RSPCA will be in touch; being unpleasant to two respectable gentlemen going about their lawful business; oh, and breaking the nose of a Hackney Carriage Driver, licence number ... er ...?'

'Four free free,' the cabby managed, his nose spreading slowly over his face.

'There's only ... um ... seven o' you,' another rough shouted.

'Sergeant,' Lestrade turned to the man at his right elbow, 'tell these gentlemen all about Metropolitan Procedure One Three Eight, would you?'

'Yessir, certainly, sir,' the sergeant cleared his throat. 'Metropolitan Procedure One Three Eight states that in the context of crowd control no police action shall be undertaken unless the said police outnumber the said crowd eight to one.'

'Especially ... ?' Lestrade reminded his man.

'Especially on Mondays.'

'You're bluffin',' a rough growled.

Lestrade pointed to the roof of an adjoining building. Against the pearly haze of the February sky a lone helmeted bobby straightened from his hiding place.

The Inspector pointed again to another building where a young rookie rather spoiled the triumph of the moment by smiling down at him and waving. He pointed a third time and yet another boy in blue emerged from roof railings.

'Three sides of the square surrounded, gentlemen,' Lestrade said. 'Which leaves the side behind you - the one that faces the City whence I suspect most of you came. Constable,' he turned to the man on his left, 'be so good as to recite for these gentlemen Metropolitan Procedure Eight Two Nine.'

The constable cleared his throat. 'Metropolitan Procedure Eight Two Nine clearly states that no foot action of the police vis à vis a crowd situation is to be undertaken without the use of the Mounted Division and said Mounted Division is to be equipped with extra long truncheons and if need be, lances.'

'Lances!' the crowd muttered, stumbling backward.

'If you put your ears to the ground gentlemen,' Lestrade said, 'you will probably catch the cad ... cade ... rhythm of their hoofbeats galloping along the Tottenham Court Road in this general direction as I speak. You will also catch frostbite on account of the snow, but that's a small price to pay for Social Democracy, isn't it?'

'Er ... Inspector Lestrade, sir,' the sergeant tapped his superior's shoulder.

'Yes, sergeant, I'm a busy man. What is it?'

'Shouldn't we oughta tell them about Metropolitan Procedure Three Nine Two, sir?'

'Oh, now, that's a bit extreme, sergeant,' Lestrade frowned.

'The baby Howitzer, I mean. You know we aren't allowed to use it within half a mile of the Palace.'

But the crowd hadn't waited to hear more. First one, then knots of three and four melted away from the back. Then the whole black-coated rabble began to run, fanning out of the square by every available orifice and covering their heads with their hands to avoid the missiles being rained on them by the scores of policemen above.

'I think this puts the lid on Rousseau's concept of the General Will, Clarence, don't you?' Lestrade heard a fleeing rough call.

'I do, Arfur, I do. Maybe the lumpenproletariat aren't ready for the barricades yet. Next September do you?'

'Better make it the September after, Clarence, if it's all the same to you. I've got that Emmanuel Kant to get frough yet.'

'There's no need to be unpleasant to what I feel is essentially a well-meanin' body of philosophers, Arfur.'

And the voices echoed away through the sidestreets that twisted to the East End.

The Inspector turned to his sergeant. 'You'd better get your three blokes down from there before they freeze to death.'

'Yessir. Very good, sir,' the sergeant waved his boys down.

'It's a good thing we happened upon you, sir, off-duty an' all. What is all that guff about Metropolitan Procedures? We ain't 'eard of 'em in C Division.'

'Neither had I until five minutes ago,' Lestrade winked at him, 'but you remembered your lines well, sergeant ... er ... ?'

'Regan, sir. This is Constable Carter.'

'You'll go far, lads.'

'Lestrade!'

'Ah,' the Inspector turned to the wrecked hansom. 'Mr Gladstone, sir, I trust you aren't injured.'

'Damn you, Lestrade, for your confounded cheek!' Holmes snapped.

'Ah,' he tipped his bowler, 'you must be Mr Morley.'

'Please, Lestrade,' Holmes shuddered. 'It's been a ghastly enough day without being taken for a Liberal. Besides, no attempts at satire, please. You haven't the wit for it.'

'Oh, come now, Holmes,' Watson flustered, 'I mean, damn it all, Lestrade here probably saved our lives. A moment later...'

'A moment later and I'd have had my quarry,' the Great Detective sneered. 'As it is, the Count is long gone by now - halfway to the Docks, I shouldn't wonder. Why is it, Lestrade, that just as my vast intellect is about to produce dazzling results, your great flat feet come tramping all over the place?'

'Luck, I suppose,' Lestrade said.

Holmes closed to his man. 'Keep out of my way, Lestrade, that's all I ask. London isn't big enough for both of us.'

'I say, Holmes,' Watson chortled, 'that's rather a cliché isn't it?'

'No, it isn't!' Holmes snapped. 'I leave that sort of thing to your friend Conan Doyle. Cabby!' the driver lifted a battered head out of a handkerchief. Luckily for him, it was his own head and still marginally attached to his neck. '221B Baker Street and double quick time.'

'Right,' the whip snaked out and the hack jerked forward, happy to feel the presence of the hames in action again. 'But what about my door?'

Even the assorted clutch of constables blanched at Holmes's reply to that one.

Lestrade eased back the serpentine of the twelve-bore. 'Sergeant, you'd better have one of your men return this to Mr Wesson the gun-smith. Thank him for allowing us to borrow it. For the spent cartridge he'll have to sign in triplicate.'

'Very good, sir. Er ... sir ... I hope, on the acquaintanceship of a few moments you won't presume it forward of me, but ...'

'Yes, man, spit it out.'

'Well, I was just wondering, sir, where did the cartridge go? Only there's blood all down your leg and on the snow where you've been walking.'

Lestrade glanced down. 'Oh yes,' he said, 'so there is,' and he toppled forward in the slush.

Across the road from where a group of constables were lifting an unconscious Inspector on to their shoulders prior to the solemn walk to Charing Cross Hospital, a gnarled old woman dragged her gammy left leg down the steps of the grand old house in the corner. Her back slewed to the right and she grinned at the leaden sky through gappy teeth. Chuckling as she went and tucking the forged papers under her arm, she made her way to the Docks.

2

Assistant Commissioner James Monro stared out over the darkling city, the river at Hungerford Wharf brown between the white banks. Not since his native Scotland had he seen such snow in February. And in all his twenty-seven years in Bengal, not so much as a flake of the stuff. He turned at the rattle at the door. 'Come,' he bellowed in the stentorian Scots calculated to terrify rookies and members of the Press. An unshaken detective limped in, hobbling with the aid of a stick.

'Shot yourself in the foot again, Lestrade, I gather,' the Assistant Commissioner said.

'The leg, sir,' the Inspector had the neck to correct him.

'Well, take the weight off it and sit ye doon ... Not there!'

Lestrade's good knee had only barely bent when it snapped straight again. 'Sorry.'

'No, no,' the Scotsman was softer. 'I should be apologizing, laddie. We're all a little on edge this morning. It's a new directive from on high. That chair's reserved for Chief Inspectors and above.'

'Ah.'

'That's yours,' Monro pointed to an altogether shabbier piece of furniture, the one Lestrade recognized as having housed Mr Howard Vincent's pet iguana before the founder of the Criminal Investigation Department had forsaken the Yard for an altogether higher place. Now man and lizard lounged on the back benches of Her Majesty's House of Commons. Lestrade winched himself down.

'How old are you now?' Monro fixed his man with a tilt of his pince-nez.

'Thirty-two, sir, last month.'

'Thirty-two, eh?' the Assistant Commissioner found himself grinning stupidly. 'Well, well ... Well,' he cleared his throat, shaking himself out of some half-forgotten reverie. 'When you're forty-six or so, no doubt that chair will be yours. Now, to the matter in hand. The Commissioner has asked me to pass on his warmest congratulations for the act of unsur-passed crowd control you executed in Hanover Square on Monday last.'

'Thank you, sir,' a smile of self-satisfaction crept over the parchment features.

'I wouldn't do that just yet, were I you, laddie,' Monro whirled to a pile of papers on his desk. 'Smile, I mean. Y'see this pile of papers?' Lestrade did.

This is only a fraction of it. Lost Property downstairs is choc-a-bloc and the basement, well, you can't see a stick of Fenian dynamite for the correspondence.'

'About what, sir?'

'Well, mostly, demands for resignations of the entire detective branch, a total disbandment of the uniformed men, a retraining programme which I estimate will cost nearly three million pounds and will end in April 1947 and several suggestions as to what Colonel Henderson can do with the rest of his sadly limited career. Not to mention a timely reminder that when a police officer was killed in the line of duty in 1833 the jury returned a verdict of justifiable homicide.'

'What will the Commissioner do, sir?'

'Damned if I know, laddie. Whatever it is, he won't be doing it at Scotland Yard.'

'You mean ... he's going?'

'Man, he's gone. One of his last acts was to ask me to see you personally. But of course he hadn't seen all this, had he?'

'Perhaps it's just as well, sir,' Lestrade nodded sagely. 'Better he didn't find out.'

'Och, awa', I'm not talking about these. I said it was mostly to do with what an appalling job the Metropolitan Police did on 'Black Monday' as the damn'd papers are calling it. These eight however, have to do with an appalling job you did on that self same occasion.'

'But...'

'Och, there are no buts, laddie,' Monro leaned back, his hands locked behind his head. 'Not in the Metropolitans. It's all relative, y'see. Relative to the complete crassness and abject inactivity of the rest of the Force, your slick operation and quick thinking was splendid stuff indeed. But I have a letter here from a lady who says 'that a policeman wrought havoc in her hoose by putting his size tens through her skylight. Another from a member of the League Against Loud Noises for the totally unnecessary discharge of a shotgun. A bill from the London Hackney Carriage Company for damage done to one of their vehicular contrivances which you could and should have prevented. Etcetera, etcetera. Oh ... and a rather curious note from a gentleman named Sherlock Holmes accusing you of baulking him of his prey. Do you know this Holmes? White Hunter is he?'

Lestrade shrugged. 'Never heard of him,' he said with a face as straight as a poker.

'Well, I've got a directive', Monro sighed, 'from our new lord and master, General Charles Warren, the likely next appointee as Commissioner of the Metropolitan Police. Hasn't even got the job yet and he's giving orders.'

'A soldier?'

Monro clicked his teeth. 'Ach, I can see why you're a detective-inspector, laddie,' he grinned approvingly. 'I foresee there'll be a mite more saddlesoap and blanco at the Yard than you and I are used to. The new directive says that I am to suspend you for causing a public nuisance in pursuance of your duty. What do you have to say to that?'

Lestrade's mouth flopped open.

'Exactly what I thought you'd say,' Monro nodded. 'So,' he carefully buried Warren's directive under the pile of paperwork. 'You'd better hobble over to Mr Rodney's. He's got a wee job for you. I'll tell the Generalissimo when he arrives that his new directive got here just too late for me to reach you.'

'Mr Rodney?'

'Aye, you know the one. Assistant Commissioner in charge of traffic. Chap with mousy hair and a habit of forgetting who the bloody hell you are.'

'But I'm a detective,' Lestrade said, still bewildered by it all.

'Aye, laddie. And if you want to stay one, you'll get your back-side over to Traffic and talk to Mr Rodney.'

'Oh, no,' Lestrade shuddered. 'It's not that torso they found under the Opera House last year, is it?'

Monro chuckled. 'Aye, it's funny how the old Assistant Commiss-ioner is obsessed wi' that, isn't it? And him not even old Assistant Commissioner (Crime). Still, there's none so peculiar as middle-aged policemen. You'll be one yersen one o' these days, laddie.'

Mr Monro always became heavily vernacular when he had term-inated a conversation. Lestrade clawed his way to his feet, checking that the iguana hadn't left anything indescribable on his trousers.

'I'll see myself out,' he said.

'Out' of course was something of a misnomer. Old Scotland Yard suffered from being far too small and every day, irritated coppers glanced along the new Embankment towards the Mother of Parliaments where the Opera House that was to house their new headquarters rose steadily, brick by brick. Why, they all asked themselves as they climbed over the saddles of the Mounted Division balanced precariously on the stairs, was it all taking so long? They had no idea that every workman on the site spent his waking hours between tea-breaks arguing the toss over the Dialectic and how long it would be before the huddled masses stopped huddling and brought about the Rise of the Proletariat.

So the journey to the office of Assistant Commissioner (Traffic) Rodney took Lestrade eight minutes. Agreed, it was only on the next floor, but he had to negotiate the shoeboxes of the Criminal Record Office and he did have a gammy leg. His inspectorly tap on the glass-panelled door elicited the traditional Assistant commissionerly response, '... Er ...'

'Inspector Lestrade, sir. You sent for me.'

'I know I did,' the Assistant Commissioner bridled. Rodney was an elegant man the wrong side of fifty-three. He had grown his Dundrearies in a more hirsute age when facial adornments were the mark of authority and the old Queen, God Bless Her, had only been on the throne a mere forty-four years. Faced with the incredible efficiency of Lestrade, Rodney did the most decisive thing of which he was capable - and indeed for which he was renowned - he plonked himself down in his leather chair. Not for nothing was he known the length and breadth of the Yard as Rodney the Plonker.

'Now then, Abberline, I'll come straight to the point.'

'Lestrade, sir,' Lestrade reminded him.

'What?'

'Inspector Lestrade, sir.'

'Yes, well, there are more pressing matters. Monro says you're his best man.'

'That's very flattering, sir.'

'What is that - gout?' Rodney waved an elegant hand at Lestrade's infirmity.

'Buckshot, sir.'

'My God!' Rodney turned quite ashen. 'We hardly ever have these problems in ... er ...'

'Traffic, sir?'

'Quite. Now, to the matter in hand.'

'Yes, sir.'

'Mevagissey. Know where that is, Monro?'

'Er ... the West Country, sir. Cornwall, I believe.' Lestrade knew the Geography for Detectives lecture off by heart.

'Er ... is it? Oh, good. Well, catch a train then. You'll need the London and North Eastern won't you? Via Godalming?'

'I think that's the Great Western, sir, via Swindon,' Bradshaw was, after all, an Inspector's constant companion.

'Well, well, you know best. You'll report to me, won't you?'

'What about, sir?'

'Eh? Well, the murder of course. Good God, Abberline, Henderson said you were his best man. I'd hate to meet his worst.'

Lestrade hadn't the heart to tell the Assistant Commissioner that in mentioning Inspector Abberline, he already had.

'Perhaps you could be a bit more specific, sir?'

'Well, really,' Rodney sighed with exasperation. 'It's difficult to know how much more specific I can possibly be. Very well - to recap. My cousin, the Reverend Hereward Rodney was until last Thursday the Rector of Mevagissey.'

'And last Thursday?'

'He ceased to be on account of someone stove in his head.'

'Good Lord.'

'No, no, the local police have ruled out divine retribution. Whatever killed Cousin Hereward, it was not a thunderbolt.'

'Please accept my condolences, sir,' Lestrade said.

'Hmm? Oh no, I can't claim Cousin ... er ... and I were very close. I hadn't seen him since ... oh, now you've asked me. No, it's a matter of principle, you see. Honour of the Yard and all that. I wouldn't expect a plumber to take out my insides. Same with murder. Can't have the Cornwall Constabulary stomping about all over the place. It isn't decent. Get up there, Abberline, there's a good chap. Take a sergeant or something with you. And keep me informed. Got it?'

'I think so, sir.'

'Excellent!' Rodney got up, shaking Lestrade heartily by the hand. 'Well, off you go then, Monro. And I'd have the police doctor look at that arthritis of yours if I were you. Treacherous month, February. Especially on the Pennines. Good morning!'

George George had been a sergeant for more years than he cared to remember. Like his parents before him, he was not blessed with an unbridled imagination, but in the Criminal Investigation Department at the Yard in those days, that was just as well. He sat with his elbows jammed against the filing cabinets which lined the converted lavatory which was Lestrade's office. The two young men facing him were apprehensive, standing bolt upright, hair carefully maccassared, bowlers in the crooks of their arms.

'Tyrrell?'

'Yessir.'

'Launcelot Tyrrell?'

'Yessir.'

'Three years on the horsetroughs, I understand?'

'Yessir.'

'And what made you become a policeman. Tyrrell?'

'Guilt, sir, I suppose.'

'Guilt?' George narrowed his beetling brows and his centre parting widened. 'And that's sergeant, by the way. Or detective sergeant if you prefer. Inspectors and above are referred to as 'sir". Now what do you mean, "guilt"?'

'I come from a long line of assassins, sir.'

George slammed back into his chair. 'Assassins?' he repeated.

'Yessir. Walter Tyrrell or Tirel was the bloke who shot King William Rufus in the New Forest.'

'Painful,' George muttered.

'James Tyrrell was the one who had the Princes in the Tower smothered with pillows.'

'How long ago was all this?' George's detective nose was beginning to work.

'Well, the Princes were four hundred years ago, sir. William Rufus somewhat longer.'

'I see,' George sighed. 'I've never known a policeman waste police time before. Even so, I'll be keeping an eye on you, lad.'

He turned his dull, implacable gaze to the other one. 'And what long line do you come from, Green?'

'Policemen, sir. It's in the blood.'

Is it, now? Eighteen months with Lost Property. Four with Public Carriages. Six with M Division. One week with the River Police. Going for the record, are you?'

'Sir?'

'The Commissioner's Prize for the Most Moved on Policeman?'

'I've got to know my trade, Sergeant,' Green told him. 'My old dad told me to work my way up from the bottom.'

'And where, according to your old dad, was the bottom?' George asked.

'M Division, sir.'

'Well, he got that right,' George nodded. 'It says here', he peered closer over the ledger, 'that your first name is Godolphin. Misprint?'

'No, sir, Godolphin, I'm sure. My mates call me "Pad", sergeant.'

'Pad?'

'Short for "Paddington", sergeant. "Paddington" Green. Get it?'

George's face hadn't changed one iota. 'I leave the jokes to my guv'nor,' he said solemnly. 'If you're wise, you'll do the same.'

And, as if on cue, his guv'nor hobbled at that moment through the door. Luckily, it was already ajar and he negotiated it quite well, for a man in a hurry with buckshot lodged in his leg.

'Right, George. Get my Gladstone and a spare shirt. We're going west. Who are these?'

'New recruits, guv'nor. Name of Tyrrell and Green.'

'Any good?'

'Shouldn't think so, sir. I give 'em three weeks.'

'All right, that's what they've got,' Lestrade staggered to face them. 'You're Green?'

'No, sir, I'm Tyrrell.'

'Well there you are,' the Inspector said. 'Your first lesson in detective work.'

'What's that, sir?' Green asked.

'You only have at best a fifty-fifty chance of being right. And as for getting your man, well ... Now, to more important matters. Mr George here has a reputation second to none for the quality of his bevy. You, Green, are doubtless acquainted with the mechanics of a steam kettle, Metropolitan Police for the use of?'

'Yessir.'

'Good man. Tyrrell, have you got your bowler hat allowance yet?'

'Yessir.'

'In your pocket?'

'Yessir.'

'Right, that's the second lesson in detective work - never admit to a senior officer how much money you're carrying. On the corner, just beyond The Clarence you'll find Messrs Singh and Song, Purveyors of Darjeeling and China Tea to the Metropolitan Police. They also do a mean line in Bath Olivers. Mr George and I have some planning to do, so while we're at it - Green, the tea. Tyrrell, the biscuits.'

'Very good, sir,' they chorused.

'And welcome to Scotland Yard, gentlemen, as ever in the forefront of the relentless fight against crime.'

There really wasn't much planning they could do. It was no hardship for two bachelors to throw their meagre belongings into respective Gladstones and make for the train. Snow delayed them beyond Wimbledon and Lestrade dozed fitfully, his outstretched leg in the second class carriage giving him gyp, while George thumbed through the February edition of *Good Housekeeping*, where an article written by a Mrs Hudson of Baker Street entitled 'Living With Two Men' was rather less salacious than he had hoped it would be.

Beyond Wimbledon, the level snow gave way to a thaw in the form of nasty, driving rain. And at Swindon, where they changed platforms in the steam and the smoke to take Brunel's damned broad gauge, there were leaves on the line and a delay of three hours. So they called it a day and stayed at The Bell. George was paying.

Thursday dawned wet and mild, but in the tangle of wrought iron and glass that was Swindon Central, it was wetter and milder than ever. At least George kept himself in trim by periodically hurtling off down the platform chasing Lestrade's errant bowler, whisked from his head now and then by recalcitrant gusts. But the same wind had blown away the leaves and the Yard men rattled south-west to Exeter.

From here it was pony and trap, and two soggy, dispirited detectives, noses streaming with seasonal mucus, had to be helped down and into the cheerless hostelry whose creaking sign said it all - The Happy Traveller. While their Donegals and bowlers dripped and steamed in front of a lacklustre fire, the Yard men were downstairs in the ironically-named Snug, partaking of the village's delicacy, Mevagissey Duck.

'This is off, guv,' George sniffed his second forkful. 'Smells of fish.'

Lestrade's nose joined his sergeant's. 'Ah, it'll be the winds,' he observed. 'Eat it, George and don't look a gift meal in the mouth ... You have got your wallet, haven't you?'

'Mr Lestrade?' a voice caused them both to look up. Before them crouched a wizened old fellow with his collar on backwards. Only the Easterlies through which he had trudged had removed the cobwebs from his orifices.

'The same,' the Inspector narrowed his eyes. 'Mr ... er ...?'

'Austin. Lemuel Austin. I am ... was ... Mr Rodney's curate.'

'Really?' The man had to be the oldest holder of that office in the country. 'Won't you join us?'

'How kind,' the little old boy slid back a chair with a practised hand. 'I don't usually frequent public houses, of course,' he turned to the surly figure of his host. 'A pint of your best, Jack,' he trilled and then to Lestrade, 'I understand from Mr Smith that you wish to speak to me.

'Mr Smith?' Lestrade repeated.

'Sergeant Smith, from St Austell. He's our local detective, I suppose.'

'Well, you're way ahead of us, Mr Austin,' Lestrade admitted. 'Oh, by the way, this is Sergeant George.'

The ancient curate extended a bony hand. 'Charmed, sir.'

'Would you like to tell us what happened?' Lestrade asked.

'Well, it was a little before Evensong two Sundays ago. I had cycled over from Black Head as was my wont.'

'Black Head?' George had abandoned the dubious duck in favour of taking notes.

'It's a fair point,' the curate explained. 'About six miles away as the guillemot flies.'

'The guillemot?' George was out of his depth. They didn't have guillemots in Bermondsey. Blackheads were ten-a-penny.

'A large sea bird, sergeant. I collect their nests.'

'You do?' George and Lestrade exchanged glances.

'Yes, it's a hobby of mine. Talking of which, I don't suppose either of you gentlemen has ever seen a hobby nest?' He rubbed his hands eagerly, straining forward in anticipation.

'I've seen a hobby horse once,' George said, and noticing how crestfallen the old curate was, added, 'not relevant, I suppose?'

'Can we get back to The Day In Question?' Lestrade asked. It was doggedness like this that had elevated him to Inspector after only thirteen years on the Force.

'Oh yes, I'm so sorry,' Austin's wrinkled upper lip disappeared into the froth of Jack's best. 'When I get going on nests, I'm like a little terrier.'

'Er ... the Sunday before Evensong?,

'Yes. The third before Septuagesima. Well, you may have noticed I'm not as young as I was and I came over a little peculiar by the lych-gate. I had to stop and relieve the pressure on my cycle clips.'

'And?'

'And I saw the Bishop.'

'The Bishop?'

'The Bishop of Exeter.'

'Where?'

'Coming out of the church. Or at least I assumed it was he.'

'Why?'

'Well, he wore gaiters and a top hat with strings.'

Lestrade mused over his half, undoubtedly from its taste, of Jack's second best. 'Did you see his face?'

'No, not actually.'

'Forgive us, Mr Austin,' Lestrade said, 'but we are, as yet, unfamiliar with the toxology of the churchyard. Would the Bishop have had to pass you to reach the road?'

'Ordinarily, yes,' the curate said.

'And extraordinarily?'

'Well, he didn't. He disappeared between the yews and hopped over the wall.'

Lestrade and George exchanged glances.

'Er ... this wall,' the sergeant asked, 'how high would you say it was?'

'Ooh, eight or nine feet at that point.'

'And how old is the Bishop of Exeter?' Lestrade asked.

'Oh, slip of a lad,' the curate said. 'Seventy-one.'

'Forgive us,' Lestrade smiled, 'we're new here. Is it usual for seventy-one year old Bishops to hop over nine foot walls in Cornwall?'

'Habitually, no, but I happen to know that His Grace believes that Fitness is next to Godliness. It was the theme of his Diocesan address last March.'

'Do you have that, sir?' George asked.

'What?' the curate was confused.

'The Bishop's Diocesan Address. I rather think we'll need to talk to him.'

'What happened next?' Lestrade asked.

'Well, I waved and said "Hello, Your Grace".'

'And?'

'That was the odd thing. He didn't respond.'

'Perhaps he didn't hear you,' Lestrade proffered.

'Perhaps not. But I happen to know that he has the finest auricular capability west of Bodmin Moor. I was in Truro cathedral once when a chorister broke wind in the North Transept.'

'Really?' Lestrade was outraged. Whatever was the world coming to?

'His Grace got wind of it and flew down the whole length of the cathedral before swinging the lad round by the cassock. Muscular Christianity. It was poetry in motion.'

'And on the third Sunday before Septuagesima?'

'I went into the church, to light up and so on. And I found him.'

'The Rector?'

The curate nodded. He was paler now and took refuge in his landlord's best, gulping down the amber nectar with alacrity.

'I realize this is painful,' Lestrade said'

'Not half as painful as it must have been for him,' the curate shuddered.

'Could you bring yourself to describe what you saw?' the Inspector asked.

'The Reverend Rodney was lying slumped over the eagle lectern. His blood was running down over its chest feathers. Not much left of the back of his head.' He finished the glass with a swig.

'He was dead of course.'

'Or very nearly so. I fancied I heard a gurgling sound, but it may have been the plumbing.'

'The plumbing?'

'We have a little pantry in the Vestry. Mr Smith is under the impression that the Rector was attacked there.'

'He is. Why?'

'Bloodstains, I think he said. I must admit I didn't notice. I lifted the Reverend down - no easy feat for a man whose cycle clips are killing him - and administered the last rites.'

'Did you see anyone else in the church?'

'No. But frankly I didn't wait around. For all I knew, there was a maniac lurking in the shadows. The gas lighting isn't all it should be. I pedalled like a thing possessed to the Verger's. He sent his boy for the police.'

'That would be Sergeant Smith?'

'That would be Constable Widger, our local bobby.'

'What did he do?'

'Panicked.'

'What?' It was George's turn to be outraged.

'He said he'd never seen a body before and wasn't sure of the procedures. I've know Tom Widger all his life. Curiously squeamish for the son of a Cornish poacher.'

'You went back to the church?' Lestrade asked.

'Oh, yes. I reminded Tom of his duty and led him to the lectern.'

'Led him?' Lestrade thought he'd misheard.

'Well, he wouldn't open his eyes.'

'And when he did?'

'He passed out.'

'So you had two bodies?'

'In a manner of speaking, yes. What could I do? I had Evensong in a few minutes. I dragged the Reverend Rodney into the Vestry and propped him in a corner of the pantry. I jammed him against the wall with the table and propped his back up by sticking a mop up his vest-ments. The door doesn't fit too well. I thought if anybody saw through the gap they'd assume he was taking tea rather than sprawled dead.'

'What about the constable?'

'The Verger hauled him outside and ran him round the churchyard a few times. He soon came to.'

'And you went ahead with the service?'

'Why, yes. When two or three are gathered together, you know, Inspector ...'

'How many were there at the service?'

'Two or three.'

Lestrade's eyebrow raised and the curate saw it.

'Well, it was a vile night,' Austin remembered. 'The rain had already started by the time I reached the church the first time. Widger and the Verger nearly drowned out there. Besides...'

'Besides?' the policemen chorused.

'Well, you'll find out anyway,' the curate said. 'The Reverend Rodney was not the most popular of men. His congregation had been dwindling of late.'

'Any special reason for that?' Lestrade asked.

The curate shrugged. 'None that I can think of,' he said.

'Where is the body now?' George relicked his pencil stub. It tasted a damn sight more appetizing than his dinner.

'Grave number three one nine. Just left of the path.'

'Ah,' Lestrade frowned. 'No chance of a quick re-opening of the coffin, I suppose?'

The curate looked horrified. 'Certainly not,' he said. 'For that you'd need either the permission of the Bishop or a magistrate's order. I doubt you'll get either.'

'So do I,' Lestrade realized.

'To that end', the curate fished about in his stipendiary bag, 'I wondered if these might be useful?' He scattered a host of sepia photographs on the table.

'What are these?'

'Various snapshots of the Reverend Rodney. They say these

devices can capture the soul of the dead. What do you think, Inspector?'

Lestrade glanced at the clock in the corner. 'It's nearly dusk, Mr Austin. I make it a rule never to think after dusk. Which one is Mr Rodney?'

'There,' the curate pointed to the first of the photos. 'Third from the left in this snapshot.'

'The one standing next to that serving girl?'

'Yes, that's him. Ever smiling. Ever beaming.'

Lestrade squinted at it. The leer on the dead Rector's face presented an altogether different picture of him.

'Here he is on a village outing to Torbay,' the curate said.

'Oh, I know it's a bit like coals to Newcastle, but even folk in a tourist village need an away day now and again.'

'Hm,' Lestrade mused, 'he appears to be helping that young girl down from the coach. Or is he helping her up?'

'Or is he helping himself?' George muttered.

'Ah, always the gentleman,' Austin smiled. 'You know, I can't for the life of me think why the parishioners began to stay away in droves from his services.'

'Perhaps his sermons were on the lacklustre side?' George suggested.

'Where was this one taken?' Lestrade asked.

'Oh, that was the Mevagissey Board Schools confirmation class of 'eighty-four.'

'And is he ... confirming this girl? The rather pretty one with the hour-glass figure?'

The curate adjusted his pince nez. 'I can't really make this out. There appears to be a flaw in the film.'

'What? Just where his hand is, you mean?' Lestrade asked.

'Yes. It was a hobby of the Reverend's of course.'

'I can see that,' Lestrade nodded. 'Er ... what was?'

'Photography. He got various people in the parish of course to take these, but he had a darkroom in the Rectory. Made Julia Margaret Cameron look decidedly average, I can tell you.'

'On second thoughts', Lestrade slid his plate away, 'it's not too late after all. Perhaps you could take us to the Rectory, Mr Austin?'

'Oh, of course. I'll just get my bicycle. Oh dear, I'm not sure I can give you *both* a lift.'

Lestrade couldn't accept Curate Austin's crossbar on account of his gammy leg. And George couldn't on the grounds that even at the advanced age of thirty-one, he hoped to be a father one day; Mevagissey's cobbles might well put an end to all that.

So it was that all three men trudged through the night of driving rain, wrapped in wet mufflers against the maelstrom. The puddles were ankle deep in places and passers-by hurrying home to the huddled houses on the hill stared in frank amazement at the two Lunnon gen'lemen walking the wet cobbles arm in arm.

'Oh, it's all right,' the old cleric called cheerily to each one. 'They're policemen.'

He left them at the Rectory gates. Old Mrs Riviera - known to all and sundry as the Cornish Riviera - was on her way to that great tourist resort in the sky and what with the Rector having gone before, all manner of parochial tasks fell on old Austin. He pedalled into the night.

The Rectory was a great black pile in the darkness framed by dripping rhododendron bushes and silent sentinel cedars. Its windows, like sad eyes, watched them come, hobbling up the drive, orphans of the storm.

'Well, put it in, man,' what with the wind, the rain and the pain in his leg, Lestrade was within hailing distance of the end of his tether. George was fumbling with the key the curate had lent them. It rumbled in the lock and the door swung wide.

'Aaarggh!' George knew his guv'nor's scream anywhere.

'Found something, sir?' he called into the pitch blackness of the hall.

'Yes,' Lestrade hissed, 'the umbrella stand. Why didn't you bring a bullseye, dammit?'

'Sorry guv. Hang on.' There was a fumbling of Lucifers and a scrape of sulphur and George stood there, beaming triumphantly in the match's flare, 'Ooh, I don't like that.'

Lestrade agreed. A rather revolting old goat stared down at them from a snowy landscape, looking sheepish. There was another one of the Rector a little higher up. Ever a man of infinite resource, George lit the oil lamp on the table and wandered through the cold, silent house humming, subconsciously no doubt, 'Lead kindly light'.

Lestrade stumbled in his wake.

'Where did the curate say the darkroom was, guv?' George asked.

'Off the bedroom at the top of the stairs.'

'Right. Well, here are the stairs.'

'Go on then,' Lestrade snapped, listening to his Donegal dripping on the carpet.

The lamp caught each brass stair rod like a flash of lightning. At the top a great black bear snarled at them in silence, the oil glow sharp on his beady, wicked glass eyes. A family of moths flew out of his fur at the policemen's approach.

'This one then,' George opened the door.

A bachelor's bedroom, single bedded, stark; and a hideous framed thing emblazoned with the motto 'God Is Not Mocked'.

The sergeant took in the sickly green of the washstand, the matching bowl and jug and the ecclesiastical fol-de-rols draped over the towel rail.

'His second-best,' Lestrade said.

'How do you know that, guv?' his sergeant asked.

The Inspector shrugged, 'I don't. But wouldn't a Rector wear his Sunday best for the Third before Septuagesima? That's the one he died in. What's that door over there?'

George tried it. 'It's locked, guv.'

'That's never stopped you before,' Lestrade observed.

'Shoulder job?'

'Why not?' the Inspector shrugged. 'I don't suppose the Rector will complain.'

'What about the sequestrators?'

'Just rub some liniment on them,' was the senior man's advice. 'They'll be all right.'

That was good enough for George. He squared up to the thing, pawing the carpet like a bull with a personality problem and hurtled against the frame. Lestrade wasn't sure whether it was wood or bone splintering, but there was an almighty crash and the Inspector trod carefully over his prostrate partner and carried the lamp into the gloom. Around the walls of a small alcove were row upon row of glass phials, each one labelled in leaf of gold, dazzling in the flickering lamplight.

'Nitrate of silver,' Lestrade read aloud.

'I'll be all right,' a voice moaned.

'Tincture,' the Inspector read on, running the lamp around the shelves.

'No, really,' the voice droned. 'It's nothing, Dislocation. Think nothing of it.'

'Stop complaining, George,' Lestrade answered unfeelingly, scanning more bottles of Windsor brown and midnight blue.

'You knew when you joined that the job had its ups and downs.

On your feet. Tell me, did you go to that lecture on Photography for Policemen?'

'No, guv. I'd just broken my arm if you remember, tackling that Jehovah's Witness in Threadneedle Street.'

'Ah, the old lady. Yes, I did warn you she was a wrong'un.'

'You did, guv'nor, you did. I just wasn't prepared for the brick in her handbag. Hello, hello, hello.' George was more or less upright by now, standing at his guv'nor's elbow. He had, with the instinct of a born snooper, flicked open a little cabinet drawer. He was glad it was too dark for Lestrade to see that he was blushing.

'Well, well, a little parish peccadillo if I'm any judge,' the Inspector peered over the sergeant's shoulder, the one that appeared to have dropped an inch or two. 'Isn't that the girl in the photo of the outing to Torbay?'

'I don't know, guv. I can't make her out from that angle.'

Lestrade glanced at the bottles again. 'Developing nicely,' he said.

'How old would you say she is?'

The Inspector shrugged. 'Fifteen, sixteen. I haven't seen a chemise that short since ... well, never you mind when.'

'This', George produced another one, 'is the serving girl in the group photo. I didn't recognize her at first without her clothes on. My, but she's a strapping lass.'

Who was she strapping, that's the question.'

'Yes, I don't care for that glint in her eye. Look, sir, there's dozens here.'

The sergeant was right. Dozens of scantily clad girls, not one of them over twenty, in a variety of lewd poses. There was no doubt about it, the Reverend Rodney had an eye for detail.

'No chance of taking these back for the lads, I suppose?' George asked.

Lestrade gave him an old fashioned look. 'The inside of that locker door of yours is full enough already,' he told him. 'Besides, tomorrow you and I have got some other doors to knock on. I want names to these ... er ... faces. Get yourself another lamp, George.'

'What am I looking for, sir?'

'Letters, articles of clothing. Anything else that links the Rector with these girls. I have a shrewd suspicion that his interest in them wasn't entirely ecu ... ecu ... ecumenical.'

The sergeant stumbled into the passageway, clutching his aching shoulder. That was easy for the guv'nor to say.

Widger and Smith came with the sunrise. One was a big copper, square of frame, as were all the sons of Polgooth. It was Constable Widger that came as a surprise, however. The curate had known him all his life. Curious then in a dynamic, go-ahead constabulary that the constable too was the wrong side of sixty.

'Sixty-three, sir,' he told the Yard men, standing before the empty grate in the Reverend Rodney's library, 'last Thursday.'

'Congratulations,' Lestrade said. 'Tell me, Widger, how well did you know the Rector?'

'As well as can be expected, sir,' the old man said. He was crimson of face, with a cheery grin and a little toothbrush moustache.

'How long had you known him?'

'Ooh, ever since he arrived sir. 'Bout ... ooh ... nigh on eight yearn.'

'What sort of man was he?'

'Man of the cloth, sir.'

'Yes,' Lestrade tapped his fingertips together as though in prayer. 'I am aware of his occupation, Constable. What manner of man was he?'

'I didn't have much to do wi'im, sir.'

'You're not a churchgoer then?'

'Methodist, sir,' Widger said. 'I goes to chapel over at London Apprentice.'

'Where?'

'It's a village, sir,' Smith offered, 'two miles north of here.'

'Did the Rector have any enemies?' Lestrade asked.

'Not that I know of, sir,' Widger said.

Lestrade was less than impressed with this example of Cornish Constabulary. His buttons were bright enough, but he saw nothing, heard nothing, knew nothing. Not altogether the most helpful man to have at your elbow.

George came in with the tea. For all his bruised shoulder, here was a copper - resourceful, dependable, brave. He'd smashed the lock on the Rector's tantalus and he and his guv'nor had partaken of some excellent brandy before the sun was up. It streamed in now through the leaded panes as the sergeant was mother with the bevy he'd half inched from the Rector's kitchen.

'The Bishop of Exeter,' Lestrade turned his attention to the Cornish detective. 'What can you tell me about him?'

'Name of Cordon,' Smith told him. 'Hubert Gordon. Signs hisself Hubert Damnoniorum.'

'Tall man?'

'Average.'

'Elderly?'

'Average.'

'I've heard he's seventy-one.'

'Very like.'

'Fit?'

'Average.'

Lestrade reached for George's tea like a man clutching at straws and going under for the very last time. 'Could he, in your opinion, stove in the head of one of his rectors and hotfoot it over a nine foot wall?'

Smith pondered awhile. 'Not all the way from Matabeleland he couldn't.'

'What?'

'Matabeleland. That's where His Grace is now.'

'For how long has this been the case?' Lestrade asked.

'Near on three months,' the sergeant said. 'I know because I saw him on the platform at Exeter and he said to me "Well, Smith, wish me luck." And I said "Why's that, Your Grace?" And he said "'Cos I be off to Matabeleland on a fact finding tour and mission of goodwill. See you in March". That's what he said.'

'And you're sure he's gone?'

'Well, we had a postcard from there at the station.'

'Is that usual?' Lestrade's eyebrow rose.

'Of course, sir,' Smith replied. 'We're all his flock, you know. Aren't we, Widger?'

'You'll have to speak for yourself, sir. I'm a Wesleyan deep down.'

Smith shrugged. 'You don't seriously suspect His Grace, do you, Mr Lestrade?'

'I seriously suspect everyone at this stage of the enquiry, Smith. Even you and Widger here. Right,' he threw a scattering of sepia photographs onto the library table, 'who are they?'

'My God!' Smith's eyes widened. 'Widger?'

'No, sir,' the constable was confident. 'They're not me.'

'Clearly not,' sighed Lestrade, 'unless you've had fairly drastic surgery lately. I want to know the names of those young ladies. Now.'

'Ar well,' the constable fumbled in his top pocket for a flimsy pair of spectacles, 'this yer'n,' and he shook his head, 'this is Daisy Porthluney from Trenarren way. This one - my, how she 'ave grown - is Hannah Tresilian. This one... she've left now. Went away to Lunnon if I remember right. 'Er name were Emily Carrick. 'Er dad's a carter in they parts.'

'Yes,' mused Lestrade, 'the Rector was clearly interested in "they parts" himself. Have either of you seen these photographs before?'

The Cornishmen shook their heads.

'What about this?' Lestrade handed over a slim volume that had lain on the table in front of him.

Widger read the title aloud: '*The Lay of the Last Minstrel.* What is that, sir?'

'Well, if my memory serves me correctly, it's a poem by a bloke called Scott. Only it isn't. See for instance, page 38.'

The constable flicked to it. 'The page seems to be torn, sir,' he said.

'Teethmarks,' proffered Lestrade. 'Paragraph three, line six.'

Widger's eyes widened and his spectacles plummeted off the end of his nose. 'That's not possible, is it?' he asked. 'Not in Corn'all at any rate.'

'It's an obscene publication, sergeant,' Lestrade filled Smith in as the Cornish detective took a look for himself. 'There's a false panel in the wall behind me and at the rear of *The Parish in Fact and Fiction* and the sixteen volumes of *Canon Law: The Evidence*; there are another half dozen like that. They are all to do with older men who seduce young girls. Printed in Holland on some particularly nasty stationery. The Last Minstrel seems to have been particularly well endowed.'

'Well,' Smith tilted his regulation bowler to the back of his head, 'I'll be a clotted cream. Whoever'd have thought it of the Rector?'

'Somebody did,' Lestrade said. 'And somebody killed him for it.'

That day was very much like the last, the wind groaning with the trudging policemen up the winding streets and bobbing the little fishing boats on the heavy grey surface of the harbour below the town. Several times during their enquiries, Lestrade and George pondered where the wind came from. But as sure as God made little pygmies, they both knew where it was going to.

By nightfall, even the cheerless gloom of The Happy Traveller had charms of its own and the gen'lemen from Lunnon huddled over the flickering grate as though their lives depended on it.

'Right then, George,' Lestrade said, massaging his gamminess, 'Daisy Porthluney, from Trenarren way, I believe.'

'Yes, sir,' George toasted his blue feet, 'rather more of a way than I had imagined in fact.'

'You took a trap?'

'Oh, I found the house all right. But she wasn't in. Some deranged old relative told me Daisy and her dad were down at the cave.'

'The cave?'

'It's a cleft in the cliff, sir, formed by years of geologized corrosion.'

'Yes, thank you, sergeant. I knew I'd regret missing the lecture on Rock Formations for Policemen. What were the Porthluneys doing in a cave?'

'Well, that was the curious thing, guv.' George was wringing out a sock so that the fire hissed and spat. 'They appeared to be humping crates until I came along and then they started tapping the roof.'

'Tapping the roof?'

'Old Cornish custom I assumed, at first, naturally.'

'Naturally,' Lestrade nodded, frowning.

'But it turned out they were fossil hunting.'

'I see. And the crates?'

Well, they used them to stand on, so they could reach the ledges.'

'Ah. Who was there?'

'Well, I only saw the Porthluneys, man and girl, but judging from the scraping of barrels deeper in the cave, there must have been more of them.'

'Barrels?'

'They're a bit taller than the crates, it expires, so they're even better for standing on.'

'I see,' Lestrade was not convinced. 'Well, to the matter of the Rector.'

'Ah,' George fumbled for his notebook. 'Now that was a different kettle of fish. As soon as I told them who I was, they got quite agitated. Old man Porthluney started screaming how tapping rocks wasn't against the law and whathaveyou. When I pointed out I wanted to ask the daughter about Rodney, he quieted down.'

'What did the girl say?'

'Nothing.'

'Nothing?'

'The old man didn't give her a chance. Did all the talking for her. Yes, the Rector was very kind to her. Yes, he'd taken photographs of her - of all her confirmation class at various times. Lots of vicars did that, apparently . There was nothing in it.'

'So he didn't appear to mind?'

'No,' George said. 'Even when I showed him the snaps we'd found. Said he didn't know anything about it, but he expected they'd be what was called "artistic".'

'Hmm,'Lestrade mused. 'A model of tolerance and liberalism then, our Mr Porthluney.'

'Apparently so. How did you fare, guv'nor?'

'The Tresilians were a different matter,' Lestrade stretched himself out. 'Mr Tresilian was killed at sea three years ago. Or rather at the shore. I couldn't get much sense out of his wife. Inbred, I shouldn't wonder. Something about barrels falling on him. That's why I queried it when you mentioned barrels. I can't for the life of me see how you can be killed by barrels at the water's edge.'

'Unless it's dark, of course,' George reflected.

'On a wild night, you mean?' Lestrade asked.

The sergeant nodded.

'But then what would he be doing at night, in a storm, on the beach?'

The strange Western ways had clearly baffled the Yard men.

'Anyway, I too showed the photos to Mrs Tresilian.'

'And?'

'She just looked at them. Know what she said?'

'No.'

'"Ain't she a beauty, my Hannah?"'

'That was it?'

'That was it.'

'What about the girl?'

'Ah, well, she was a little more forthcoming than yours, apparently. She told me the Rector was always taking photographs, not to mention liberties, of all the local girls.'

'Poor little things,' George mused. 'Cut up, was she? Crying? Consumed with guilt and shame?'

'Not a bit of it,' Lestrade said. 'Offered to lift up her frock for sixpence.'

'Really?' George was aghast. 'You didn't .

'Please, George!' Lestrade was affronted. 'You know I don't carry small change. Did you send the telegram to Tyrrell and Green?'

'Yessir, but I have to say their chances of finding this Emily Carrick in London are about four million to one.'

Lestrade nodded. 'Even so,' he said, 'no stone unturned. Mr Rodney will have our guts for garters if we don't explore every ... er ...'

'Avenue, sir?'

Lestrade winked. 'Quite right, Abberline.'

'I don't get it, guv,' George was staring into the embers. 'Two girls for certain - more possibly - well, three if you count Emily Carrick - all being interfered with by the Rector - and nobody seems to give a tinker's damn.'

'You forget, George,' Lestrade said, 'this is Cornwall. There's none so queer as folk, especially fishing folk. Ours not to reason why.

A cheerier fire altogether crackled in the hearth of 221B Baker Street. The taller of the two men was rosining his bow in an absent-minded sort of way when he glanced up and said to his colleague, 'Have you ever wanted to murder anyone, Watson?'

The good doctor's left hand lost its grip on his newspaper. 'Me, Holmes? Good Heavens, no ... although, er, I did once, of course.'

Holmes continued to rosin without breaking his stride. 'I wasn't referring to your professional incompetence on the operating table, my dear fellow.'

Watson bridled, stung, not for the first time in his life, by his companion's lack of tact. 'Neither was I, Holmes,' he blustered, 'I was referring to Afghanistan, back in '78. Kill or be killed it was, of course, in those days. Pathans everywhere you looked. There we were, my orderly and I, with nothing but a dollop of laudanum and a Webley Mark Four. Or was it Three?'

I'd love to saunter down memory lane with you, Watson,' Holmes said through gritted teeth, 'but I fear the Pax Britannica isn't what it was.'

'Oh, there I must disagree with you, Holmes,' the doctor rumbled. 'Volume six on endocrinal complaints in the rationally disadvantaged was second to none.'

'Hmm,' Holmes mused, 'you wrote that, didn't you?'

'Oh,' Watson blushed, 'a fumbling, inept artifice if I say so myself.'

'Yes,' Holmes agreed. 'Unfortunately you weren't the only one to say so. I seem to remember *The Lancet* was less than kind.'

'Editorially, they're a joke, Holmes,' Watson assured him. 'What do a bunch of surgeons know about medicine?'

Holmes arched an eyebrow. 'You have a point there,' he demurred.

'However,' Watson cleared his throat. 'Talking of murder, I could murder a pint at this precise moment.'

'Of good Cornish cider, Watson, I'd wager.'

'Cornish?' Watson was a little confused. 'Oh, very well, but why Cornish, pray?'

'Ah, well quipped, Watson,' Holmes chuckled, although it was immediately obvious from the doctor's face that he had failed to quip for some time.

'Er ... you've lost me, Holmes,' he confessed.

'Ah, wishful thinking, old man,' the Great Detective beamed. 'Do you absorb nothing from the pages of *The Thunderer*, old fellow?'

Watson scanned the paper in question, re-gripping it anew. 'South American mining isn't what it was and the bottom seems to have fallen out of rubber.'

'No, not the article on the world crisis in incontinence pads. Page sixteen, fourth column.'

Watson riffled to it. 'Rector of Mevagissey bludgeoned to death in his own pulpit. Good Heavens! Didn't I read that in the *Church Times* yesterday? *The Thunderer* must be slipping.'

'I don't doubt it,' Holmes commented, his elegant fingers executing a quick pizzicato on the strings. 'Any news source with an editor named Buckle can hardly be worth the paper it's printed on.'

Watson ignored the mixed metaphor and the lack of syntax, knowing as he did that his companion's brilliance shone elsewhere. 'Isn't Lestrade on that one?' He read on.

'Who?' Holmes yawned.

'Yes, by Jove, he is. Listen to this ...'

'I've read it, Watson.'

'"Inspector Sholto Lestrade of Scotland Yard arrived on Thursday last in the company of Sergeant George ...'

'I've read it, Watson.'

'"The Reverend Hereward Rodney is a distant cousin of Assistant Commissioner Rodney..."'

'I've read it, Watson,' Holmes screamed, so that the veins stood out, throbbing with pure genius, at his temples.

'Sorry, Holmes,'Watson mumbled.

But Holmes was already in control. 'What does it say - sergeant now, is he, Lestrade?'

Inspector, Holmes,' Watson corrected him. 'Play the white man.'

Holmes snorted. 'Right. A little exercise for you, my dear fellow. Close your eyes.'

'What?'

'Your eyes, Watson, close your eyes.'

'Oh, very well,' Watson did as he was told.

'Now, page three of *The Thunderer*. I calculate you read it exactly eight minutes ago.'

'Er ... oh.'

'What was on it? No, no, keep your eyes shut. It'll help concentration.'

'Er ... there was a rather ravishing picture of a girl.'

'No, that was the *Sun*, Watson; last Friday's issue. She was Mary Clary, voted Miss Billingsgate for the fourth year in succession. Do concentrate, please.'

'Um ... it wasn't that story about the Chinese ambassador?'

'No, that was page eight, second column and in any case it has nothing to do with murder.'

'Oh, murder,' Watson clicked his fingers. 'It was that review of Lord Hartington's speech before the Select Committee on over-crowding of the shipping lanes off the Isle of Wight.'

'No,' Holmes corrected him. '"Solent Abuse" was second column on page four.'

'Got it!' Watson's eyes flicked open. 'Er ... "Spy Network Uncovered in Rangoon".'

'No, dear fellow,' Holmes was patience itself, 'that was the fifth column. You want the first. Although at least now you're on the right page.'

'Er ... um,' Watson had reached the end of his span of concentration. 'No, it's no good. Give up.'

'South Mimms,' Holmes hinted.

'Ah, of course,' the doctor ejaculated. 'Squire Ralston, bludgeoned to death ... oh, my God.'

Yes, Watson?' Holmes leaned forward.

'Well, something of a coincidence, surely, Holmes. First the Reverend Rodney, now Squire Ralston. How many bludgeonings can there be in the space of a fortnight?'

'And how many bludgeoners carrying out their vicious trade in an area the size of England?'

'Er ... give up, Holmes,' Watson said again.

'No, Watson, it's not a conundrum, my dear fellow, merely a philosophical introspection.'

'Do you suppose Lestrade is involved in South Mimms too?'

'I hardly think so, Watson. First, there is no mention of him in the item concerned. Second, I happen to know that the good Inspector is less than popular with the Herts Constabulary and third, *The Thunderer* seems a little more up to date on this one. It happened the day before yesterday - barely time for Lestrade to down his breakfast pasty and get to a railway station.' He consulted the grandfather in the corner. 'With luck, we'll be half a day ahead of him.' And he flung down the bow and swept from the room.

'But we haven't been engaged, Holmes!' Watson called after him.

'Of course we haven't Watson,' the Great Detective replied above the rumble of 221B's plumbing. 'People would talk.'

'I mean, no one has taken us on to solve a crime.'

'Tosh and fiddlesticks, Watson,' Holmes re-emerged with foam all over his face and a cut-throat in his hand. 'I'm not having some blockhead from the Detective Branch solving cases ahead of me.' and Watson didn't at all care for the gleam, either on Holmes's razor or in Holmes's eye. 'By the way,' the Great Detective paused, 'that doctor friend of yours, what's his name? Lives in Southsea?'

'Conan Doyle.'

'That's the chappie. Is he still pestering you about writing some damned novel about me?'

'Indeed he is, Holmes,' said Watson enthusiastically. 'He even has a working title - ***A Study in Scarlet***.'

"What is he', frowned Holmes, 'a novelist or an interior decorator?'

Well, he's a doctor at the moment, Holmes,' Watson told him, ever a stickler for accuracy.

But Holmes had gone. 'Mrs Hudson,' Watson heard the Great Detective bellow, 'where the deuce is my Harris tweed deerstalker?'

And a muffled lowland-Scots answer came from the kitchen. 'You're the Great Detective, Mr Holmes, you find it.'

'Where away, Holmes?' Watson called. desperately ferreting under cushions for his Webley Mark Whatever it Was.

'South Mimms, old fellow,' came the reply. 'The game's afoot.'

'Yes,' groaned Watson, 'I feared it might be.

3

'Have you seen this, guv?' George shook a nasty little pamphlet at his Inspector. The Great Western locomotive lurched at that moment, rattling east and said pamphlet embedded itself momentarily in Lestrade's right nostril.

'What is it?' the Inspector rearranged his moustache.

'*Punch*, sir - the *Charivari*.'

'Ah, yes,' Lestrade mused. 'Guaranteed to get right up my nose. In what way have they outraged your constabulary sensibilities this time?'

'Well, it's this,' George fumed, 'this so-called "Song for Scotland Yard".'

'Hum me a few bars, I'll try and pick it up.'

'For instance .. .' George cleared his throat.

'Er ... you're not going to sing, are you sergeant? Only I remember with a little less than delight the Police Revue of last year.'

'Ah,' George turned an odd shade of cerise. 'Perhaps the oratorio was a little ambitious.'

'Just say it, then,' Lestrade advised.

'I won't bore you with the rest, guv. It's this coupling that gets me - "Policedom's honour is at stake, Policedom from its drowse must wake." What a bloody cheek!'

'Hm,' nodded Lestrade, 'we'll close that rag down one of these days.'

'And look at this - "The Police of the Future".'

Lestrade peered at the upside down picture of an officer in riot gear, armed with a wicker-work shield, a spiked quarter-staff, water tank and hose pipe and 'mob-persuaders' - spikes on knees.

'I like the bags of money for bus fares idea,' he nodded approvingly. 'Let's hope none of our more zealous colleagues get hold of the electric-wires-up-the-sleeves gadgets. Enough people are shocked by police behaviour already.'

'You know the *Pall Mall Gazette* called the Yard a dodo the other day?' George bridled.

Lestrade held an appalled hand to his forehead. 'Oh, tell me it isn't so,' he groaned.

'Well, guv,' George jutted his jaw forward a few times, 'I'd just like a few minutes alone with these bloody editors, that's all.'

'Yes, yes,' Lestrade smiled, 'but they'd only have more ammunition for charges of police brutality. Let's get back to the matter in hand, shall we?'

George shrugged and threw the *Charivari* out of the window.

'Mevagissey, then, sergeant,' Lestrade lolled back, closing his eyes. 'Tell me all.'

'An old world fishing village, sir,' the sergeant summarized, 'narrow streets, alleyways as devious as its inhabitants, most of whom seemed to be related to each other and couldn't quite manage the Queen's English. In fact, I've got to be honest with you, I haven't exactly understood very much over the last four days.'

'Why break the habit of a lifetime? Lestrade thought.

'The village is renowned for its capture of the pilchard, supplying Italy and the West Indies in bygone days. Apparently the record year was 1724 when over four thousand tons of pilchards were dispatched. Can you imagine that? Four thousand tons of pilchards!'

Lestrade and his sergeant sat shaking their heads in sheer wonderment.

'Fishermen on the pier head told me - I think - they caught mackerel and conger.'

'I thought that was a dance,' Lestrade frowned.

'So did I, guv,' George said. 'And when I said that very thing to one of them, he said they also caught pollocks. At least, I think that's what he said.'

'Yes, well, this is all very fascinating, George,' Lestrade yawned. 'But I rather had in mind discussing the case.'

'Ah, right you are, guv, the case. Well, the parish church is dedicated to St Peter, built on the site of an old wattle and daub oratory belonging to a monk called Moroch. The Saxons built a wooden church and this was rebuilt about 1100 by the Norman Bishop of Exeter.'

'Yes, thank you, George, I'm sure your grasp of the gazetteer is admirable, but it's the present Bishop I'm a little more interested in.'

'Ah, yes. Hubert Damnoniorum.'

'That's the Johnnie.'

'In Matabeleland.'

'According to Detective Sergeant Smith.'

'Seems a good man.'

'Salt of the earth. What did you make of Constable Widger?'

'Moron, wasn't he?'

Lestrade nodded. 'A fair bet,' he agreed. 'Now, the Reverend Rodney.'

'Right. Hereward Sacheverell Rodney. Educated Charterhouse and King's College, London. Bachelor of Divinity, Third Class, 1864. Curate at Congleton for three months. Left rather abruptly.'

'Do we know why?'

George raised an eyebrow, 'I could make an educated guess, sir.'

'Indeed. And after Congleton?'

'Six months at Godalming.'

'Left abruptly?'

George nodded. 'Seems to have gone through parishes like you and I go through stations.'

'When did he get the Mevagissey job?'

'Eight years ago. Popular at first. Congregation dropping off lately.'

'All right, then. Married?'

'No.'

'Housekeeper?'

'A Mrs Bunn.'

'Yes, you talked to her, didn't you?'

'I did, sir. Your leg was playing you up at the time.'

'It still is, sergeant,' Lestrade didn't have to be reminded. 'Can we get on with this, please?'

'Funny woman. Intensely loyal to the Rector, of course.'

'Didn't know about the young girls?'

'Not a clue.'

'Nor the dirty books?'

'Never seen them.'

'Nor the photographic darkroom?'

'Didn't know he had one.'

'Even though the ancient curate knew all about the Rector's hobbies?'

'Curious, isn't it?'

'What did you make of this Bunn, then? Was she in on the procuring?'

George considered the possibility for a moment. 'Couldn't procure a ham,' he decided.

'All right, then. Mrs Bunn, loyal or stupid or both. There's none so blind as those that will not see. Let's look at the murder itself.'

'Well, Smith was right - about it being committed in the Vestry, I mean.'

'How do we know?'

'There were still blood traces up the walls and in the cracks of the tiles, as though Rodney had been dragged.'

'And?'

'And although the curate found him draped over the lectern, he couldn't have been killed there.'

'Why not?'

'Because when you propped me in that position, guv, and proceeded to hit me over the head with that candlestick, the eagle fell over ... and so did I.'

'Ah, yes,' Lestrade commiserated slightly. 'How is the neck?'

'Was that before or after the eagle had landed, sir?'

'Well, well,' Lestrade made light of it. 'It established a truth, George. That's important in a murder enquiry. Besides that, a little discomfort is neither here nor there.'

'Well, it's here and there, actually, sir,' George could not leave it alone.

'Cause of death?' Lestrade forged on.

'Blunt instrument, to the back of the head.'

'Yes, and that's as far as it goes. The post mortem report was marginally worse than useless.'

'Was it?'

'Of course. There was no speculation as to weapon, number of blows delivered, angle of attack. Nothing. Let's face it, George, we just got there too late. However ... motive?'

'Ah, that's easy. The Reverend Rodney had a more than ecclesiastical interest in various young girls of his parish. He seems to have liked them between fourteen and eighteen.'

'And yet?'

'And yet, despite photographic evidence, the parents of two of them don't seem to give a tinker's damn about it.'

'And yet generally the Rector's congregation was falling off, perhaps as a reaction to his provacities. Which means?'

'Which means that the girls' parents are lying or somebody else knew more than they did.'

'The Carrick girl,' Lestrade nodded. 'Family moved away to London. Not usual, I wouldn't think.'

'Not?'

Lestrade shook his head. 'No. The old man is a carter. Carters stay put. Oh, they might move parish by parish. He might have gone to St Ewe or even Bodrugan's Leap. But London? That's like you and I moving to the moon, George. What do you think our chances are of Tyrrell and Green finding them now?'

'Three days ago', George computed with that grey-celled differencing machine of his, 'I said four million to one. Now, let's see, Wednesday,' he checked his half hunter, 'half past ten ... hmm... six and a half million to one.'

Lestrade nodded. It was a reasonable ratio.

'What about this other one, sir? Where is it again?'

Lestrade ferreted out the crumpled telegram that had arrived that morning. 'South Mimms, George. It's a village in Hertfordshire. You can do your gazetteer bit later. It seems the local squire is dead.'

'Why are we on this one, guv? We've got our hands full in Cornwall.'

'Cause of death, sergeant,' Lestrade told him. 'Viz and to wit a blunt instrument. Only this time, we've still got a corpse above ground. Or we will have if this damned train ever reaches Swindon. Oh, by the way, if the officer in charge of the case in Hertfordshire is one Chief Inspector Edward Towgrass, you leave the talking to me.'

Chief Inspector Edward Towgrass stood on the gravel drive in front of the hideous Queen Anne building that was Ralston Hall. The Ralstons of South Mimms had come over with the Conqueror but had fallen on slightly harder times after the Great Railway Boom of the 1840s. They had put their trust in bonds of the East Kent and Cross Channel Railway Company, floated, if that was the right word, by Monsieur Felon of Le Havre. After that it had been downhill all the way. First the Colney Hatch properties had gone, then the Verulamium Estate. Now all that was left was South Mimms itself and Ralston Hall. The family had slipped a long way since South Mimms's only famous son, Arthur Young, Improving Landlord, had first whispered 'Turnips' in the ear of the then Squire Ralston. That had been in 1793. The now Squire Ralston lay under a drugget on his bed in the Blue Room where the underpaid, dwindling body of retainers had carried him.

Towgrass, with uniformed constables at his elbows, narrowed his eyes as the speck which was his own station wagon grew larger on the road. He spat out the wad of tobacco he was chewing and summoned his men forward. His lantern jaw had already set firm by the time the vehicle rattled and rolled to a halt in front of him. He took one look at the ferret-faced man in the Donegal and bowler and snapped at the driver up on the box, 'Burden, you miserable bastard, who said you could use the station wagon to pick up civilians? Oh, it's you, Lestrade. Didn't recognize you without a gammy leg.'

That very limb made its appearance at that moment as stick, then Inspector, clambered out and on to the ground.

'Towgrass,' Lestrade smiled through gritted teeth. 'This is

Sergeant George.'

Towgrass nodded, ignoring the man's outstretched hand. 'I wonder how I knew it would be you?' he said.

Lestrade shrugged. 'We just go where we're sent. What have you got?'

'Plenty of expertise as it is,' the Hertfordshire man told him. 'Without the Yard sticking its nose in.'

'Well, well,' said Lestrade. 'So much for police co-operation. I have my orders, Towgrass. Let's just get on with this, shall we?'

The Chief Inspector clicked his fingers and his constables dashed ahead to open the main doors, ancient oak set with studs. He led the Yard man through a wide hall, freezing cold and damp, up a swirling staircase to the first landing. Here a grandfather clanged half past three. The day was nearly over and no sign of spring.

'Shall I serve tea, Mr Towgrass?' a voice called from below.

The Chief Inspector half turned. 'Fussock, the butler,' he explained.

'He's only being sociable,' Lestrade said.

'Yes. In the library,' snapped Towgrass. 'The corpus delicti is in here.'

Towgrass swept aside the drapes of the four poster and whipped back the sheet.

'George, pass me that candle,' Lestrade ordered.

The sergeant did.

'Perhaps you could light it?' the Inspector suggested.

'Oh, right, sorry guv,' and the room was filled with the scraping of Lucifers.

'I see the standard of sergeants hasn't improved in the Metropolitans,' Towgrass sneered. 'Unlike my man Spatchcock. He'll go far.'

'Your man Spatchcock? Where's he?' Lestrade asked.

'I told you. Gone far. He's back in St Albans. He found the body.'

'Did he?'

'Routine surveillance.'

'You were surveying Squire Ralston?'

'No. Spatchcock was on Artificial Waterways. He'd done Brocket Hall and was working his way south.'

'Uniformed man?' Lestrade checked.

'At the moment. But I'm toying with transferring him to the CID. He'll make a reasonable detective in twenty years or so.'

Lestrade looked at the dead thing on the bed. 'What's all this, then?' he asked.

Towgrass leaned back against the ottoman and folded his arms. 'You tell us, Mr World's Second Greatest Detective.'

Lestrade sensed George tensing but he patted the man's shoulder and hobbled alongside the deceased, hovering over him with his candle like some crippled ghoul. 'Very well,' he said. 'The deceased was aged what, fifty-five, sixty?'

'Fifty-seven,' Towgrass specified. 'Last Monday. There was a party.'

'Well nourished,' Lestrade commented. 'Inclined to obesity.'

'Fat,' Towgrass insisted, 'I'd say.'

The Inspector hauled on the right arm and the Squire gave him the cold shoulder. A mass of congealed blood lay dark on the pillow and the pennies dropped off his eyes. 'Back of the cranium stoved in,' Lestrade said. 'By a blunt instrument. At least three blows, but it's difficult to tell with all this blood. Hold this candle, George. Don't wobble, man. You've seen murder victims before.'

'Sorry, sir. It's so cold up here.'

'Family's in debt,' Towgrass said. 'They're only lighting fires on the ground floor.'

'One question, Towgrass,' Lestrade said.

'Only one?' the Chief Inspector chuckled. 'Still, it's early days.'

'Why is the late Squire wearing an apron?'

'Ancient Order of Buffaloes,' Towgrass said. 'He was Head Bull or something. They've got strict orders for laying people out.'

'What, with blunt instruments, you mean?'

Towgrass crossed to the window where the defunct fountain lay like a green bowl on the gravel below. 'If you're considering whether the Ancient Order expelled the late Squire in a fairly permanent way, it has already crossed our minds. We are less than fifteen miles from London, Lestrade. This isn't the back-woods, you know.'

'Any leads?'

'None. Yet. But Spatchcock is, as I told you, in St Albans as we speak, checking out the local lodge.'

'You give your uniformed men a lot of rope,' Lestrade observed.

'I told you,' Towgrass turned back to his man, 'Spatchcock's one of us. He'll be out of blue serge by the weekend.'

'You say this Spatchcock found him?'

'He did.'

'Details?'

'You'll need to talk to him, Lestrade...'

There was a tap on the door and a constable appeared. 'Beggin' your pardon, Mr Towgrass.'

'Yes, Chester, what is it?'

'It's Lord Verulam and the Hertfordshire Hunt again, sir.'

'My God! What now?'

'They've got a fox cornered in the Reverend Litchen's graveyard, sir.'

'Well? I always thought Litchen was a hunting parson.'

'Oh he is, sir, but the dogs have been diggin' up graves and widdlin' over tombstones. There's a hell of a stink.'

'Yes,' sighed Towgrass, 'I expect there is. What's Litchen doing about it?'

'Wielding his twelve-bore, sir.'

'Oh, Christ. Lestrade, I can't think of a man I'd like to have less on this case than you. But until I'm Chief Constable I suppose I'm stuck with it. Try not to upset anyone, will you, or it'll be my bollocks on a plate as well as yours.'

'Friendly sort,' grunted George when he'd gone, constables snapping to attention on the staircase. 'You and he go back a little way I gather?'

'We do,' nodded Lestrade, peering closer at the Squire's head wound. 'Some power behind this,' he observed.

'And you're not going to tell me about it, are you.

'I am not. What do you reckon he weighs?'

'Towgrass?'

'Ralston. Do try to stay on the track, there's a good sergeant.'

'Sixteen, seventeen stone. Why?'

'I'm just wondering how much fight he put up. Hold this nearer his fingernails, will you?'

The candleflame hovered near the dead man's hands, the flickering light licking his apron with luminous shafts in the near darkness.

'No skin,' Lestrade muttered. 'No sign of a struggle.'

'No warning,' George said. 'Just a quick thwack from behind.'

'Or several.'

'Or several,' the sergeant echoed.

Lestrade checked his half hunter. 'Quarter to four, sergeant,' he noted. 'Everything stops for tea.'

Fussock the butler stood like a lamp-post in the corner of the room. Lestrade had taken in the late Squire's reading matter. Like most of the gentry plagued by dwindling financial fortunes he appeared not to have bought a single book since 1849. So that meant that Mrs Beeton was missing, not to mention *Origin of Species* and *My Life Already* by Baron Rothschild. A shame really, because the Rothschildren wrote a rattling good yarn.

'Well, Mr Fussock ...' the Inspector began as the taller man solemnly lit the oil lamps.

'Just Fussock, sir,' he intoned, a veritable martyr to catarrh.

'Very well,' said Lestrade. 'How long have you served Squire Ralston?'

'Forty years and more, sir. Ever since he was sent down from Oxford.'

'Sent down? Why?'

'Not for me to say, sir. I believe there were some irregularities at Brasenose.'

That came as no surprise to Lestrade.

'I was born on the Verulamium Estate, sir,' the lackey volunteered. 'As was my father before me. Generations of Fussocks have served the Ralstons.'

'I see. And what manner of man was Osbaldeston Ralston?'

'He was the nineteenth in the line, sir.'

'Yes. That wasn't quite what I wanted to know. Who is to be the twentieth?'

'Twentieth equal, sir'.

'Equal?' Lestrade looked at George, but he was having trouble with his pencil stub.

'Ian and Kelvin, the young masters, sir. They're twins.'

'But one must be the elder ... mustn't he?' Lestrade's knowledge of such things was not encylopaedic. After all, he'd never given birth to twins in his life.

'Ah, yes, sir. Young master Ian was the firstborn. But the Squire in his will stipulated that they should inherit equally.'

'You're very privy to your master's financial arrangements,' George commented.

'I witnessed his last will, sir.'

'His last?' Lestrade said. 'Were there others?'

'No sir. I meant as in his last will and testament.'

'Yes, I see. I see. Was he a fair master, the Squire?'

'I always found him so, sir. When he was sober.'

'When he was sober?' Lestrade repeated. 'And that was ... ?'

'1873 if I remember. Mr Gladstone promised to repeal the income tax.'

'That led to a bout of sobriety?'

'No, sir. It was Mr Gladstone's breaking his promise that led to that.'

'I see. So the Squire was a drunk?'

'A drunk; no sir. Merely drunk. You wouldn't know unless you were dancing with him.'

Lestrade glanced at George, who, characteristically, glanced back. 'Which you did?'

Fussock looked affronted. 'Never, sir,' he assured the policeman. 'Oh, except possibly on the night of the news of Prince Albert's death. The Squire could never abide the fellah.'

'I see. I hope you're writing all this down, George.'

'Oh, every word, sir.'

Lestrade crossed to the leaded panes. He could just make out before the dark line of elms the pale expanse of the lake which the fourteenth squire had had drained and in which Sergeant Spatchcock had found the body of the nineteenth squire. 'Tell me about the night he died,' he said.

'He was celebrating, sir,' Fussock told the Yard men. 'What he called a ... oh, dear!'

'Yes?' Lestrade sensed a break in the man's speech pattern, a catch in his voice. He'd seen guilty men crack this way before.

'What he called a killing, sir - on the Stock Exchange.

'By which he meant?' the Inspector closed to his man.

'A rather large amount of money, sir, usually by buying low and selling high.'

'I see,' Lestrade bluffed. To him, the City was a closed book - a book that bore the curiously lacklustre title 'So You Think You Know All About Speculation?'.

'So Mr Ralston had cause to celebrate. Go on.'

'He decided to throw a party. It had been some time, I must say, since Ralston Hall had seen such frivolity. The last time must have been when Lord Palmerston died.'

'Which would be ... ?' young George asked for the record.

'In keeping with the Master's hatred of Liberals,' Fussock explained.

'No,' said George, 'I mean, when did it happen? When did Lord Palmerston die?'

'1865.'

'God, man,' Lestrade said, 'that's twenty-one years ago. Are you telling me there hadn't been a party at the Hall since then?'

'No, sir. If it hadn't been for their respective clubs, the young masters wouldn't know what a party was. We below stairs had to check Mrs Beeton for the protocol, I can tell you. And we had to borrow her from the lending library in Potters Bar.'

'You made a guest list of course.'

'Of course, sir. Mrs Beeton is very particular about that.'

'How many were there?'

'Only one Mrs Beeton, sir. Unique, that woman.'

'No. Guests, Fussock, guests. Do try to stay with it, man. I realize you've had something of a shock.'

'Here we are, sir,' the old man produced a crumpled paper from his pocket. 'I'm afraid it's a little the worse for wear.'

'Yes, well, aren't we all?' Lestrade snatched it from him.

'What this?' he frowned.

'It's the guest list,' Fussock explained.

'If it is, it's written in Egyptian.' Lestrade shook the paper at him. It showed a square with a series of connecting lines inside it, like a plan of some long-forgotten maze.

'Ah, sorry, sir,' Fussock blustered. 'That's not the guest list.'

'Clearly not,' Lestrade handed it back. 'Do you have the guest list?'

'No, sir,' Fussock decided after much pocket-searching. He spent so long in his right trouser pocket that George decided he must have a hole there. 'I fear not.'

'Well,' Lestrade threw himself jadedly down on the battered old leather of the armchair, 'perhaps you can remember a few of the names you sent invitations to while my sergeant writes them down.'

'It was the County Set, sir.'

'County set? You mean the Hertfordshire gentry?'

'Yes, sir. I remember that specifically because it was quicker to send young Davy by hand than to post them. Now that Sir Rowland Hill has gone ...'

'Yes, I know,' Lestrade commiserated, 'the end of civilization as we know it. How many invitations did you send out?'

'Sixty-eight, sir, if I remember aright.'

'And, if you remember aright, how many came?'

'Five.'

'Five?' Lestrade and George chorused.

'Ah, well, sirs, you mustn't forget that there hadn't been a party here since Lord Palmerston died.'

'How could we?' Lestrade wondered aloud. 'As a matter of

interest, Fussock, do you remember how many came then?'

'Eight. It should have been nine but the Bishop of Llandaff went down with cholera at the last moment.'

George shook his head. 'The lengths some people will go to to avoid a social engagement!' he realized anew.

'Right,' said Lestrade, 'the five guests. Let's have 'em.'

'Well, there was young master Ian and young master Kelvin.'

'Ralston's sons.'

'The same, sir.'

'You mean there were only three genuine guests?'

'Put that way, I suppose so, sir, yes.'

'Well, put it any way, Fussock, and give me their names.'

'Right you are, sir. There was Squire Cotterell over Braughing way, young Miss Ratcliffe from St Albans and Mr Hands from Hertingfordbury.'

'The gentlemen were unaccompanied?'

'Oh, yes sir. As you'd expect.'

Lestrade's eyes narrowed on an inspectorly glint. 'We would?' he said quietly.

'Well, it was ... oh dear, this is disloyalty and no mistake, but you'd find out anyway. Squire, he had something of a reputation.'

'With women, you mean?' George asked.

'Not so much with them as in front of them, sir,' Fussock explained.

'What?' Lestrade was perplexed.

'He lacked the social graces, sir. And of late, things had got worse.'

'In what way, worse?' Lestrade was afraid to hear the answer.

'Well, he'd pick his nose, sir,' Fussock explained. 'What began as a discreet tweak with a napkin while he pretended to retrieve a fallen fork became an index finger buried to the knuckle in an obfuscated nostril. And he'd break wind, particularly in the evenings after his favourite dish of Gentleman's Relish and anchovies. Twenty years ago he'd wander into the Orangery or at least scowl at one of the dogs. Latterly, he'd simply raise a cheek and let rip. Then, there was the spitting ...'

'Yes,' Lestrade held up an already horrified hand, 'I think we get the picture, Fussock, thank you. So no women. And yet this Miss Ratcliffe came.'

'Yes, sir. That was odd.'

'Miss Ratcliffe?'

'Her coming. And indeed her going.'

'Tell me more,' Lestrade commanded..

'Well, sir, the invitation was actually addressed to her father, the Admiral.'

'Admiral Ratcliffe?' George was a stickler for accuracy.

'The very same, sir.'

'You'll find him in Hart's *Navy List*, George,' Lestrade waved the butler on.

'Ah, not any more, sir.' That's why Miss Ratcliffe attended the Master's party and not her father.'

'Dead?' Lestrade ventured.

'Not a week since, sir,' Fussock told him. 'No sooner had I sent young Davy off on his bicycle than the Master read it in *The Times*. Laughed till he broke wind, he did.'

'What happened to him?' Lestrade asked.

'Oh, he was all right after a while, sir, when the air had cleared.'

'No, I mean the Admiral.'

'Oh, he keeled over on the deck of HMS *Pointless*, sir. Heart.'

'Do I gather, then, from Squire Ralston's reaction to the Admiral's death, he didn't care for the man?'

'Bitter enemies, sir, from years ago. Hanged if I know why.'

'And yet he invited his bitter enemy to a party?'

'And the others, sir - he didn't care for Squire Cotterell or Mr Hands either.'

'We'll get to them later. Why did you find Miss Ratcliffe odd?'

'Well, first, sir, that she came at all. Pretty as a picture, she was. Very becoming, isn't it? Black on a woman? The only one I've not known it suit was old Lady de Vere's maid.'

'Why so?'

'She was black too, sir. Sort of disappeared in a way. But Miss Ratcliffe, she was very becoming. No sooner had I got over the shock of her arriving, what with her dad barely cold, when I announced her and she and the Master went off in here, sir. Into the library.'

'What was odd about that?'

'Well, it was the noises, sir,' Fussock shifted from foot to foot, the embarrassment of it clear in his mind.

'Gentleman's relish and anchovies?' George enquired.

'No, sir. The shouting. I've never heard language like it.'

'The squire was annoyed?' Lestrade asked.

'He was, sir, but it was Miss Ratcliffe to whom I was referring.

It would've made a rating blush. I had to send Mrs Fussock below. She'd have had one of her flushes if she'd stayed.'

'When did Miss Ratcliffe leave?'

'It would have been about half past nine, sir. She'd been there nearly half an hour. It was what she said to me as she left; I'll never forget it.'

'What was it?' Lestrade asked.

'Well, sir, she looked me in the eye, this slip of a girl and she said to me - 'If I were a man, I'd have called that conniving bastard out tonight. You'd be scraping him off the lawn tomorrow." Not very ladylike, is it, sir?'

'No, Fussock,' Lestrade agreed. 'But then, neither is murder.'

The doors crashed back at that moment and two men of Lestrade's vague age hurtled in, arguing furiously. At their first sight of the policemen, they stopped.

'Who the devil are these two, Fussock?' the taller one demanded.

Lestrade and George clambered to their feet and stared in disbelief. Were it not for the difference in height, the two could pass as brothers.

'Ah, young Master Ian, young Master Kelvin, this is Inspector Lestrade and Sergeant George from Scotland Yard.'

'The Yard, eh? Well, you're a threat late, gentlemen. All right, Fussock, get out. And take Master Kelvin with you, will you; it's way past his bedtime.'

'Just bugger off, Fussock,' Kelvin snarled at his brother. 'But make sure there's nothing sharp lying about for Master Ian. You know he isn't allowed sharp objects.'

The brothers Ralston squared up to each other, their white scarves tangling and their topper brims colliding.

'Gentlemen, please!' Lestrade was referee for the evening.

'Mind your own business!' the Ralstons snapped in unison. Even their voices were identical.

'Murder is my business!' Lestrade thundered.

The brothers grim broke apart, Ian to the brandy, Kelvin to the Scotch.

'Well,' Ian was the first to break the silence, 'what have you found out? Who killed my father?'

'Our father,' Kelvin reminded him.

'That's all we need,' moaned George, 'The Lord's Prayer.'

'Who is this oaf, Lestrade?' the younger brother by a few minutes demanded. 'I don't care for his impertinence.'

'Neither do I,' Lestrade admitted. 'But this is not germane to a murder enquiry. Master ... Kelvin, is it?'

'It is.'

'When did you see your father last?'

'This morning,' Ralston said. 'And I didn't like the look of him.'

'No,' Lestrade tried all the patience he could muster, 'I mean alive; when did you last see him alive?'

'Hm,' the younger Ralston frowned, clutching his cut glass. 'It would have been at that so-called bash of his - last Saturday.'

'The night he died,' Lestrade said.

'He was perfectly all right when I left him,' Kelvin insisted.

'You were there, Dog-breath, you saw it.'

'I saw nothing, dear boy,' Ian glided past in icy fraternity.

'But had I been near the lake shortly after midnight, I'd have seen you bending an iron bar over the old bastard's head.'

'You'll take that back, you lying swine!' Kelvin grabbed his collar, but George was faster and separated them.

'All right, all right,' he muttered. 'Move along there.'

'You seem very sure, Mr Ralston,' Lestrade turned to the elder Master, 'about the time and manner of your father's death. Now let's all sit down calmly and discuss this, shall we, like rational human beings?'

'Not likely!' snorted Kelvin, but he sat down anyway.

'Impossible!' Ian retaliated, but he did likewise.

'Good,' Lestrade perched on the cold arm of a Chesterfield between them. 'That's much better. Now, Mr Ralston. How do you know the time of your father's death and what was used to kill him?'

'I don't,' Ian said. 'That was what the police told us. And bearing in mind this is the Hertfordshire Constabulary we're talking about, my father was probably riddled with Cherokee arrows in the middle of the afternoon.'

'Do I assume you gentlemen don't live here at Ralston Hall?' Lestrade asked.

'Good God, no,' snorted Kelvin. 'I haven't lived here since I was thirteen. Charterhouse, Trinity, anywhere but here. Still, it's all mine now.'

'Bollocks it is!' Ian bellowed. 'There's a will somewhere and I'll find it if I have to raze this hell-hole to the ground.'

Lestrade's quietly waving arm seemed to pacify them, at least for the moment. 'So you both came to his party?'

'Yes,' said Ian. 'The invitation spoke of a killing ... Perhaps he was inviting us to his?' he said as though the thought had only just occurred to him.

'We wanted to make sure, Inspector,' Kelvin said, 'that we got our share. You see it was perfectly in keeping with our father to disinherit both of us, if he felt so inclined. He'd threatened it often enough.'

'So we came just to make sure whatever extra he'd got from the City came our way.'

'Sooner rather than later in your case, eh, Ian?' the younger Ralston sneered.

Lestrade interrupted the riposte. 'Did either of you see a Miss Ratcliffe that night?'

'Rather,' leered Ian. 'Rather a corker, I thought.'

'She told father where to stick it in no uncertain terms,' Kelvin recollected.

'They had a row?' Lestrade checked. In a policeman's world, confirmation was next to godliness.

'Fair made the glass shake in the orangery. Mind you, the old bastard had it coming.'

'What was the row about?'

'No idea,' Ian shrugged. 'But that doesn't matter. The old bastard had it coming.'

'Just a moment,' Kelvin broke in. 'Are you suggesting that Jane Ratcliffe killed father?'

Lestrade looked at the terrible twins under his eyebrows. 'It had occurred to me,' he rumbled.

'Oh, come on,' Ian chuckled. 'We've known Jane Ratcliffe since she was in nappies.'

'Does that mean she's incapable of murder?' Lestrade asked.

'Incapable, no,' the elder Ralston contended. 'But young broth and I play the stock market, Lestrade, and we usually win. We're used to calculating all sorts of odds and the reckoning in the City is that a gentleman not a million miles from this room is the guilty party.'

'Fussock!' George snapped his fingers with the joy of a man who's discovered the end of a rainbow.

'Rubbish,' Kelvin mumbled. 'Fussock hasn't an antisocial bone in his body. Besides, he was utterly devoted to the old skinflint whose surging loins produced us - God knows why. He'd virtually ask the old man if it was all right to breathe.'

'Well, there you are,' George wouldn't let go of it. 'Mr Lestrade and I worked on the Despatch Case last year. The murderer turned out to be just such a sycophant. Grovelling, bobbing, toadying. Then one day he went for his master's eyeballs with a pair of sugar tongs.'

'No, I wasn't referring to Fussock, sergeant,' Ian said coldly.

George stroked his considerable chin. 'Well, allowing for the fact that Mr Lestrade and I are pure as the driven in this matter, unless this amounts to a confession...'

'... which it does not.'

'Then you must mean .

All eyes turned to the younger Ralston.

'For God's sake, not even Scotland Yard can be that stupid!'

Kelvin roared, 'I just told you, Ian and I were together when I saw Father last.'

'Come, come, brother dear,' Ian sneered. 'We only have your word for that; the word of a charlatan and mountebank of the worst water.'

'You lying bum roll!' the younger Ralston was on his feet again.

'Please, Misters Ralston,' Lestrade mediated once more. 'Mr Ralston senior', he turned to the elder by several minutes, 'where was your father when you saw him last that night?'

'He was in the Orangery. This was a little after eleven thirty.'

'Did you notice anything odd about him?'

Ian shrugged. 'Only the smell,' he said. 'I suspected the ptarmigan patties.'

Lestrade always did. That's why he'd never tried one. 'What did you do then?'

'I didn't fancy the drive back to town and the last train had gone. I called it a day and slept in the Green Room.'

'That's ...' Lestrade tried to get his bearings.

'At the back of the house, next to Father's.'

'Overlooking the lake?'

'That's right.'

'You didn't, I suppose, happen to look out of your bedroom window a little after midnight?'

'Sadly, no,' Ian said. 'Had I done so, however, we all know who I would have seen, iron bar in hand.'

'I slept in the Pink Room,' Kelvin ignored the slur. 'Like pea brain here, I thought it too late to go back to town.'

'What time did you retire?' Lestrade asked.

'About one, I suppose.'

'After your father's demise?' Lestrade arched an eyebrow.

'After the police say he died, yes, but you must remember, Inspector, his body was not found until dawn the next day.'

'By Constable Spatchcock?'

'Is that his name?' Kelvin yawned. 'Forgive me, but all you police chappies look alike.'

'Yes,' nodded Lestrade, without smiling. 'It's the pointed head that does it. Is it Fussock's custom to lock the house at night?'

'Tyndall does that, the under-butler.'

'And he did it that night?'

'I've no idea,' Kelvin said. 'You'll have to ask him.'

'We intend to,' Lestrade told him.

'Actually, all this is pointless,' Ian suddenly said, crossing to freshen his glass.

'Why so, cretin?' his brother asked.

'Because, after you and I spent that perfectly pointless half an hour with old Lammergeyer ...'

'Old Lammergeyer?' Lestrade interrupted.

'Benson Lammergeyer,' Ralston explained, 'the family solicitor at St Albans. Limited Intellect here and I went to sort out Father's finances once and for all.'

'No help?'

'None whatever,' Kelvin cut in. 'Benson Lammergeyer is to soliciting what Dan Leno is to Greek Tragedy. Actually, it's not the old fossil's fault. Father, it transpired, owed more money than the National Debt. No, the reason that it is pointless is that I expect the murderer', and his beady eyes swivelled sideways to his brother, 'to be brought to book by the weekend.'

'Now that we're on the case, you mean?' George nodded.

'Now that I have hired a team of private detectives,' Ian smiled.

'No!' Kelvin roared. 'Who?'

'Do you think I'd tell you that?' Ian snapped.

'Well,' his little brother bridled, 'they're bound to be inferior to the team I've hired.'

'You've hired!' Ian shouted. 'Where did you find them?'

'St Albans,' his brother smiled.

Ian frowned. 'Is one of these detectives of yours tall, with an aquiline nose and a deerstalker hat?'

'Fortunately, no,' said Kelvin. 'He is squat, has a small moustache and is on the portly side. I wasn't fooled by his appearance, though. Under his overcoat bulged a Webley Mark I if I'm any judge.'

'Er ... gentlemen,' Lestrade interrupted, 'did I understand that you have each engaged a team of private detectives?'

'We did,' the brothers chorused.

'How many in your team, Mr Ralston?'

'Two,' Ian answered. 'I never saw the other man.'

'And in yours, Mr Ralston?'

'Two,' Kelvin told him. 'Likewise, I did not meet his partner.'

Lestrade shook his head. 'Gentlemen, I fear you have hired the selfsame team.'

'What?' the Ralstons roared in unison.

'The tall one with the nose and the silly hat is Mr Sherlock Holmes. His partner in crime, as it were, the short one with the gun - and I shall be checking his licence for that, by the way - is his confidant, Dr John Watson.'

There was a stunned silence.

'Well,' said Ian, 'I've got to hand it to you, Lestrade. Your powers of detection are phenomenal.'

'Which is rather what I suspect Sherlock Holmes told you his were. Am I right?'

'Brilliant!' Ralston eulogized.

'Elementary,' Lestrade shrugged. 'It's what he tells everybody. Actually, I'm not sure he should be walking about. Presumably that's where Watson comes in, sees to his medication and so on.'

'Well, there you are,' Kelvin said. 'Trust you to pick some deranged idiot, brother.'

'It looks as though we'll have to rely on the Yard after all,' Ian fumed. 'It's a bit bloody dishonest of this Holmes and Watson to offer their services to us both. They must have known we were brothers. They must have colluded.'

'I've no evidence about that,' Lestrade said. 'I've always assumed they have separate bedrooms at Baker Street. Besides, it's the sort of thing that would appeal to Mr Holmes, the intrigue of being briefed by identical brothers. I always said he was mad as a speckled band.'

Lestrade got to his feet. 'Sergeant George and I will need to talk to you again, gentlemen. Please give him your town addresses. I need to talk to the rest of the staff.'

The Ralstons had been right about one thing at least. Old Benson Lammergeyer was no help at all. That was because his office was shut and all the caretaker knew was that he was in the South of

France and wouldn't be back for some time because he had retired. The rest of Squire Ralston's staff were as much use as a colander in a flash flood. Only Mrs Fussock shared her husband's doting on the dead master. Everybody else hated his guts.

A weak February sun sent its rays flat against the south east facets of the Abbey, its solid Norman tower marking the spot where Alban, the first Christian martyr, had so fatally upset his garrison commander. Lestrade and George had spent the rest of the morning locating the Woolpack, the hotel where Holmes and Watson were staying, and then booked into the Pea-Hen.

They decided against the George in case it caused confusion.

They found Constable Matthew Spatchcock on his old beat along Fishpool Street, the one he used to have before they transferred him, temporarily, to Artificial Waterways. He was plodding along at two and a half miles an hour on the raised pavement where the medieval pilgrims had padded north to the city's western gate long years ago. He was a little older than Inspector Towgrass had led them to believe and years of sampling McMullen's best when he was stationed at Hertford had caused him to let out his belt a notch or two. There were introductions all round.

'So you found the body, Spatchcock?' Lestrade asked.

'I did, sir. Not a pretty sight, I can tell you.'

'Tell us about it.'

'Well sir, in the dawn's early light I thought the Squire 'ad 'ad another island built. Then I realized it was movin', driftin' with the tide so to speak.'

'It's not a tidal lake up at the Hall, is it?'

'Not exactly, sir,' Spatchcock said, 'seein' as 'ow the sea is near on fifty miles away. It's just the flow of the river. The fourteenth squire 'ad it widened by Capability Brown and deepened by Possibility Adams, Dredger to 'Is Late Majesty King George IV.'

'Ah, yes, you were on Waterways, weren't you?'

'Until two days ago, sir, yes. I knows the Avon and Kennet like the back o' my 'and. Still, I'm not sorry to be orff o' all that. Didn't do much for my feet I can tell you. An' the missis is pleased - no more darnin' an' lancin' chilblains.'

George had no idea that people darned chilblains, but then he'd never served time in the Hertfordshire constabulary.

'So checking the lake at Ralston Hall was routine, then?' Lestrade asked.

'Yes, sir. First port of call of the day. Fair shook me up, I can tell you. I mean, prams, bath chairs, the odd dead dog or cat but a 'uman bein', we only ever 'ad one o' them on the Avon and Kennet. Some old bloke who got tipsy and fell in. That weren't pretty neither. Got sluiced to death he did.'

'What did you do when you found Squire Ralston?'

'Blew my bloody whistle - oh, beggin' your pardon, sir. Do you think they're any better, these whistles? I'm a simple man myself. I likes the old rattle.'

Lestrade nodded. Nostalgia wasn't what it used to be, but deep down he too preferred the rattle of a simple man.

'Well, it was 'alf an hour before somebody came. Old Mellors, the Squire's gamekeeper. Together we fished him out.'

'What did you make of the state of the body?'

Spatchcock shrugged. 'I'm no detective, sir,' he admitted.

'Chief Inspector Towgrass speaks highly of you,' Lestrade told him.

'Well, sir,' Spatchcock tipped his helmet to some passing ladies, 'that's nice of him, sir, but I knows my place.'

'Your best guess, then,' Lestrade harried his man. 'Was the water frozen?'

'No, sir. For all it was a raw night, the frost had cleared by mornin'. But the Squire 'e was like a lump o' rock.'

'Rigor,' said Lestrade.

'Thank you, sir,' Spatchcock smiled proudly. 'I does me best. No, 'e was stiff as a pig's pego in the Spring, sir - oh, beggin' your pardon.'

Lestrade waved the agricultural simile aside. 'What was he wearing when you found him floating?'

'A dinner jacket, sir. White tie and tails.'

'You went through his pockets?'

'No, sir.' Spatchcock stopped patrolling. 'Why on earth should I do that? I know'd who 'e was.'

'What about the wound?'

'Ooh, nasty sir, that. The back of 'is 'ead was stove in. I dunno by what, but somethin' 'eavy.'

'Inspector Towgrass seems to think it was an iron pipe.'

'Well, there it is then, sir,' Spatchcock walked on, a Yard man at each elbow.

'Did you find it?'

'What's that, sir?'

'The iron pipe?' Lestrade's gaze met George's over the constable's helmet.

'No, sir. Mr Towgrass 'ad divers down in the lake for a couple of days, but we didn't 'ave the happaratus and the blokes was gettin' fearful cold. 'E called it off.'

'Did you know the Squire, Constable?'

'Only to wave to, sir. I'd only met 'im once or twice, on the waterways patrol, you know.'

'Constable, I wanted to talk to you,' a young lady in a black day dress with a matching muff and parasol had crossed the road to them.

'Oh, mornin', Miss Ratcliffe,' the constable saluted. 'I was so sorry to 'ear about your old dad, Miss. Didn't suffer, I 'ope.'

'No, Constable,' she smiled. 'He went as he would have wished to go - unconscious.'

The constable nodded. 'Oh, may I introduce...'

'No need, Constable,' Lestrade interrupted. 'You're a busy man, what with your beat and everything. Off you patrol now. I'm sure we can answer Miss Ratcliffe's questions.'

'I'm sure you cannot, sir,' she watched Spatchcock's dark blue frame march steadily into the distance of Verulamium where elms wreathed the mill. 'And I'll thank you not to use my name until I know yours.'

Lestrade looked at her. She was, as the Ralstons had said, a corker. Her golden hair was swept up under the feathered black of the hat and her eyes shone in the noonday sun with a reflective brilliance. For all her mourning, there was a smile that played elusively around her lips. It made Sergeant George adjust his tie.

'I am Inspector Sholto Lestrade,' he told her, 'Scotland Yard. This is Sergeant George.'

'I see,' she said. 'But I fail to...'

'We've been assigned to the case of the late Squire Ralston,' Lestrade explained.

'Bastard!' the Yard men heard her hiss.

'I beg your pardon?' Lestrade frowned.

'He was a bastard, Inspector,' she said levelly. 'Forgive me, but I have a rendezvous in town. Will you walk this way?'

George for one didn't have the anatomy to walk anything like that way, but walking with Miss Ratcliffe was certainly preferable to patrolling with Spatchcock.

'Do I gather you were not altogether fond of the late Squire, Miss?' Lestrade asked.

'I would cheerfully have shot him,' she told him frankly.

'Or bent an iron bar over his head, Miss?' George threw in.

'No,' she said. 'It would be a lie if I said otherwise. Someone else did that for him. And if I ever meet him, I'll shake him by the hand.'

'What was the cause of your dislike, Miss Ratcliffe?' Lestrade asked.

'He swindled my father, Inspector. Cheated him out of some consoles - the old man's life savings.'

'I understood that your father was an admiral,' Lestrade said.

'So he was. But he retired years ago. I was the youngest in the family by a long way. My brothers and sisters are all married and living overseas.'

'You're not married, Miss?' George took the opportunity to confirm.

'No, sergeant, I'm not and before you come out with some appalling claptrap like "I can't imagine why not", it's because I have yet to meet a man who is my equal in terms of intellect. I believe I may this afternoon.'

Both Lestrade and George took that to mean each of them and they swept on through the open park of Romeland where only the swish of the headmaster's cane from the school in the old gatehouse marred the late morning.

'My father had always dabbled,' she told them. 'Even as a midshipman under Codrington he was always gilt-edged. He'd known Osbaldeston Ralston since they were cadets together. The vicious old reprobate had always secretly hated my father. He was always egging him on into dangerous speculations and risky investments. Usually, my father avoided him, but of late, well, I don't know. I suppose he got greedy. But stupidly he still trusted Ralston. He was a loving, trusting man. And Ralston killed him for it.'

'Literally?' Lestrade asked.

'Oh, no,' her face was hard and cold. 'Ralston didn't have the brass neck for that. He simply robbed my father blind. It was the shock that killed him.'

'How much money are we talking about', Lestrade asked, 'if I may ask?'

'You may ask, Inspector,' she said. 'It was over one hundred thousand pounds.'

Lestrade had turned as pale as Jane Ratcliffe. So had George George. 'I see,' he said.

They had stopped outside the Woolpack Hotel.

'So you went to have it out with Squire Ralston at his party?'

'Some party!' she snorted. 'I've had more fun having my appendix out. There were two old duffers mouldering in a corner and those unspeakable children of his.'

'The boys Ian and Kelvin?'

'Twisted offspring of a degenerate line,' she said. 'I knew I'd get no help there. Do you suppose they did it? Killed their father, I mean?'

'I'm afraid we rather had the same thought about you, Miss Ratcliffe,' Lestrade confessed.

She shook her head smiling. 'No,' she said, 'I gather there was too much of his head left for. it to have been me. I tell you, gentlemen, that Saturday night was about the only time I've ever wished I was a man. Now, if you'll excuse me', she swept up the steps, 'I have a meeting with the World's Greatest Detective.'

'Who?' chorused Lestrade and George.

'I believe he calls himself Sherlock Holmes,' she said. 'I have retained him to trace my father's fortune. It's not the money, you understand, but the principle.'

'Yes, well,' Lestrade grinned in the chilly air, 'one of those Mr Holmes has in plenty.'

4

They had found him in the street as the first dawn of March lifted over the Villas of Lisson Grove. He lay sprawled on the flight of steps that led to the cellar of the King Arthur, a gent in his late forties, nattily attired in astrakhan coat and wideawake. His wallet was gone and what had probably been a gold tie pin had been ripped from its moorings. As Lestrade and George looked down, they saw his false teeth lying on the pavement and the railings above him daubed with his blood.

'Yesterday, South Mimms; today, Marylebone,' the sergeant muttered, only now coming to terms with the cold and the hour.

'Isn't that why you joined?' the Inspector asked him 'to see the world? Notebook, George. I'm only going to be able to bend this leg the once.'

He crouched as best he could while above him a clutch of constables was busy tying the blue cordon and moving on the odd nosy party who happened to be stirring with the lark. Lestrade eased back the coat flaps. 'Fully clothed,' he said. He fumbled through pockets. 'One ticket for the Lyceum. What's on, George? You're a theatre-goer.'

'Er ... *Babes in the Wood*, sir. Still the panto season.'

'Oh no, it isn't,' Lestrade countered.

'Oh yes it is,' George stood his ground.

Lestrade continued the search. 'Aha.'

'A clue, sir?'

'No, I haven't got one. It's a letter of rejection.'

'What, some woman's turned him down?' George looked at the pulverised head. 'Most determined suicide I ever saw.'

'No, not that kind of rejection. It's from a publisher, turning down an author.'

George shook his head. 'Still the most determined suicide I ever saw.' He clicked his tongue. 'Not the end of the world, I wouldn't have thought, having a book turned down.'

'I don't know,' Lestrade said, having harboured no literary ambitions at all. 'I seem to remember you being a bit cut up last year when they didn't use your Disraeli sketch for the Police Revue.'

'Ah, that was different, guv. That was sheer waste of talent.'

'No wallet,' Lestrade had moved on, tilting the corpse as best he could. 'No watch. The tie's ripped. Whoever did this probably tore it off to get at the pin.'

'Simple hit-and-run, then,' George assumed.

'There's never anything simple about murder, George,' Lestrade reminded his partner. 'You know that. And Tom Berkeley's not a man to send for the Yard for no purpose.'

The Inspector of that name was alighting from a station wagon above them as Lestrade spoke.

'Pass me those teeth, will you? If there's a gold one still in the gum, we've got to get our thinking caps on. Who found the body?'

'Up here, sir,' a constable called from the railings.

Lestrade hobbled up to him with the aid of George and the deceased's left leg.

'Mr Dickson, sir, a carter.'

'Mr Dickson ...' Lestrade caught sight of Tom Berkeley ducking under the cordon. 'One moment, if you please. Tom, how long's it been?'

'Too long, Sholto,' the Inspectors shook hands. 'Been in the wars again?' He threw a glance at Lestrade's leg.

'"Black Monday",' he said.

'I heard about that,' Berkeley said. 'Bloody fine bit of policing.'

'Thanks. How's the family?'

'Mildred says - and I quote - "When are you coming over to finish that dinner, Sholto Lestrade? The custard's nearly cold!"'

'God, yes. I was called away, wasn't I? A rape in Coldharbour Lane. When was that?'

'Three years ago.'

'Ah. How's little Fanny?'

'Not so little these days. Do you know, she was twelve last week?'

'Get away!'

'Pretty as a picture.'

'I'm sure of it. She'll be courting any day now.'

'Not until I've vetted him first. Anyway, you know you're the only man in her life, Sholto.'

The Yard man slapped him across the shoulder. 'Go on with you, I'm old enough to be her father!'

'Yes,' laughed Berkeley. 'So am I. Now, to business. Bad one, this. As soon as I got the word, I thought of you. You made good time.'

'Better than you think. We were actually in St Albans when your telegram arrived, passed on by the Yard. It pains me to say it, but we do have the best postal service in the world, you know.'

'You'd better have a look at this, sir,' the sergeant called from the steps.

'Tom, you know George George.'

'Yes, how've you been, George?'

'Better, sir, thank you.'

'Bit of an altercation with a locked door at Mevagissey a couple of weeks ago,' Lestrade whispered to his old friend.

'Playing the whingeing detective at the moment.'

Berkeley nodded. It was a rôle he knew well.

George handed Lestrade the deceased's false teeth. They lay cold and clammy in the palm of his hand, flecked with blood. Something else lay with them, screwed up into a ball between the dentures. A piece of paper.

'Hello, hello, hello,' Lestrade muttered. He passed the teeth to Berkeley. 'Pity they can't chatter any more,' he observed. He unrolled the paper ball.

'What is it, Sholto?'

'Confirmation, Tom,' Lestrade said. 'Confirmation that you're a bloody good policeman. You did right to send for us. We've seen this somewhere before.'

Constable Albert 'Nutty' Slack stood at ease on Lestrade's threadbare carpet at the Yard, second floor back. One day, when he'd been at inspectorial level for fifteen years, he might gravitate to first floor front, but by then, they'd all have moved lock, stock and truncheon, down the Embankment to the Opera House and he could really spread his wings. And by that time, as Assistant Commissioner Rodney had recently reminded everyone with a memorandum, there would be nearly sixteen million horse-drawn vehicles on the roads. Still, the roses would do well.

'I'd offer you a chair, constable,' Lestrade said, 'but as you see, we're all rather huggermugger at the moment. Can you drink tea standing up?'

'I think so, sir. We get a lot of that in D Division.'

'Been there long?'

'Sixteen and a half years, sir, come Friday.'

'And how do you like working for Mr Berkeley?'

'Well, sir ...' the constable's face darkened.

'Speak out, man,' Lestrade felt the buckshot jump in his leg.

'Well, he's the salt o' the earth, sir, o' course, but he's a bit on the little and oft side.'

'Soft? What, on the lads?'

'No, sir,' Slack was sure. 'Hard as nails on us, he is - and rightly so. No, he's a bit soft on trassenoes for my liking.'

'Ah, it's the new approach, constable,' Lestrade told him. 'Softly, softly, catchee baddie. Now, I gather Lisson Grove is in your patch?'

'It is, sir. Know it like the back of my elastic band.'

'Your report, then.'

'Well, I was proceedin' in a sarf-easterly direction .

'That's down the Grove?'

'Yessir.'

'Ah, let me stop you there, constable. Detective Green here has been busy perfecting the constabulary art of tea-making since Sergeant George and I have been away. If I may say so myself, he's not half bad at it now. Get it down your weasel and stoat.'

'Thank you, sir,' Slack took the handleless cup with alacrity.

'I can't offer you a Bath Oliver to accompany it because Detective Tyrrell has not picked up the buying of biscuits with the same aptitude. Where is he, by the way, George?'

The sergeant stuck his head around a particularly large stack of shoe-boxes. 'Said he had a lead on the Carrick girl, sir, the one from Mevagissey.'

'Tsk,' muttered Lestrade, 'fancy allowing a little thing like police work to get in the way of life's essentials. Can you bear it dry?'

'Fine bevy, sir. Thank you, Mr Green.'

'My pleasure, Mr Slack,' the detective staggered past carrying a Remington of absurdly heavy proportions.

'So,' Lestrade went on, 'down Lisson Grove way. What was your beat roster?'

'I was filling in for Henry Blenkinsop, sir. He was down wiv his young 'uns.'

'His young 'uns?'

'Scarlet fever, sir.'

'Where's his trouble and strife?'

'Gone, sir.'

'Scarlet fever?'

'Houndsditch, sir. Wiv a winder-cleaner.'

'Ah. Even so, you know the beat?'

'Oh, yessir. I pass the King Arfur eighteen times on the road.'

'At what time did you find the body?'

'A Mr Dickson sir, 'e found it. That would be about six thirty.'

'You'd been on since midnight?'

'Yessir. Bleedin' cold it was, saving your presence.'

'What did you make of it?'

'Well, there was blood all along the railings and down the step. It's my guess that whoever 'it 'im did it along Lisson Grove, rahnd abaht Number 32 and 'e didn't finally go down until the pub.'

'The gate above the steps, the one that led to the cellars of the King Arthur, is that normally open?'

'On Wednesday mornin's, sir, yes. Delivery day. Old Dave at the Arfur always leaves it open so's the drayman can get in.'

'And what time is that?'

'Varies sir, but usually abaht seven.'

'All right, now think hard, constable.'

A furrow of effort appeared on the ancient face of 'Nutty' Slack. 'Ready, sir.'

'What time did you pass the Arthur before you bumped into the carter, Dickson?'

'That would be abaht ... ooh, six fifteen, sir.'

'You turn round below the Arthur?'

'Yessir, then proceed in a north-westerly direction.'

'Up the Grove?'

'That's right, sir.'

'So,' Lestrade tried to visualize the frog and toad in his mind. 'At the furthest point, how far are you away from the Arthur?'

'Ooh, I'd say abaht six hundred yards, sir.'

'Six hundred yards. Do you mind me asking, Slack, how old you are?'

'I'm sixty-one, sir. Retiring soon.'

'Good for you. Do you mind if we try a little experiment?'

'Sir?'

'Put your cup down and face the wall, there's a good chap. With your back to me. That's it.'

Lestrade bent down as best he could with a stiff leg and whispered into one of his drawers. George looked at him oddly.

'What did I say then, Slack?'

'You said "Put your cup down and face the ...'

'No, not then. I whispered something. What did I whisper?'

"'I'll be with you in apple-blossom time', sir.'

Lestrade smiled. 'And I didn't think you cared. One last thing, constable. You didn't, I suppose, see anybody? Lurking in the shadows, perhaps, under the stairs at the Arthur?'

'Not a soul, sir. I reckon chummie had scarpered long before I got there.'

'Yes,' sighed Lestrade, 'No doubt he had. Well, thank you, constable. I just wanted to clarify those few points from your report. Give my regards to Mr Berkeley.'

'Thank you, sir. I will, sir.' He saluted and saw himself out.

'What was all that abaht ... about, guv?' George asked.

'The Drawer Test?' Lestrade asked. 'First trick I learnt at the knee of old 'Dolly' Williamson back in the '70s, George. Whisper into a container of muffled paper and if anyone can hear you, they've got bloody good ears.'

'So, sir?'

'So that bothers me,' Lestrade chewed his pencil end. 'Hypothermical though this obviously is, George, if somebody swiped you several times around the head so hard that your false teeth fell out and your cranium caved in, wouldn't you scream, just a little?'

'The odd whisper might escape my lips, sir, yes,' George mused. 'Along with my false teeth of course.'

'Yes, perhaps it was just a whisper, then.'

'Why, sir?'

'Because if our fractured friend had screamed, Constable Slack, at six hundred yards away, would have been bound to have heard him. So would half of Lisson Grove, come to that.'

'That assumes, sir, that the deceased had full possession of his vocal cords at the time.'

'No sign of cut throat, was there?'

'No, I was thinking more of your laryngitis, sir. Lot of it about at the moment. Mr Abberline hasn't said a word in four days.'

'There's a blessing,' said Lestrade. 'All right, George. It's your shout at the Clarence in a few minutes. Before then, let's solve a crime or two. First, the ball of paper tucked neatly into the dentures of the deceased.'

'Placed there after death, sir.'

'How do we know?'

'The paper was almost dry, sir. It was a clear night, but no frost. And no trace of saliva.'

'Right, so whoever killed him left a calling card, viz and to wit the aforementioned. What is it?'

'Ah well, that's the sixty-four quid question, guv. It appears to be a drawing', and he looked at the crumpled paper again, 'of a series of squares, one inside the other.'

'And where've we seen it before?'

'In the pocket of Fussock, the butler at Ralston Hall, sir. He gave it to you in loo of a guest list the other day.'

'You sent the telegram?'

'An hour ago, sir. But I don't like it.'

'Sending telegrams? Fairly harmless pursuit, surely?'

'No, sir, tipping Fussock off. He'll do a runner, sure as eggs is eggs.'

'No he won't, George,' Lestrade perused the green board with its flappings of paper. 'It isn't that simple. Fussock had difficulty standing, I noticed, never mind stoving in the skull of two men twenty miles apart on two successive nights.'

'Are you not including the Reverend Rodney in the killer's list, guv?'

'I don't know,' Lestrade said. 'I had a word with Will Tattenham in the canteen over breakfast.'

'The bookie? What was he doing here?'

'His usual. Helping us with our enquiries. I asked him what were the chances of more than one person being responsible for these killings.'

'What did he reckon?'

'Well, you know Will. He wanted to know angles of blows,

positions of bodies, directions of blood stains, distances between crimes, etcetera, etcetera.'

'And then?'

'Then he said - "Two hundred and sixty-nine to one".'

'Well,' George raised both eyebrows, 'there's a comfort.'

'Come on,' Lestrade growled. 'We've faced worse odds than that! Remember the Pillow Case?'

'Do I ever! Sixteen thousand and forty-three to one.'

'The Justin Case?'

'Er ... Forty four thousand and eight.'

'The Case of the Lengthening Odds?'

'Er ... No, I've forgotten that one.'

So had Lestrade. 'Even so, you catch my drift. What's this?' he found a memorandum on his desk, tucked away under his teacup.

'Oh, that came while you were having a pee, sir. It's from Assistant Commissioner Rodney.'

'But he's got our report on his cousin.'

'This is on the Opera House torso, sir. Any breakthroughs, he wants to know.'

Lestrade aimed the missile carefully at the bin and missed. 'No,' he said. 'None whatever. But we're on to the bastard who knifed the Duke of Buckingham, tell him.'

'When was that, guv? Must have been before my time.'

'Mine too. 1625. Right, George. My throat tells me your shout at the pub is imminent. Let's assume that Rector Rodney is the first of the three. Let's look at the victims. Common ground?'

'All men,' George said. 'All middle aged.'

There was a pause.

'Is that it?'

'Well, we don't yet know who the third man is, sir.'

'No, that's true,' Lestrade said. 'But this', and he held up the letter he'd half-inched from the latest corpse, 'would seem to whittle it down to two. In effect, from the fact that there is no postmark on the envelope and that the envelope was sealed in his pocket, I think it whittles it down to one.'

'It does?'

'The letter is addressed to a Mr Archer of the Minories. It is written by a Mr Batchelor, of the *Quiver* magazine. It's my guess that our friend of the crushed cranium is the latter.'

'... And his murderer is Mr Archer!' George's fingers clicked at the sudden brilliance of it.

Lestrade sighed. 'I'll tell you what, George. That's enough sleuthing for one morning. You can buy me several drinks at the Clarence and then we'll go and see what the Minories look like in the spring, shall we?'

The Minories in the spring looked like the Minories at any other time of year. The raw cold and snows of February had given way to the gustier squalls of March, but the tall tenements precluded the wind and the Yard men found Number 89 without difficulty.

A florid man with a waxed moustache and a towel over his arm appeared at the tinkle of his door bell. 'What'll it be, gents? Trim? Short back and sides? Ah,' he caught sight of Lestrade's parchment features, 'the full facial, I see.'

'No, thanks,' Lestrade couldn't place the accent. 'We're looking for Mr Henry Archer.'

''Enry!' the florid man roared, 'ow many times 'ave I tol' you? No visitors at ze chop.'

'Sorry,' a rather ashen-faced man appeared from behind a faded curtain. Standing beside the barber himself, the two of them made an effective pole.

'Five minutes,' the barber snapped. 'That's all I geeve you.'

'Five minutes, Senor Alfonso, thank you. Thank you.'

He led them down a flight of stone steps into a basement kitchen of indescribable dinginess. In front of a green, spotted mirror stood a row of wigs of varying degrees of moth. Archer took up a pair of tweezers and began to work on one, threading horse hairs back into place in the half light.

'Please forgive him his rudeness, gentlemen,' he said. 'He's from Seville.'

'Ah, yes,' George said. 'That's where the oranges come from, isn't it?'

'Got a light, Mr Archer?' Lestrade asked, clamping a new Havana between his lips.

'Please,' the wig-maker shouted, then gentler. 'No naked flames here. It's the glue, you see. We'll all go up like a tinder box.'

George had wandered off to examine the ceiling.

'I am Inspector Lestrade of Scotland Yard,' Lestrade said, 'Sergeant George here ... there ... and I would like to ask you a few questions.'

'Oh? I thought you'd come about a wig.'

Lestrade ignored this slur on his tonsure. Obviously, what with the bowler and the half light, his leonine head of hair had passed the wig-maker by.

'George,' Lestrade muttered, 'what are you doing?'

'Sorry, guv'nor,' the sergeant scuttled to his side. 'I was reminded of old Sweeney Todd, you know. Looking for the apparatus that tipped the chairs from the floor above.'

'Yes, well, let's keep this within the bonds of plausibility, can we?' Lestrade said. It had been a long time since his days in the old H Division; he'd forgotten how many steps there were in Fournier Street. 'Mr Archer, do you know a man named Byngham Batchelor?'

The Inspector saw the wig-maker turn paler yet. 'Yes,' he said.

'In what capacity?'

'He ... was nearly ... might yet be my publisher.'

'Your publisher?'

'He works as an editor for the *Quiver*. Look, if it's about "The Flowers That Bloom In The Spring Tra La" I can explain.'

Lestrade eased himself down into a leather swivel. 'I wish you would,' he said. George put stub to paper, perched on the pile of old, well-thumbed *Graphics* in the corner.

'Well, it was more or less my story,' Archer's fingers fidgeted with the curls of the wig he was working on.

'More or less?' Lestrade's eyebrows raised a notch.

'Well, let's say it was an adaptation.'

'You submitted it to Mr Batchelor?'

'For inclusion in the April edition, yes. Oh dear, does this mean he doesn't like it?'

'Is it usual for editors to send Scotland Yard detectives if they don't like authors' work?'

'Well, no ... er ... I shouldn't think so. I'm rather new to all this.'

'Tell me, Mr Archer,' Lestrade pulled a letter from his inside pocket, resting the gammier of his legs on a handy stool, 'all modesty aside, how would you describe "The Flowers That Bloom In The Spring"?'

'Tra La,' George added.

'As my colleague so rightly says,' the Inspector smiled.

'Well, I don't know. It had its moments, I think. It's a little difficult...'

'You wouldn't, for example, call it "quite the most appalling piece of trash I've seen in twenty three years"?'

'Er ...'

'Nor yet "Reminiscent of the early Stevenson - George Stevenson"?'

'Um ...'

'Perhaps "Codswallop of an unprecedented type. Never have I seen such dreadful sentence construction, so weak a plot, such undelineated characters. The denouement is like chewing a wet rug." Familiar so far?'

Archer had sat down, visibly shaking, 'Perhaps it needs a little beefing up,' he said, but he even failed to convince himself.

Lestrade dropped the letter into his lap, 'Tell him, George,' he said.

'The body of Byngham Batchelor was found in Lisson Grove this morning,' the sergeant said, leaning towards his man. 'His head had been smashed in from behind. There was an awful lot of blood.'

'Oh my God!' Archer's voice was barely audible.

'Where were you, Mr Archer, at about six fifteen this morning?' Lestrade asked.

'Er ... here, in bed. I live at the back of the shop. Through there,' he pointed to a beaded curtain that led into a tiny alcove, barely big enough for a single bed.

'Were you alone?' Lestrade asked.

'Oh yes,' Archer said, obviously shocked that Lestrade could have thought otherwise.

'So we only have your word for that, don't we?' George said, cracking his knuckles in the time-honoured tradition.

'Um ... look,' Archer summoned up his courage from somewhere. 'You don't think I had a hand in this, do you?'

'A hand?' Lestrade chuckled. 'Oh no, Mr Archer, it's not your hand that interests us, it's your foot. Would you raise your left boot please?'

'My ... ?'and he did so.

'Oh dear,' Lestrade peered at it closely. 'What size do you take, Mr Archer?'

'Er ... size eight. Why?'

'Well, as my sergeant so gratuitously informed you a moment ago, there was an awful lot of blood at the scene of the murder. And going off in a south-easterly direction, as it were towards the Minories, was the crimson track of a size eight boot.'

The Yard men watched the epiglottis rise and fall, quickly followed by its owner, as the barber's assistant cum wig-maker crashed gracefully to the floor.

"Ey,' an accented voice called from above, "Enry, what ees going on? Your five minutes, zey are up. Gentlemens up 'ere want a shave.'

'All right, Senor Alfonso,' Lestrade called. 'Keep your hair on.' Then to George, 'all the same, these bloody Italians. Take advantage of the moment, George. Have a shufti around friend Archer's boudoir. There may be something that will help.'

'Right, sir,' George stepped over the prone prose-writer, 'I didn't know about those bloody footprints, by the way. D'you think we can nail him on that?'

'I shouldn't think so,' Lestrade rummaged through drawers. 'I made them up. Well, you never know. I've got confessions with less than that before now.'

'What are we looking for guv?' George felt compelled to ask.

'A miracle, sergeant,' sighed Lestrade, lighting his cigar with his own lucifer. 'A bloody miracle.'

It didn't of course compare with the Great Fire of Tooley Street; still less with the four-day conflagration that began in Pudding Lane and ended with Sir Christopher Wren laughing all the way to the bank. Even so, the blaze that began mysteriously in the basement of Senor Alfonso's Barber-And-Something-For-The-Weekend Shop in the Minories was one of the celebrated events of that year. No one, thankfully, was hurt. Senor Alfonso himself managed to drag his unconscious assistant to street level before the macassar-oil went up and the florid old Spaniard told the *Daily Standard* that it was just as well. If the fire had started any earlier, two Scotland Yard detectives on a routine enquiry might have gone up with the building.

Instead, by the time the bells were clanging and the brigade was thundering its way along Flower and Dean Street, those selfsame detectives were in Fleet Street, at the offices of the *Quiver* magazine.

'Ambrose Matters,' a rather dour individual stood before them.

'Er ... does it?' Lestrade felt constrained to ask.

'No, no,' a flicker of disbelief disturbed the clear eyes. 'I mean, I am Ambrose Matters.'

'Ah, of course. Inspector Lestrade and Sergeant George, Scotland Yard.'

'Ah, yes, poor Byngham. Of course, I half expected it. Will you take tea, gentlemen?'

'Thank you no, sir,' Lestrade answered for them both. 'But personally I'd kill for a seat.' He transferred his weight from one leg to the other.

'Yes, of course. How crass of me. It can be a terrible thing, gout. Killed an old uncle of mine.'

The detectives lowered themselves into the leather of the chesterfield. George whipped out his notebook , CID for the use of.

'Did I hear you correctly, Mr Matters?' Lestrade checked, 'that you "half expected" the murder of Mr Batchelor?'

'Well, you know how it is. A young life cut short in the bloom of manhood's pride.'

'I would put Mr Batchelor at forty-eight or so,' Lestrade said.

'Well, there you are. He'd had one brilliant success, but was on the way to another with his latest piece.'

'Forgive me, Mr Matters,' the Inspector said, 'but I understood that the late Mr Batchelor was an editor.'

'A sub-editor, yes. The Quiver can only have one editor, Mr Lestrade - without wishing in any way to be pretentious; *moi.*'

'So he was a brilliantly successful sub-editor?'

'As sub-editors go, he was competent; no more. But as a writer, in his own right, he could have been another Wilkie Collins - Dickens even.'

'Wilkie Collins?' Lestrade was unfamiliar with that name. Dickens of course was a household word.

'The crime writer and novelist. Funnily enough, Byngham had been to see him last night at his house in Blandford Square.'

'That's around the corner from Lisson Grove, guv,' George chirped.

'Thank you, sergeant,' hissed Lestrade, 'ever my faithful gazetteer. Do you know why?'

'Why yes. Mr Collins had been kind enough to submit a piece for the magazine. He doesn't get about much any more so Byngham went to him - oh, a few minor editorial changes.'

'What sort of man was Byngham, Mr Matters? Was he, for instance, married?'

'No, no,' the editor lit a cigar, but declined to offer one to his visitors. 'Batchelor by name and bachelor by nature.'

Lestrade raised an eyebrow. 'He ... er ... didn't... er... incline, did he?'

'Incline?'

'Well, what I mean is, did he have preferences?'

'If you mean was he a pederast, Mr Lestrade, why not come straight out with it?'

'Very well,' said Lestrade, now that the air had cleared. 'Was he a pederast?'

'How dare you suggest such a thing!' Matters roared. 'The *Quiver* is a family magazine, Mr Lestrade, lovingly conceived in the ethic of Protestant work and Christian brotherhood. I leave it to Truth to employ all manner of deviants. You only have to look at Henry Labouchere ...' he stopped suddenly, leaning back and the purple veins ceased to throb in his forehead. 'But I digress. Byngham Batchelor was as straight as a die - I'd stake my reputation on it.'

'Forgive me, Mr Matters,' Lestrade changed tack. 'But we policemen don't get much time for reading - other than criminal record sheets that is. What is the great success that Mr Batchelor had?'

'It was two years ago,' the editor said. 'We published it in serial form first and then Blackwoods turned it into a book. Instant bestseller, of course. It was called *Record-globe*, an exciting parallel to our own universe but set at some indefinable time in the future.'

'Weird,' commented George.

'Brilliant,' countered Matters. 'It made Messrs Blackwood very rich men.'

'And Mr Batchelor,' Lestrade added.

'That too, of course. But Byngham was never interested in money, Mr Lestrade. "Ars Gratia Artis" was always his motto.'

Ever a chap of the first declension only, Lestrade had no choice but to accept that. 'I believe you mentioned his latest piece?'

'Indeed,' Matters fumbled through a drawer at his elbow. 'Here it is. A short story for the magazine. I have no doubt that he intended to flesh it out for a full-blown book. It's nothing short of a masterpiece, even better than his first and in a totally different style. For some reason, Byngham didn't like the title. He was very insistent that we should change it. But I think we'll keep it as it is for the April issue - "The Flowers That Bloom In The Spring... "'

'Tra La,' George added.

'How on earth did you know that?' Matters frowned.

'Intuition, sir,' the sergeant told him.

Lestrade took the manuscript, immaculately typed on a Remington. 'This has been immaculately typed on a Remington,' he observed.

'It's the way publishing's going, Mr Lestrade,' Matters said. 'I predict by 1992 we won't accept any more hand-written manuscripts; the processing of words is just too complicated. Mind you, I was quite happy to accept this in Byngham's own hand, but he wouldn't hear of it. Said it would strain my eyes, didn't want to be a burden, etc etc. That was the sort of chap Byngham was.' He trumpeted editorially into a handkerchief. 'We shall miss him round here.'

'Was he a kind man, Mr Matters?'

'Kind?' Matters echoed. 'Kind and considerate in the extreme.'

'If, for instance, he had to reject a writer, turn down a piece, he'd do it gently?'

'"The quality of mercy is not strained", Inspector. You've no idea the rubbish sent in to us by members of the public, but it is my policy, as it was Byngham's, to deal gently with the idiots. Funnily enough, I had a puerile piece from a policeman the other day - a Constable Walter Dew, I believe. Know him?'

Lestrade and George shook their heads.

'Just as well. With a style like his, his only hope of publication is to catch a famous murderer. Which is what I presume you gentlemen are hoping to do.'

'In theory, sir,' Lestrade nodded.

'Well, I wish you luck, gentlemen. A good man like Byngham Batchelor could have had no personal enemies, but there must be thousands out there who envied his fame. Good morning.'

And they saw themselves out.

Night came to the city as it did with extraordinary regularity. The lamplighters shouldered their poles and trudged home through the gutters, while the gay whirl of Theatreland opened up and the streets became congested anew with cabriolets and landaus and gigs. A routine Thursday, March 1886. Monro was still in his Heaven and all was nearly all right with the world. Even the new Opera House was showing signs of being finished before the end of the century. Its bricks rose waist high in the black of the evening.

'Right then, Tyrrell,' George lolled back in the guv'nor's chair now that the guv'nor had gone home. 'Tell me again about Emily Carrick.'

'Well, I never saw her, sir ... er ... sarge.'

'No, I realize that, lad, but even so.'

'Well, Pad and I ... that is, Constable Green and I sorted through nearly four thousand carters, sir.'

'Yes, yes, you'll get no medals for that around here, sonny. It's routine policework. Paper, paper and more paper. And when you've finished that, it's the shoeboxes. Sixty-three thousand known felons operating in the Greater London area. And when you've sifted that lot it's the shoe leather - miles and miles of bleeding pavements; not to mention your bleeding feet.'

'Quite. Well, anyway, sarge, having done all that, we located the Carricks at Number 24 Jacob's Street, Bethnal Green.'

George rocked back, aghast. 'You went into the Nichol? On your own?'

'Well, Pad... er... Green was with me, sarge. Why? What's the Nichol?'

'It's a collection of streets in that Godforsaken parish, lad,' the sergeant told him. 'Old Nichol, New Nichol, Half Nichol. The Met only patrol there in fours. You had no trouble?'

'None, sir.'

George reached for the hipflask in Lestrade's top drawer, reserved for just such moments as these. 'Well, you're bloody lucky, son. The last man the guv'nor sent in there had to have his right leg off.'

'Blimey!'

'That's right,' George swigged. 'Wouldn't have been so bad, but he'd already lost his left one at Sebastopol. Which reminds me', he put the flask away, 'I'd better leave off this before I end up legless too. What about the Carricks, then?'

'Well, he was a bit funny, the old man.'

'In what way?'

'He wouldn't talk to us at all. So we had a go at his missus. Well, in between the tears, it perspired that her daughter...'

'Emily.'

'Emily ... she was expecting an unhappy event.'

'The Reverend Rodney's unhappy event?'

'Nobody'd say. I got the distinct impression, sarge, that the Carricks are Godfearing people who couldn't abide the shame of their only child being in the family way out of wedlock.'

It's common enough,' George shrugged, ever the guardian of the nation's morals. 'This is 1886 for Christ's sake.'

'Ah, but the Carricks are of the Methodist persuasion, sarge. That makes the difference.'

'If you say so. So how did you find out about the girl?'

'A neighbour - in the tenement below. She said two huge blokes in white coats came and took her away one night soon after the Carricks had moved in.'

'Took her away to where?'

'She didn't know, sarge. But the wagon they bundled her into had "Colney Hatch Asylum" painted on the side.'

'It's common enough,' George shrugged again. 'If you was to have a shufti through any asylum in the country, you'd find half the inmates were wayward girls like Emily Carrick, Tyrrell.'

'But she's not a loony. sarge,' the rookie protested.

'Neither are you,' countered George, 'but you work for the Metropolitan Police. Enough said?'

'Er ... I suppose so, sarge.'

'Right.' George tapped the side of his nose. 'The guv'nor will want that report in triplicate before you go home tonight. Savvy?'

'Savvy, sarge,' the constable moaned.

'Right then. Best be at it. Oh and Tyrrell...'

'Yes sarge?'

'Well done. Good bit of basic policework. I'm proud of you boys.'

'Thanks, sarge,' and the constable almost skipped out of the guv'nor's office.

'That's it,' George mused half to himself. 'Make 'em laugh, make 'em cry, make 'em work.'

Lestrade took the pretty way home via Number 38 Blandford Square, just around the corner from Lisson Grove. The door was opened by a fresh faced woman of about Lestrade's age, perhaps a shade younger.

'Not today, thank you,' she said, having decided that whatever Lestrade was selling, she'd already got plenty of it. She hadn't reckoned with the foot in the door, however, *Metropolitan Police Manual*, page sixty-one.

'Aarghh!' Lestrade had used the wrong leg.

'My dear man,' the woman caught him as he staggered. Beneath those mutton-chop sleeves bulged a deceptively powerful pair of biceps. 'Are you all right?'

'I think so,' Lestrade hobbled into the hallway. 'Inspector Lestrade, Scotland Yard.'

'Oh, I see.' She showed him into a drawing-room, heavy with flock, photographs and fussy furniture. 'Well, I'm afraid if it's literary advice you want, you'll have to make an appointment. Mr Collins doesn't see just anyone, you know.'

It was Lestrade's turn to see. 'I see,' he dutifully said. 'And with whom do I have to make an appointment?'

'With me,' she said. 'Oh, I do apologize; I'm Elizabeth Graves. My mother isn't in at the moment, but she's the Woman in White.'

'Oh, good. May I make an appointment, then?'

'Of course,' she consulted a diary on a table. 'Perhaps the

eighteenth of the month?'

He consulted his half-hunter. 'Perhaps in two minutes?'

'Really, Mr ... um ... Lestrade, I don't think ...'

'Ah well, Miss Graves, that's where we differ. You see, I do.'

'But Mr Collins isn't well. He's in bed.'

'No matter,' beamed Lestrade. 'Even with a gammy leg, I can manage the stairs.'

'No, no,' she said. 'If it is a matter of some urgency .

'It is a matter of total urgency,' Lestrade assured her.

'Very well,' and the frost positively crackled as she left the room.

He waited, accompanied only by the ticking of the clock, for some minutes, taking an opportunity to place his foot higher than his head. Then the door opened and he nearly fell off the armchair with shock. Miss Graves had returned and, as Lestrade had expected, she was not alone. What he did not expect at all was that the person with her was sitting in her arms, like a rather outsized baby. But the baby had a massive head to counter his tiny pale hands and slippered feet, with one bulging right temple and a correspondingly depressed left, as though someone had had a damned good try at kicking his head in. His beard was nearly to his waist and he squinted at Lestrade through rimless, opaque spectacles.

'Lizzie tells me you're from Scotland Yard,' he wheezed.

Lestrade staggered to his feet, 'Correct, sir. You are Mr Wilkie Collins?'

'I believe I am.' She put him down on the sofa and arranged cushions around him. 'You're sure you're a detective?' he checked.

'There are those who would question it,' Lestrade confessed, 'but it's what they pay me for.'

'Ah, no, it's just that I haven't seen the *Graphic* today. Have you?'

'Er ... no,' Lestrade returned to his chair. 'Should I have?'

'Well, no, I suppose there's no reason why you should. Only I have to check every day, you see.'

'In the *Graphic*?'

'In every newspaper.'

'You follow current affairs, Mr Collins?'

'No. I have to check that no-one's written my obituary.'

'Er ... is that likely?'

He leaned forward, peering at the Yard man. 'You have no idea what it's like,' he said. 'The abject terror of it all.'

'Er ... quite. Of what all?'

'Of reading of your own death. It's quite ghastly.'

'I'm sure it is. Now, Mr Collins ...'

'Lizzie,' the crime writer interrupted, 'what time is it?'

'Half past eight, Wilkie,' she said. 'I'll bring them through,' and she swept away.

'I believe you had a visitor last night,' Lestrade said.

'Who told you that?' Collins tried to bury his huge head under a blanket.

'Er ... well, actually it was Mr Ambrose Matters of the *Quiver*.'

'How does he know?' Collins whispered. 'My God, I didn't know it was common knowledge.'

'Well, I don't know about common .

'Of course,' Collins checked that the coast was clear by squinting severely right and left. 'Lizzie says it's the laudanum, you know.'

'Does she?'

'But I know she's real.'

'Lizzie?'

'The green woman,' Collins hissed, on the edge of something akin to hysteria. 'She of the tusked teeth.' It was obviously Wilkie Collins's lot in life to be surrounded by women of various hues.

'She was certainly here last night,' he took off his glasses and wiped them on his blanket. 'On the stairs.'

'I see,' Lestrade said, shifting a little less easily than he did. 'I was referring to your other visitor - Mr Batchelor of the *Quiver*.'

'Ah, yes. Lizzie saw to him. Didn't you, my dear?'

The young lady had returned with a tray full of bottles. 'What, Wilkie?'

'You saw to Mr Batchelor.'

'Indeed,' she threw a withering glance at Lestrade. 'He didn't have an appointment either.'

'What had he come to discuss?' Lestrade asked.

'He wanted to pick Mr Collins's brains on a detective novel he was writing. I made him an appointment for the seventeenth of the month.'

'I fear he will have to cancel,' Lestrade said.

'Why so?' Collins asked.

'I thought you read the papers every day, sir,' the Inspector reminded him.

'I only flick through them for the sight of my own name,' Collins said. 'What else can be of import?'

'The death, by blunt instrument, of Byngham Batchelor, Mr Collins. It was widely reported in all the Evenings.'

'Oh my God,' the firelight flickered eerily on the writer's glasses. 'Blunt instrument,' he muttered. 'What would Sergeant Cuff have done?'

'Who?' Lestrade asked.

'No one,' Collins said quickly, rocking gently back and forwards. Lestrade noted that his legs failed to reach the floor. He turned to his secretary. 'Thank you, Lizzie. I'll manage the doses tonight.'

'No, Wilkie,' she warned, but she went all the same.

He reached across for a bottle and helped himself. 'For my neuralgia,' he wheezed. 'What is your hypothesis on Mr Batchelor then, Inspector?'

'We aren't allowed to hypothesize at the Yard, sir,' Lestrade said. 'Tell me, does the name Hereward Rodney mean anything to you?'

Collins was on his second bottle. 'For my arthritis,' he explained, his eyes like bags of blood. 'No,' he said, 'not a thing.'

'How about Osbaldeston Ralston?'

The great crime writer shook his huge head. 'This is for my gout,' he said. 'I think I'll lay off the colchicum and morphine tonight. Mustn't overdo it.'

'Or perhaps this,' Lestrade passed over a piece of paper with a concentric design on it.

Collins peered at it, raising his spectacles. 'Those people,' he said. 'Who are they?'

'They have all died by violent means in the last three weeks,' Lestrade told him.

'By the same hand?'

'I don't know, but I fear the list is merely provincial at the moment.'

'Have you counted the letters?'

'Pardon?'

Collins put down the paper and slurped from a blue glass bottle. 'Spot of laudanum, Mr Lestrade?'

'Er ... isn't that poisonous?'

'Rubbish. And it's not true about my man Hellow dying after taking half my dose. He had a seizure, that was all.' Collins's eyes began to roll in his head. 'It could happen to any of us. In fact', and he leaned forward confidentially, 'it will happen to me if ever my feet reach the ground.'

'I see,' Lestrade said. 'Er ... you asked me if I'd counted the letters.'

'Yes. Of the names of the deceased. *Hereward the Wake* was

it? Not a very good book, that. I did say that to Charles, but he never could take criticism. Probably went home and whipped his wife - you know these Canons of the Church of England.'

'Hereward Rodney,' Lestrade said, not having understood a word of the mystery man's last few sentences.

'Fourteen,' muttered Collins. 'Got a mind, you see', he tapped his bulging temple, 'like a differencing machine. That's why papa put me to work all those years ago with Messrs Antrobus, the Tea Brokers.'

Lestrade hadn't realized it was possible to break tea. Fast and wind, yes. But not tea.

'Who were the others?'

'Er ... Osbaldeston Ralston,' the Inspector said.

'Eighteen,' Collins nodded. 'And the third?'

'Byngham Batchelor.'

'Sixteen. That's your average. That's your clue. It's something to do with sixteen,' Collins shut his eyes tight. 'One six, six one, one sixth, one sixteenth. This has something to do with numbers, I'm sure of it. Tell me, Inspector Whicher was before your time I suppose, at the Yard.'

'Yes, sir, but my old dad worked with him on the Constance Kent case.'

'My old dad was a bastard,' Collins said. 'Saw me in the tea trade, in the law, anywhere but where I was happy.'

'And where's that sir?' Lestrade asked.

'Here,' Collins tapped his little blue bottle. 'Right here,' and he chuckled wheezily.

'Does that design mean anything to you, sir?' Lestrade asked.

'This?' Collins scrutinized it again. 'It's a maze, isn't it? Hampton Court?'

Lestrade looked again. 'Too simple?' he suggested.

'How dare you!' Collins hissed. 'I'll have you know that *The Moonstone* is the finest detective story in the English language. Do you know what I earned in the financial year beginning April 1863?'

'No, sir.'

'Er ... neither do I now, but it represents a lifetime's salary for you, Lestrade.'

'I didn't mean to criticize your theories, sir,' Lestrade said. 'I merely meant that Hampton Court Maze is more complicated than that design would comply.'

Collins leaned back on the sofa, his rocking less pronounced, his stoop less in evidence, his little white hands clasped under his barbed wire bristle of beard. 'Numbers,' he hummed, almost tunefully. 'The clue to this case lies in numbers.' And he began to snore.

The Inspector tiptoed towards the door, watching out for a green woman with prominent incisors. In the hall Lestrade glanced back at the literary genius wheezing in his laudanum haze, swathed in blankets and he was very, very glad that *he* wasn't anybody's detective creation.

5

'I see head lice are in the news again,' Dr John Watson only consulted *The Thunderer* for the medical page.

'Head wounds are more our stock in trade at the moment, my dear fellow,' his companion said. 'Mrs Hudson!'

The little woman of that name bustled into the drawing-room. 'Yes, Mr Holmes?'

'Is everything packed?'

'It is, sir. Where away this time?'

'The wilds of Wales, Mrs Hudson. A particularly revolting little village called Blaenllechau in the Rhondda Vach.'

'That sounds pretty wild to me, Mr Holmes. I've put in an extra shirt. And doctor, your bag.'

'So are you, Mrs Hudson ... oh, I do beg your pardon,' the good doctor rarely gave vent to his personal feelings, especially at the expense of his syntax, but he was still reeling from the brilliance of Holmes's Welsh pronunciation. And he was still wiping Homes's spittle off his dressing gown. 'I still feel, Holmes, that we're letting Miss Ratcliffe down rather badly. You promised to look into the financial affairs of her father.'

'Where were you yesterday, old fellow?' Homes sipped his second coffee of the morning.

'Er ... Whymper's, Holmes, having my brolly re-ferruled.'

'Quite. And while you were there, I was at the Stock Exchange.'

'Good Lord, were you really?'

'I have said 1 was, doctor. Surely you don't want a second opinion?'

'Er ... good lord, no, of course not.'

'Admiral Ratcliffe had, to cut an exceedingly long financial story short, been swindled by Osbaldeston Ralston. Not once, I gather, but on several occasions. And the Admiral was not his only victim.'

'Look here, Holmes, you don't think Miss Ratcliffe bashed in his cranium, do you? Pretty little thing like that?'

'Since we have not been able to view the corpse, Watson,' Holmes said, 'I have no idea how pretty Ralston's cranium was. But in answer to your question did she kill him? the answer is an emphatic "No".'

'But she had the motive, surely?'

'So did half the bulls and bears in Throgmorton Street.'

'Ah,' mused Watson, finishing his kedgeree, 'the mark of the beast.'

'No,' said Holmes. 'She simply wasn't strong enough, old fellow. If the description of the wound given to us by the Ralston brothers is accurate, that would have taken some strength. Miss Ratcliffe reached your tie knot, that makes her five foot two. Her right hand, when I shook it, was small and sparse, with little metatarsal vigour. I have no reason to assume that her left was any different, unless of course she exhibits herself oftentimes in a freak show. Any more coffee, Mrs Hudson? My nerves are shot to pieces this morning.'

The little woman called something muffled from the kitchen.

'No, we're looking for a man,' the World's Greatest Detective assured his friend.

'Speak for yourself,' Watson bridled. 'Oh, I see. One of the Ralston brothers, then? But they're our clients too, Holmes. Isn't it just a teensy bit dishonest, acting for them both? Especially since each one says the other did it.'

'Dishonest, Watson? No,' Holmes ran an elegant finger the length of his elegant nose. 'I prefer the word "delicious". You remember the Affair of the Gallstone?'

'The priceless ruby half-inched from that country house?'

'The same. A routine business, very much below my intellectual par, were it not for one thing.'

Watson thought hard - rare for a doctor in Gladstone's England. 'Er ... the identical pair of Nubians,' he beamed.

'Exactly,' Holmes permitted himself a smile. 'But my mention of the Gallstone reminds me that Lestrade went to call on Wilkie Collins three nights ago.'

'Wilkie who?'

'Collins, Watson. He is a writer of detective fiction, unlike your friend Conan Doyle, who clearly is not. He wrote a book called *The Moonstone*.'

'Oh, yes, but I thought he was dead.'

'No, merely his talent,' Holmes said. 'Although I must say, there was one thing in *The Moonstone* he got absolutely right.'

'The intricacy of plot? The attention to detail?'

'The stupidity of the Metropolitan Police. Now why do you suppose Lestrade should visit Collins, whose best work was done twenty years ago? He's been a virtual recluse since his American tour in '73.'

'I suppose America does that to a man.'

'What if I tell you that Wilkie Collins lives in Blandford Square?'

'What if you do?' shrugged Watson. It clearly hadn't helped.

'It is within blunt-instrument-throwing-distance of Lisson Grove,' Holmes sighed, 'where the body of one Byngham Batchelor was found four days ago.'

'Ah! I see. So you think that Lestrade thinks that this Wilkie Collins...'

Holmes held up his hands in horror. 'No, Watson, no. But I would have given Mrs Hudson's right arm to have been a fly on the wall. What does Lestrade know that we don't?'

Watson didn't have to think long about that one. 'Nothing at all, Holmes,' he said. 'Surely? Nothing at all.'

'Blaen where?' Lestrade asked.

'No, guv, I don't think its Blaenwhere. It's Blaenllechau.'

'It sounds like the Blaen leading the Blaen, if you ask me,' Tyrrell said.

Nobody had of course and six hostile eyes looked at him oddly. Lestrade muttered to George, 'I'd watch that one if I were you. Got ideas above his station.'

The station to which they embarked was Cardiff, staying at the Angel in the shadow of the Marquess of Bute's attempt to rebuild the great Norman castle of Robert Fitz-Hamon. From there it was pony and trap up the twisting roads of the Rhondda Vach where the rows of miners' cottages lay under their blankets of mist and rain and the smoke of the pits wreathed the pit wheels, standing like monolithic monsters against the treeless heaps of slag.

'There was a time, min,' the driver told them, 'when a wiwer could travel from one end of the valleys to another an' never touch the groun'.'

'A Wiwer?' George repeated.

'Oh, sorry. That's my Welsh Standard Three comin' back to me after all these years. Squirrel to yew, butty,' and he hauled in his reins outside the Workmen's Hall. 'That'll be ninepence three farthin's.'

'George,' Lestrade tottered down from the cart and left the luggage and the tip to his inferior. Well, that was what sergeants were for.

Their timing was immaculate. The Coroner's inquest was nearly over as the Yard men squeezed their way into the smoke filled room. Top-hatted gentlemen lined the front, interspersed with ladies in feathered hats and muffs. Near the back, where Lestrade sagged against a freezing radiator, grimy miners with cloth caps, ragged scarves and moleskin trousers did as they were told by hard-faced women in headshawls. Around the edge of the room, the sombre dark blue and enlivening silver of the Glamorgan Constabulary made up the lunatic fringe.

'Mr Lestrade, is it?' a portly plainclothesman elbowed his way towards him.

'It is,' the Inspector said.

'Detective-Inspector Mortimer, Pant-y-Grdl CID.'

Lestrade shook his hand, 'You called us in.'

'Well, I thought I'd better, seein' as 'ow it's who it is that's dead.'

'Where's the body?'

'Up at the 'ouse. Wanno see it?'

'In the fullness of time.'

'Excuse me,' a full-bodied voice bellowed. 'This is a Coroner's Inquest; more, it is ***my*** inquest. I will not have casual conversation during it. Matters are too grave. Who are you, sir?'

'Detective-Inspector Mortimer, Mr Pryce, Pant-y-Grdl CID.'

'Not you, Mortimer. The other one - you, sir, face like a ferret.'

'Do you mean me?' Lestrade felt constrained to ask, although he had heard the description before.

'Of course,' the Coroner bawled. 'I shudder to think what the odds are against two men with ferret-like faces talking at my inquest.'

'Pity it isn't an inquest ***on*** him,' Lestrade hissed to Mortimer. 'Inspector Lestrade, sir, Scotland Yard.'

'Oh, yes,' the Coroner was not good at climbing down. 'Well, you're a mite late.'

'Minor havoc at Chepstow,' Lestrade explained. 'Wye flooding.'

'Why indeed,' muttered the Coroner. 'Well, as I was saying - there is only one conclusion to which this inquest can come, namely that Mr John Nathaniel Wallace Lionel Guest met his end at the hand and behest of person or persons unknown. I don't think you need to leave the room to discuss that, do you, Mr Jenkins?'

The foreman of the jury stood up, 'Well, I...'

'Excellent. And is that the verdict of you all?'

'We ... er . . .'

'Good!' the Coroner's gavel came down with a crack. 'This inquest is closed. Good morning.'

'Well,' said Lestrade, 'now that the case is over, perhaps we can start to investigate it. Mr Mortimer, what is the quality of the local brew?'

'So-so,' was George's comment on the local brew - 'Prince of Ales' it most certainly was not. But then, George was a Londoner and he had his loyalties. Anyway he'd hardly got a half down his neck at the Blaenllechau Working Men's Club formed years earlier by thirsty miners determined to beat the licensing laws of their 'dry' county, when the Pant-y-Grdl station wagon arrived and the policemen, Welsh and English, rattled up the twisting labyrinth of streets, slowing to allow innumerable sheep and their new-born offspring to cross in front of them. They alighted on a windswept, barren hillside, where the soil was black and and a thin covering of grass and heather had been cropped short by the untended flocks. Led by Mortimer, they clambered over derelict dry-stone walls at crazy angles on the hillside.

'Here we are, then.' Mortimer stopped before a quarry of Rhondda-grey granite that generations of miners had hacked out of the hillside to build their squat little terraces. 'Is this where yew foun' the body, Myrddin?'

A round little policeman with thin lips and even thinner hair under his helmet answered him, 'Not precisely, sir. It was a little lower down. Aye, by there.'

'You found the body, Constable ... er?' Lestrade asked, wiping the sheep currants off his shoe.

'Er, not precisely sir, no. And that's Williams, by the way; Constable 491 Myrddin Williams.'

'So who did?'

'Dai Evans from Tylerstown.'

'What was he doing up here?' Lestrade asked. 'Is he a farmer? Quarryman?'

'Peepin' Twm,' Williams said.

'Peeping...?'

'Twm. Yew know,' Mortimer explained. 'Yew must 'ave 'em in England, mun. Blokes who like watchin' courtin' couples ... courtin'.'

'And this is a place for courting couples, is it?' Lestrade found that hard to believe. They were miles from anywhere and the wind was whistling something shocking.

'Well, aye,' Mortimer assured him. 'Yew've only got to look at the view, mun. Breathtakin', innit?'

Lestrade and George did as they were bid. In both directions stretched identical rows of miners' terraces, like tall cloches under the rain. A lazy, leaden river, black with coal and grey from the sky's reflection, meandered silently through their centre and the trucks of coal and slag came and went endlessly. Beyond all that, across the valley from them, the same bare precipices and desolate wilderness, dotted here and there with sheep.

'All right,' Mortimer said, 'I'll grant yew, Porth isn't much to write home about, but down there, between the slag heaps - Pontypridd - the jewel of the Rhondda.'

'D'yew play, Mr Lestrade sir?' Constable Williams asked.

'Not a note,' Lestrade admitted.

'I believe the constable was referrin' to rugby football, Mr Lestrade,' Mortimer said. 'It's a second religion to us 'ere in the valleys. Oh, after religion of course.'

'Oh, sorry, Mr Lestrade, sir,' Williams said. 'I was forgettin' yew was an Englishman. Do yew 'ave a Glee Club up at Scotland Yard, Sergeant?'

'I believe we do,' George said. 'But you wouldn't catch me within a hundred yards of it. Audiences have no soul these days,' he glared at Lestrade, who looked away.

'Oh, pity,' Williams said. 'Yew've got the look of a baritone.'

'An' yew'll 'ave the look of a soprano in a minute, Myrddin, if you don't shut up,' Mortimer snapped. 'The Inspector 'ere 'aven't come to listen to yewer prattle. 'E've come to listen to mine.'

'Thank you, Inspector. Is there a rock whose lee we could shelter behind? My old riot wound's playing me up again.'

'Over by 'ere, Inspector,' Williams called and all four men squatted in the windless side of the quarry face. Lestrade carefully removed the pointed bit of a sheep's skull from his backside before spreading George's Donegal flaps and sitting on them.

'Very well, then,' he said. 'Assume I know nothing.'

The men of the Glamorgan Constabulary had already made such an assumption. 'The name of the deceased', said Mortimer, 'was John Guest. 'E was a very big man roun'yer.'

'Round where?' Lestrade checked. After all, he had not seen the body yet and didn't want to miss anything.

'Roun' yer,' Mortimer explained. 'In the valleys. 'E's one of the Guests, see.'

'*The* guests?' Lestrade was on alien territory.

'Duw, yew must 'ave 'eard of the Guests, mun,' Mortimer assured the Yard man. 'The Guests, the Crawshays, the Hills and the Homfrays 'ave these valleys sewn up. All from Merthyr, of course, but they've spread now as far west as Port Talbot and as far north as Abergavenny. Ever taken the hills up to Abergavenny, Myrddin?' he asked the constable.

'No, sir.'

'Lovely. Lovely. Lovely. Especially in the spring. Ah, to be in Abergavenny, now that spring is yer.'

Lestrade's clearing of his throat brought Mortimer back to the reality of the situation, 'Yes, well, as I was sayin' - John Guest. 'Ead of a cadet branch of the family. Owned the Yns-y-Bwl collery. 'E's well out of that, min'.'

'Why do you say that?' Lestrade asked.

'Trouble,' Mortimer tapped the side of his not inconsiderable nose, 'What they call nowadays "employer/employee relationships". I dunno, when I was a boy, it was all master and servant. Then along comes ol' Gladstone with his every man comin' within the pale of the constitution...'

'Aye,' corroborated Williams.

'I don't think 'e was includin' people like yew, Myrddin,' the Inspector said.

'Guest knew about this?' Lestrade asked.

'What, Gladstone?'

'The bad feeling at his pit at ... er .

'Yns-y-Bwl,' Mortimer found it for him. 'Oh, duw, aye. 'E caused most of it.'

'How?'

'Short wages, long hours, no compensation. Yew'd think there'd never been a Mines Act at all to listen to Sioni Guest for 'alf-an-hour.'

'So you were the first policeman on the scene, Constable Williams?'

'That's right, sir. Ol' Dai Evans come into the station last Thursday afternoon.'

'What time was this?' George was taking notes.

'Well, now the whistle 'ad gone for the middle shift, so it would 'ave been about three o'clock.'

'What did he say?' Lestrade asked.

'Tol' me 'e'd found a body. Or rather'e tol' me and Sergeant Owen. Sarge turns roun' an' says to me, "Myrddin, Dai 'ave found a body up at the quarry at Blaenllechau." "Get away," I says to 'im.' "I'll give the orders,"'e says to me, so I turn roun' an' say...'

'Yes, thank you,' Lestrade raised his hand. 'So when you got here, what?'

'Well, on the way up I asked ol' Dai 'ow come 'e was up the mountain by yer when 'e should 'ave been down Number Three.'

'Number Three?' Lestrade repeated.

'Collery,' explained Mortimer. 'Number Three Pit. They've all got numbers, see. Like bein' in the bloody police, innit?'

'And what did he say?' Lestrade asked.

'Well, e' may be a pervert, ol' Dai, but 'e's an honest one. 'E said 'e was spyin' on this couple, see. 'E - the bloke now, not ol' Dai - 'e 'ad 'is 'and up this girl's frock; quite springlike wasn't it, Inspector, last Thursday?'

'Not bad,' Mortimer remembered.

'Anyhow, with the valleys bein' so crowded all the time, you've got to take yewer chance while you can. So what's a bit of goosepimples by comparison with a bit of 'ow's yewer gransha?'

'And then?' Lestrade was sitting on a damp Donegal, albeit someone else's and he'd just put his hand squarely in some sheep currants. He sensed his patience was becoming an increasingly rare commodity.

'Well, the bloke 'eard 'im - ol' Dai now. So 'e oiks 'is arm out from the girl's unmentionables an' comes after Dai.'

'And what does Dai do?'

George, ever the cultured policeman, thought she was Queen of Carthage, but he felt the ***bon mot*** inappropriate and licked his pencil stub instead.

'Runs like buggery,' Williams explained. 'Loses the bloke somewhere up above and 'ides in 'ere. Nearly fell over Mr Guest. 'Ell of a shock for 'im, fair play.'

'It's foul play we're talking about, Constable. Did you touch the body?'

'Oh, aye,' Williams said proudly, 'I'm not squeamish. 'Ad two brothers killed at Tynnewydd. A bit o' blood never 'urt nobody.'

'Unless you've lost it,' George commented.

'Do you remember how he was lying?'

'Er ... oh, duw. On 'is back, was it? Or on 'is front? No, I tell yew a lie. It was on 'is side.'

'He was dead, I suppose?' Lestrade checked.

'Oh, duw, aye,' Williams confirmed, chewing the chinstrap of his helmet, 'as a dado. Most of 'is 'ead 'ad gone yer at the back and 'is eyes were bulgin'.'

'Did this bloke who was chasing Dai see the body?'

'No,' Mortimer said. 'But Dai saw somethin'. Didne, Myrddin?'

The constable looked blank. 'Did 'e, sir?'

'Well, aye, mun,' Mortimer reminded him. 'As ol' Dai come into the quarry, Mr Lestrade, 'e saw a bloke makin' away over by there.'

'Over by ... where?' Lestrade tried to follow the pointing finger.

'Through that gap in the wall.'

'Could he be our man?' Lestrade asked.

'Could be.'

'Would Dai know him again?' the Inspector asked his colleagues.

'Dai wouldn' know 'is own mother,' Williams moaned.

'Unless it's cuddlin' 'e can't see it at all.'

'But 'e did say that the bloke got tangled up in the barb wire, Myrddin, didne?'Mortimer prompted.

'Oh, duw, aye, sir. I'd forgotten that. Dai did say, Mr Lestrade, that the bloke got caught up in the barb wire.'

'Over here?' Lestrade staggered painfully to his feet and braved the biting wind again to reach the broken wall.

'Aye, just by there.'

The eagle-eyed detective peered at the wire. There, caught on its murderous spikes, was a small, wet piece of blue cloth. 'What do you make of this, George?' he asked his sergeant.

George squinted closer. 'Piece of blue cloth, guv,' was his deduction. 'Wet.'

'Yes, thank you, George. Tell me, Constable Williams', the uniformed man had joined them by now, together with his inspector, 'did you or any other constable pass through that gap?'

'Through that gap, Inspector?' Williams chuckled, patting his sizeable midriff. 'Maybe twenty years ago.'

The Guest house was a huge Gothic pile, of the same Rhondda grey stone, faced and hewn to perfection, as the cottages that clustered below it on the hillside. The policemen were shown into a drawing-room full of men wearing black.

'I am Inspector Lestrade,' he introduced himself, 'Scotland Yard. This is Sergeant George. These gentlemen', he waved vaguely in the direction of the local police, 'I believe you know. Would I be right in assuming you are all Guests?'

'No, mun,' Mortimer whispered. 'Some of 'em live yer.'

'I am Ranulf Guest,' a balding man with immaculate silver Dundrearies crossed the tiger skin rug to Lestrade. 'The man done to death was my eldest son. I want to see his murderer.'

'So do I, Mr Guest,' Lestrade said. 'But I fear these things take time.'

'Time, man?' the eldest Guest bellowed. 'We are all living on borrowed time, Lestrade. How long have you been here?'

Lestrade consulted his half hunter. 'About four hours,' he said.

'Long enough. You, Mortimer ... and you, Lestrade. Come with me.'

The old man took up a gnarled stick with a heavy end and tottered through an ante-room. The mourning family stayed where it was, eyeing George and Williams with something akin to contempt. The Welsh constable closed to the English sergeant. 'It's at times like these', he muttered, 'I wish I was in 'afod keepin' a fish shop.'

And George, though not remotely aware of where Hafod was, concurred.

A tall, square miner with shoulders like Davenports stood in the corner of the library, an ill-fitting collar constricting his neck and a cloth cap in his hand.

'Mortimer,' Guest said, 'I think you know Will Dodd?'

'Indeed I do,' Mortimer's eyes narrowed. ''E put two of my boys in the Infirmary last year.'

'My pleasure, Mr Mortimer,' the miner grinned.

'Dodd, this is Inspector Lestrade, from Scotland Yard.'

'Oh, a real Peeler,' Dodd nodded at him.

'Scotch, gentlemen?' Guest asked. 'My brandy I keep for my friends.'

They all sat down at his behest as the paterfamilias poured the drinks.

'I think I should tell you, gentlemen, that Dodd here is not all he seems. He is what in my father's day was called an *agent provocateur*.'

Lestrade and Mortimer looked at each other. Neither of them had expected a French Connection.

'You know, Mortimer,' the oldest Guest went on, clamping himself at last into a library chair, 'if Dodd's double existence were to become public, his life would not be worth a tinker's damn.'

The Inspector nodded.

'For that reason, I must swear you to secrecy. An *agent provocateur* is only useful if he is alive. Did you notice anything on your way in?'

Lestrade and Mortimer looked at each other again. The old man sighed and hobbled to the window. 'Clear view of the drive,' he grated, then limped to another. 'You can see the stables from here.'

Indeed they could. As much as Lestrade appreciated the tour of the house, other matters were perhaps more pressing. 'Mr Guest ...'

The old man ignored him. 'Up here, Lestrade,' he pointed with his stick towards the adjoining wing. 'What do you see?'

'An adjoining wing,' Lestrade observed, grateful now that he had attended that lecture on Architecture for Policemen.

'On the roof, man,' Guest snapped.

'Er...' Lestrade squinted in the gathering dark at the gargoyle. 'Is that a wild man?'

'Furious,' commented Guest, 'the wild man or wode house as they are called, of the Guests. But behind it, man, what do you see?'

Lestrade squinted again. 'It looks like ... another man. Not so wild this time.'

Mortimer squinted as well. 'Bugger me,' he muttered as he took in the dark blue uniform with the white facings, 'it's the Glamorgan Yeomanry.'

'The Yeomanry?' Lestrade repeated. 'Devil of a place for annual exercises, Mr Guest.'

'Annual exercises be buggered,' Guest growled. 'Captain Dance's Cowbridge Troop are working for me.'

'Working for you?' Lestrade turned to his man. 'In what capacity?'

Guest chuckled grimly. 'Tell him, Dodd.'

The big miner placed his cap on the polished mahogany of the billiard table's rim. 'There's a small war about to start, gentlemen,' he said. 'In the form of a deputation from the Yns-y-Bwl Collery. Is yewer clock right, Mr Guest?'

'On the button,' Guest glanced at his grandfather.

'They'll be yer in about ten minutes.'

'I don't see . . .' Lestrade began.

'I told yew,' said Mortimer. 'Employer/employee relations'. I warned yew, Mr Guest. I said there'd be trouble. 'Course, I didn't reckon on Dodd yer.'

The miner grinned. 'No one ever does, butty,' he said.

'Dodd's information is that the man who killed my son is coming up here to talk about wages and hours.'

'You know who it is?' Lestrade asked.

'I got a pretty shrewd idea,' Dodd said.

'Well, who?' Mortimer asked.

'"Happy" Lewis.'

'Isaac Lewis? Never!' Mortimer said.

'Why "Never", Mortimer?' Guest turned on him.

'Look, Mr Guest,' the Inspector blustered a little. 'I've known "Happy" since 'e was a boy. So, come to that, 'ave yew.'

'You've known Will Dodd for a few years too,' Guest reminded him. 'And you had no idea he was working for me did you?'

'Well, no, I...'

'What evidence do you have' Lestrade asked the miner *provocateur*, 'against this man Lewis?'

''E 'ad it in for Mr Guest,' Dodd told him. 'For *any* Guest, in fact. 'E's a Socialist, see.'

'A what?'

'A Socialist,' Dodd repeated. ''E writes letters to William Morris.'

'Scum of the earth,' Guest snapped. 'They're trying to destroy the fabric of our society, Lestrade. I don't know if you see it that clearly, cocooned in Whitehall, but down here in this Godforsaken hell, it's obvious enough. Dammit, they'll want the vote next.'

'What are your plans exactly?' Lestrade asked, more aware than his host, clearly, of the Corrupt Practices Act.

Guest wandered to the door and threw it open. 'Captain Dance,' he thundered.

A young man with a monocle sauntered into the room, the shoulder chains and leek collar badges of the Glamorgan Yeomanry glistening on his tunic in the lamplight. He saluted casually.

'What are your plans exactly?' Guest asked him.

'Er ...' the good captain hesitated.

'It's all right,' Guest waved a hand at Lestrade. 'He's one of us.'

That came as something of a surprise to Lestrade, but he let it pass.

Captain Dance closed to the corner of the room and took an old sheet off a table. There stood a perfect scale model of the Guest house.

'Here', his Oxford accent was like cut glass, 'is a perfect model of the house. We are here,' he pointed his swagger stick at the lower ground floor. 'I have men here ... here ... and here to act as lookouts. At a given signal, the men from the stables, armed with carbines, will take up positions here ... here ... and here,' the stick's pointer flew hither and yon.

'Once the targets are assembled in the drive...'

'The targets?' Lestrade wasn't sure he'd heard.

'Er ... miners, aren't they, Ranulf?'

'Indeed they are, Gerontius.'

'Well, once they're assembled, we'll close in from the rear with the horses.'

'You've got horses?'

'Well,' Dance chuckled like a donkey on laughing gas, 'we are the Yeomanry, Mr Lestrade. Not good horse country, of course, the Valleys, but there it is. No, they'll just be useful in keeping the blighters in the grounds. We'll soon whisk them away behind the outer perimeter.'

'The miners?'

'Lord, no. The horses.'

'Why?'

Dance blinked. He'd never consciously thought of Scotland Yard before. In fact, he'd barely heard the name. But now he knew why they'd been dubbed the Defective Department. 'So that they don't get hurt,' he said. 'You see', he crossed to the window, 'if the horses were still in position, we couldn't use this,' and he swept another sheet off something in the bay.

Lestrade's mouth fell open. So did Mortimer's.

'What is it?' the Yard man found his voice first.

'It's a Nordenfeldt five barrel,' Dance explained. 'Better than the Gatling or the Gardner for my money. The five barrels of course are an experiment, but it's looking good. The Central London Rangers at Dartford used one three years ago and from "order" to "halt", reversing the gun, opening the limber, mounting the carriage-hopper and firing fifty rounds took twenty-two seconds. Extraordinary, really.'

'I don't believe it,' Lestrade shook his head.

'Oh, it's perfectly true, old boy,' Dance assured him. 'I can even give you the name of the troop captain if you like.'

'And how long will it take you to murder all those miners?' Lestrade asked him.

'Murder?' Guest snarled. 'Don't be ridiculous. There's an armed mob coming up that hill, Lestrade. All I'm doing is defending my property against it.'

'It?' Lestrade rounded on the old man. 'I've faced many a mob in my time, Mr Guest and it's not an "it"; it's a "them". Men, with children and wives and mothers ...'

Guest held up his hand. 'Spare me the catalogue, Lestrade. I have a wife too and she was a mother. Until one of those bastards took that from her and caved in the head of my eldest son.'

'That's why I'm here,' Lestrade said. 'I'll find your son's murderer for you, Mr Guest, I promise you ...'

'I've got my murderer,' Guest said. 'He'll be coming over that hill any moment. Right into the mouth of this,' and he slapped the gleaming steel of the Nordenfeldt, its muzzle nudging the leaded panes.

'May I remind you', Lestrade said quietly, 'that the use of private armies is illegal in this country.'

'So is murder,' Guest countered. 'But it happens anyway. Oh, I've no doubt you chaps do your best, Lestrade, but it's a poor best, a second best. No, the hangman's rope is too chancy. To get Lewis to it, I'll have to bypass an awful lot of bleeding hearts. Some social worker will point to his poverty-stricken background, his aged mother, his mewling and puking babies. They'll find a doctor who'll say he was brain-damaged falling out of his cradle. And that's before some smart-arsed counsel has a go at justifiable homicide. This way is sure,' he felt the cold steel again. 'The only pity of it is, it's too damn quick.'

There was a rap at the window. Dance threw it open and a soldier saluted briskly. 'They're coming, sir.'

'How many?' the captain asked.

'Difficult to see in the dark, sir,' the soldier said.

'I haven't time for a biology lesson, private,' Dance snapped.

'No, sir. Estimate over a hundred, sir.'

'Right, tell Sergeant Harris will you, old chap. And do your tunic up. This is the Glamorgan Yeomanry.'

'Yessir, very good, sir,' and they heard the soldier's boots crunch on the gravel.

'This is madness,' Lestrade said and strode for the door.

Instantly it was blocked by two Yeomen in bandoliers. They looked vaguely familiar.

'Meet my "family", Lestrade,' Guest said. 'Did you not notice, either, as you came in, that all my family seem rather of the male persuasion? This is no place for women and children. I am the only Guest here. Everyone else belongs to Captain Dance: correct, nephew?'

'Indubitably, uncle,' the captain clicked his heels. 'Gentlemen,' he said to the guards, 'be so good as to entertain Messrs Lestrade and Mortimer, will you? Mr Guest and I have a little entertaining of our own to do.'

'Bit like Number Two, this,' Mortimer said.

'Number Two?' Lestrade wondered what the Inspector had put his hand in.

'Collery where I worked as a boy,' the answer echoed. 'Lucky, reely. I can see in the dark, see.'

'That helps, does it?'

'Well, it would if I could pick locks.'

'Why?'

'Because', Mortimer uncoiled his legs as far as he was able, 'there's a door over by there. I'm prepared to bet it's locked. Otherwise, there wouldn't be much point in puttin' us down yer, would there?'

'What sort of lock is it?' Lestrade asked, unable to see so much as a wall.

'Druitt and Westerman, it says,' Mortimer told him.

'Droitwich.'

Lestrade was astonished. 'You can read that at this distance, in a totally dark cellar?'

Mortimer chuckled. 'They don't call me Cat's Eyes Mortimer for nothin', you know. In fact, I got to admit, they don't call me Cat's Eyes Mortimer at all, particly. It's just that Mr Guest Senior called us in to advise on security. We recommended Druitt and Westerman - oh, the Treorchy branch, of course.'

'Right, well, unless the Treorchy branch have a peculiar twist, I should be able to open that door in ninety-eight seconds.'

'Duw, duw,' it was Mortimer's turn to be astonished. 'Well, I never did.'

'Probably not,' sighed Lestrade, 'which brings me to our first problem.'

'What?'

'Knots.'

'Ah,' Mortimer heaved again against the ropes that bound him to Lestrade. They sat on the coal-dust of the floor, lashed together with their hands clasped behind them like a rather unusual pair of bookends.

'Roll to the left,' Lestrade said.

'Why?'

'Just do it, Mortimer. Or you and I will be hearing the crash of gunfire upstairs and it's not going to be a pretty sound.'

'You don't think 'e'll go ahead with it, surely?'

'Did you see his eyes?' Lestrade asked. 'Mad as a March Hare. I've seen it before. An old cove called Mullion got into the Arsenal at Woolwich when I was a sergeant. Grabbed a Gatling and threatened to blow half the workforce to Kingdom Come.'

'What happened?'

'I'll tell you about it ... some other time,' he said. 'Now, roll.'

Neither man had felt such sickening pains in all his life. Their mutual scream was drowned out by the crunch of miners' boots on the gravel above as the men of Yns-y-Bwl moved forward, their coal-grimed faces lit by their flaming torches.

The door of the Guest house swung wide.

'Is that yew, Mr Guest?' a voice called. The rest were silent.

'Who's that?' the old man demanded to know.

'Isaac Lewis, Mr Guest. We'd like a word, sir, if yew don't mind.'

'A word, Lewis?' Guest tottered towards him. 'You didn't spare my son. Why should I spare you a word?'

There were rumblings from the men at Lewis's back. He tugged off his cap. 'We were all very sorry about yewer boy, Mr Guest,' the miner said. 'But it don't change things. We've taken all we can. There's men yer behind me who've lost boys too - down the pit.'

'Aye!' A crescendo rose through the night.

'Now we know the risks we take,' Lewis said. 'Every shift, every eight hours savage amusement, but Yns-y-Bwl is ridic'lous, Mr Guest. It's just not safe, sir. 'Yewer breakin' the law.'

'So did you, Lewis,' Guest stood a dozen yards from his man now, 'when you took a pickaxe handle to my son.'

Lestrade felt the pain subside. 'When I said 'roll to the left''', he winced, 'I meant my left. 'You went to the right.'

'Oh, sorry,' Mortimer moaned. 'Tie a bloody good knot, min', don' they, the 'Yeomanry?'

'All part of their training, I suppose,' Lestrade said. 'Now, after three - roll to your right.'

This time, both detectives went the same way and lay side by side in the black grit. There was much struggling from Lestrade and then a sigh of relief from them both and their arms burst apart.

'Oh Duw, that's better, aye,' Mortimer rubbed his numbed wrists. 'Natty-from-bonky, that. Metropolitan issue?'

Lestrade clicked the deadly blade back into the brass knuckles from whence he had released it to saw through the ropes that bound them. 'No,' he smiled, 'a souvenir from Egypt - a companion of a mile.'

'I can see it would be,' said Mortimer. 'I 'ave to make do with my size 'levens in the event of trouble, but they're not much bloody good at cuttin' ropes. There's glad I am the Yeomanry didn't search yew. Yew said something about a Druitt and Westerman?'

The crowd above began to sway. Guest tottered backwards, his face to them, his head erect, a rigid silhouette against the light from his own hall.

'We just want to talk, Mr Guest,' Lewis was saying.

There was the snick of a Lee-Enfield bolt and Captain Dance was at Guest's shoulder.

The crowd stopped, the murmuring died down.

'Who's that with yew?' Lewis asked.

'Gerontius Dance,' the captain called, 'Glamorgan Yeomanry. And that gentleman behind you', he waved his swagger stick in the air, 'is Sergeant Harris.'

From nowhere, a ring of horsemen with carbines cocked had formed a line at the rear. Harris edged his horse forward and the miners struggled backwards until they were a tiny knot in the centre, Yeomanry all round their flanks and rear and a Nordenfeldt machine gun in their faces.

'What's this?' Lewis growled.

'The end, you working class bastard,' Dance trilled. 'When I drop my cane, my men will open fire.'

'Stop!' Another English accent rent the air and two rather bedraggled-looking policemen in soaking Donegals staggered though the cordon of Yeomen and into the circus that Guest was running. How were they to know that the old man had had a new duck-pond built since Mortimer's last visit, around the back of the house? Lestrade was still spitting out duck weed as he ran. 'You're all under arrest.'

There was laughter from both sides.

'Bugger off, Lestrade,' Guest bellowed. 'This is no business of yours.'

'Now, wait a minute,' Lestrade stood between the miners and the window where he knew the Nordenfeldt waited, cocked and deadly. 'This is an industrial dispute. It's not going to become a battlefield.'

'That's up to 'im, butty,' Lewis shouted.

Lestrade turned to the braying miners. 'Mr Lewis, is it?'

'Aye.'

'I am Inspector Lestrade of Scotland Yard. Do you know Inspector Mortimer?' The Welsh detective had not taken his eyes off Dance.

'Aye.'

'It has been suggested to us, that you have information relating to the death of John Guest.'

'Bollocks,' Lewis assured him.

'Perhaps, but Mr Mortimer would like to ask you a few questions.'

Lewis shrugged.

'Do you have any objections to that?'

'I s'pose not,' Lewis said warily. 'As long as that old bugger's not involved.'

'No, I assure you that Mr Guest will not be there.'

'Lestrade,' Guest thundered, 'I shall count to three. If you and Mortimer aren't out of the way by then, Dance here will open up on all of you. One...'

Lestrade hissed to Lewis, 'Put your torches out. It'll make it more difficult to see you.'

''Andier for blindin' 'orses, though, innit?' Lewis growled.

'We didn' come lookin' for trouble, Mr Lestrade, but it seems we've found it, anyow.'

'Stop!' another English voice cried out, this time from among the miners themselves. Two men forced their way to the front. One was tall with an aquiline nose probing the cold night air under the colliery grime. The other shorter with a toothbrush moustache.

'For God's sake, Lestrade, get us out of this.'

'Holmes?' Lestrade peered through the coal black. 'Watson?'

'Yes,' Lewis frowned. ''Ow come yew know these blokes, Inspector? Ianto and Dewi.'

'Ianto and ... oh, I see. Er...'

'Now, Lookyou, boyo,' Holmes attempted, 'this is all goin' a bit far, indeed to goodness, innit, look you?'

'Funniest bloody Valleys accent I've ever 'eard,' Lewis said.

'No wonder they didn' say much. Sounds like Yns-y-Bwl with just a 'int of Madras.'

'I think you'll find that's Baker Street,' Lestrade said, 'but perhaps now is not the time. Mr Holmes, Dr Watson, if you will play charades, you must expect to pay the odd forfeit. How are you at dodging machine-gun bullets?'

'What?' Holmes, Watson and Lewis chorused.

'Second window from the door,' Lestrade hissed without turning to face it. 'There's a Fordenneld gun in there, trained on us.'

'Two,' Guest bellowed.

'Oh, bloody 'ell,' Lewis wailed. 'Sod this for a game of soldiers.'

'Stand still!' Lestrade yelled as the miners began to back. He grabbed Lewis by the collar and held him fast.

'Stop!' yet another English voice cried and the casement window crashed back. All eyes turned to it. There, behind the sights of the Nordenfeldt crouched a policeman in plain-clothes. But this time, the gun was trained on Captain Dance. 'Mr Lestrade, sir, would you like to tell Captain Dance about my prowess with one of these?'

'Sergeant George!' Lestrade had never been so pleased to see his number two. 'With pleasure,' and he crossed to the good captain. 'You see, it's not only the Central London Rangers who've practised with ... one of those. Scotland Yard has been involved in trials too - all very hush-hush of course. Sergeant George here holds the Police Medal for marksmanship.'

'Huh!' Dance was contemptuous.

Lestrade closed to him, looking at him levelly. 'And he's particularly crack when he's cross,' he muttered. 'So if I were you, I wouldn't make George cross.'

The silence was audible. It was Guest who broke it, 'Gerry, you lily-livered shit. Give the order to your men.'

'Uncle . . .'clearly Dance's nerve had gone.

'If you don't, I will!' Guest bellowed, raising his stick on high.

It was Inspector Mortimer who felled him, a particularly gratuitous left hook that sent the old man sailing backwards across his polished hall to collide gracefully with an aspidistra at the far end.

'Duw,' he cradled his knuckles, 'I've been wantin' to do that these years, aye.'

'Right,' Lestrade was in command. 'You Yeomen, drop your carbines. Now!'

One by one the weapons clattered to the ground.

'You men at the back, dismount and unbuckle your swords from your saddles.'

No one moved.

'Tell them, Dance,' Lestrade snapped.

'Do as he says,' Dance had not taken his eyes off George's trigger finger.

One by one, led by Sergeant Harris, the troopers obeyed.

'Mr Lewis,' Lestrade said, 'would you be so kind as to ask your men to escort these soldiers out of the village? On no account are they to mount until ... where would you say?'

'Llantrisant,' Lewis grinned. 'It'll be dinner time tomorrow by then.'

There was laughter from the miners who jeered at the Yeomen before lining the road to the house with their torches.

Other torches, like fireflies, were approaching up the hill, accompanied by the tramp of running feet.

'That'll be Constable Williams and the Glamorgan Constabulary.' George had heard it too.

'Oh, there's proud!' beamed Mortimer. 'Well done, lads. Look lively.' And he marched off to take charge of them.

'Not exactly the cavalry,' said Lestrade, 'but it'll do. Mr Lewis, could we have a word inside?'

'Lestrade?'

'Mr Holmes.'

'Look ... er ... I know we shouldn't exactly be here, but Watson and I are working on a case.'

'The Guest Case?'

'Possibly,' Holmes bridled.

'Come off it, Holmes. We owe Lestrade here our lives - again. The least you can do is tell him what we know.'

Holmes led the Inspector a little way off. 'The man Lewis had a motive.'

'It sounds as though they all did,' Lestrade told him, 'the way the late Guest ran his mine.'

'More than that. Lewis has protested before. The last time he tried it, Guest had him beaten up. Supervised the whole thing personally.'

'Witnesses?'

'We have their names,' Holmes told him.

'Thank you, Mr Holmes,' Lestrade said. 'Leave your address with Inspector Mortimer, will you?'

'Ah well, now that our cover is blown, so to speak, I'm afraid we'll have to leave Number 16 Hafodyrydynys Street. I'm not sure we'll be as welcome with Mrs Leyshon now.'

'Just as well,' mumbled Watson. 'We've discovered that her Welsh Rarebit isn't as rare as all that.'

'Well, wherever you stay', Lestrade said, 'I'd be grateful, gentlemen, if you'd leave all this to the professionals.'

'Oh, quite, quite.' For a man who'd nearly been machine-gunned, Watson could be pretty ingratiating.

Lestrade watched as Mortimer supervised the removal of the Cowbridge Troop. He turned to Captain Dance. 'As soon as Mortimer is free', he said, 'he'll be arresting you for disturbing the peace, possibly even attempted murder. Can I trust you to wait in the library?'

Dance straightened. 'You have my word as an officer of the Glamorgan Yeomanry,' he said.

'Yes,' Lestrade was impressed. 'You'd better see to your uncle. Whichever asylum he ends up in, the staff there won't thank us if his jaw's dislocated.'

The Inspector turned to the sergeant, gently easing the muzzle of the Nordenfeldt away from his chest. 'George', he shook the man's hand, 'that was almost inspired. What happened to you and Williams?'

'Well, guv,' the sergeant grinned, 'they locked us in the attic shortly after you and Mr Mortimer left. I thought it was funny, all the Guest mourners being young and blokes an' all. When they started taking off their black togs and buckling on their bandoliers, I sensed all was not well.'

'Then?'

'Well. Williams had a brainwave. He used his belt-buckle to lever the window and we climbed down the wisteria at the back. Bit hairy up on the leads, mind you.'

'Almost as hairy as in the duck pond. What did you do next?'

'We knew we had to get help. God knows what these buggers had got planned - they're all mad, y'know. Williams scarpered to get the lads from Pant-y-Grdl nick and I started shuftying through the house. When I popped my head in here, I couldn't believe it. A bloody great machine gun. There were three blokes, two of 'em soldiers guarding it, so it was the old one, two.'

'*Police Manual*, page sixty-one?' Lestrade knew it well. 'Fisticuffs against Felons?'

'That and the poker,' George beamed, glancing at the three bodies draped around the room.

'Inspired,' said Lestrade in awe. But, tell me, all joking apart, where on earth did you learn to fire one of these?'

'Fire it?' George turned a little pale. 'How d'you mean, guv, 'fire it?'

6

'Well, duw, duw,' Inspector Mortimer sat in what passed for his office in the police station at Pant-y-Grdl. Constable Williams was being mother.

'Teisan lap, Mr Lestrade?' he asked, handing round the cake.

The Yard man glanced down. 'No,' he said, 'I always sit this way-'

'There's a thing, innit?' Mortimer said. 'I'd welcome yewer observations, Mr Lestrade.'

'I'd welcome some myself,' Lestrade told him. 'What news on Ranulf Guest?'

'Oh, he's in the Parc, now.'

'The Park?'

'Parc Willt. The local asylum for the Incurably Deranged. His family 'ave 'ad 'im committed, apparently.'

'I'd 'ave signed the papers myself,' Williams said through a mouthful of bun.

'I never thanked you, constable,' Lestrade said, 'for the timely arrival of the Constabulary.'

'Oh, that's all right, Mr Lestrade,' Williams said. 'We are, after all, 'ere to serve.'

'Captain Dance will lose 'is troop, of course,' Mortimer chewed. 'So, really, after that bit of nastiness up at the 'ouse, we're no further forward at all.'

'I wouldn't say that,' George had been silent for a while.

All eyes turned to him. 'Are you going to enlighten us, sergeant?' Lestrade asked.

'I went for a walk this morning, guv,' he said. 'A little bit after breakfast while you were interrogating Lewis.'

'And?'

'I went up to the murder scene, guv, to the quarry.'

'We're all riveted, George,' Lestrade yawned.

The sergeant passed his guv'nor a piece of paper.

'Notepad sheet, Metropolitan Police for the use of,' Lestrade correctly identified it. 'Don't tell me you found this up there?'

'No, sir, it's one of mine. It's what's on it I think you'll find interesting.'

Lestrade uncrumpled it and his eyes widened. 'Where was this?' he asked.

'On a stone face, chalked up,' George said. 'Roughly in a line with where the body must have lain. I sketched it exactly as it appeared. It's a verbatim drawing.'

'Inspector.' Lestrade passed it to Mortimer. 'Seen this before?'

'No , I don't think so,' the Glamorgan detective frowned. 'Looks like a maze or somethin'. What is it?'

Lestrade shrugged. 'A maze or something,' he said. 'But the point is that that design, or something very like it, has been found near two other bodies George and I are investigating.'

'Well, duw, duw,' Mortimer shook his head, 'there's a coincidence, innit?'

'Coincidence be damned,' said Lestrade. 'This all follows a pattern.'

'Aye,' said Williams, looking at George's sketch. 'Like a sort of ... square dance.'

'Hobby of yours, constable?' Lestrade asked.

'Oh, duw, no,' Williams chuckled. 'Not since I was in Calvaria Road Segregated Infants. Dab 'and I was, min', in those days.'

'Five bob says it wasn't on that quarry face when we foun' the body,' Mortimer said. "Ow big was it, sergeant?'

'Big enough not to be missed,' George told him.

'It was raining,' Lestrade said.

'Well, aye,' said Mortimer, to whom the pluvial state was eternal. 'Yew show me two fine days together in the valleys and I'll show yew my left nipple - assumin' I was a mason, of course.'

'Well, that's it,' Lestrade explained. 'The maze might well have been there when the body was, and it may have been drawn by the murderer. The point is that chalk would have been washed away.'

'Why redo it, then?' Mortimer pondered.

'Because', Lestrade said, 'whoever our man is who is so consistent with his blunt instrument, he wants us to know it's him; wants us to take his calling card.' He got to his feet. 'Inspector, the sergeant and I must away. We need to get back to the Yard before we forget where it is. You'll keep "Happy" Lewis under observation?'

'Oh, duw, aye,' Mortimer assured him. 'Like a bactrian under a microscope.'

But Lestrade and George barely had time to rest their backsides on the Yard benches, before a memorandum came down from Assistant Commissioner (Traffic) Rodney. It was addressed to Inspector Abberline, but Rodney's runner knew his chief's habits, so it found Lestrade after all. It read - 'Any joy with cousin Hereward? What about the torso at the Opera House? Is there a connection? What is the missing link? Get on to it soonest, Monro. And take Sergeant Henderson with you.' Clear as mud, Lestrade observed, but the memorandum from Assistant Commissioner (Crime) Monro was more to the point -'There's been another one, Lestrade. Borley in Essex.'

Borley in Essex was scarcely a village at all. It stood on a hillside overlooking the Stour which wound its way lazily through the otherwise flat country below the fenlands, making in its typically English way the squiggly border between Essex and Suffolk.

They caught the train to Bury St Edmunds and a carter's trap to Long Melford. Pausing only to sample the local ale, they followed the old fen road to the village.

Borley Rectory was a hideous building, red brick and multi-roomed with tall gables and deep shadows. It was a far cry from the mellow Cornish stone of its opposite number in Mevagissey, but this time, it was not the vicar who was dead.

'Reverend Bull?' Lestrade asked the hunched old figure who answered his bell pull.

'No,' said the figure. 'I'm Hettie, the maid of all work - and I do mean all work. Who are you and what you botherin' the vicar for at a time like this?'

'Inspector Lestrade,' he told her without tipping his bowler, 'Scotland Yard. This is Sergeant George. And we're here because we've been sent for, I gather. A man is dead.'

She scowled at him and then up at the churchyard, lying at a rakish angle above the house. 'There's a good many,' she observed from her rather peculiar angle on life.

'Who is it, Hettie?' a melodic voice called from within.

'Some coppers, Master Harry. Shall I send 'em packin'?'

'No, no, Hettie. You mustn't do that. We are all God's children. Jesus loves us, this I know, for the Bible tells me so.'

She scrutinized Lestrade carefully. 'He don't love 'im,' she was sure. A rather jolly young man with twinkling eyes and a walrus moustache bustled her out of the way.

'Luncheon for sixteen, please, Hettie. Oh, eighteen?'

'No, thank you, sir,' Lestrade said, wondering what the old crone might lace his repast with if he accepted. 'Would you be the Reverend Bull?'

'Oh, I'd love to be,' he sang. 'And all being well, when Papa goes to that great pulpit in the sky, I shall be. Until then, I am his curate, awaiting the laying on of hands. Harry Bull, at your service.

Oh, that's a little joke we have in the C of E by the way.'

Yes, Lestrade had already approximated the size of it. 'Lestrade,' he said. 'This is George.'

'Er ... George ... er?'

'Just George,' Lestrade said. 'It was the vicar we'd actually like to talk to.'

'Walk this way,' Bull said and led them through a cold mausoleum of a house, where the plumbing clanged and gurgled and they could hear Hettie crooning a dirge in the kitchen; through a dark courtyard at the back Where a few hens barely scratched a living and beyond it into a wild garden dotted with giant yews.

'You could have knocked me over with a brass lectern when Papa found the body,' Bull said.

Lestrade stopped, his shoes already caked in chicken droppings. 'Why did you say that, sir?' he asked.

'What?' Bull had lost the thread already.

'A brass lectern.'

'Oh, I don't know. Familiarity, I suppose. We have one in the church, of course, and one in the library. It's merely a figure of speech, Mr Lestrade, a quip, a *bon mot*. Nothing more. This way.'

They waded through the knee-high grass to a little wooden summer house lying beneath the arms of a curiously dead-looking elm. Spring had reached the Home Counties, but it seemed to have skipped this garden entirely. They heard the snoring long before they reached it and saw an elderly man sprawled on a bench inside, his carpet-slippered feet soaking wet, his face hidden under a copy of the *Church Times* that rose and fell as though on a tide.

'You'll have to excuse him, gentlemen,' Bull said. 'Narcolepsy.'

Instinctively, Lestrade and George took a step back, but when the younger Bull removed the newspaper, his old man was scarcely disfigured at all. 'Papa,' the curate bellowed. 'Papa.'

The old Bull leapt into a sitting position. 'Hymn Number 161,' he intoned, 'Holy, Holy, Holy, Lord God Almighty.'

'He can say that again,' muttered George. It was to no avail however. Years of hearing the organ thunder had left the Reverend Henry Bull curiously bereft in the hearing department.

'No, no,' the old man waved his hands. 'I've told you people before, if God had wanted us to have electricity, he'd have created Michael Faraday a few centuries earlier.'

'No, Papa,' the curate helped him upright. 'The electricity chappies came yesterday. These fellows are here about the murder.'

'What girder?' the old man was more confused than ever.

'I did warn you,' the curate told them. 'Give me a minute.' He sat the old man back down again and joined him on the bench. 'The body, Papa,' he said slowly. 'Old Amos.'

'Ah, yes,' the old vicar remembered. 'Bad show. bad show. But he's dead, y'know.'

'Precisely, sir,' bellowed Lestrade. 'That's why we're here.'

The vicar looked at him oddly. 'There's no need to shout, young man,' he said. 'But I fear you are too late. Our undertaking arrangements are always undertaken by Messrs Audubon of Long Melford.'

'No, Papa,' the young Bull was patience itself. 'These men are policemen. From Scotland Yard. They are trying to find out who killed Old Amos. You'd better sit next to him, Inspector, he's better when you're on his level.'

'When did you discover the body, sir?' the Inspector asked.

'Er ... ooh, it must have been Wednesday.'

'What time was this?'

The old man fumbled in his cardigan pocket for the hunter. 'It's eleven thirty-one,' he said.

'No,' Lestrade persisted. 'Not now. Then. On Wednesday, when you found the body. What time was that?'

'Ooh, it must have been about mid-morning,' Bull remembered. 'I'd come out here to the summerhouse for a snooze.'

'And where was the body?'

'Mine or his?'

'Er ... his,' Lestrade answered.

'Here,' said Bull. 'Where mine is now.'

Lestrade looked at his sergeant. 'I hope you're getting all this down, George,' he said.

'Oh, sorry, guv,' muttered George, whisking out his notepad, 'I didn't think we'd started.'

'No,' sighed Lestrade, 'I'm not sure we have. Do you mean, Mr Bull, that the body was lying on the floor of this summerhouse?'

'No, said the old man. 'Sitting. On the bench, just as I am now.'

'But dead?'

'What?'

'Old Amos was dead?'

'Oh, yes. Utterly.'

'And did you see anyone else in the garden?'

'Pardon?'

'I said "Did you see anyone else in the garden?"'

'Only Marie.'

'Marie?'

The old Rector looked at the detective. 'Tell me, young man, are you by any chance hard of hearing?'

'I?' Lestrade was thunderstruck by the wrong of it all.

'Ah, I thought so,' Bull said. 'I can always tell. You've had to repeat everything I've said for the last few minutes. Now, I hate to be unsociable, but I do have a sermon to prepare. What do you think Henry? "But I am slow of speech and of a slow tongue"?'

'You did Exodus last week, Papa,' his son told him.

#So I did. How about "He fell off the seat backward by the side of the gate and his neck brake"?'

'Ah, perhaps a little unfortunate, Papa, bearing in mind old Mr Quinlivan.'

'Ah, yes,' the old man agreed. 'I was only reading last week in the *Occupational Injuries Monthly* how common an accident that is, falling off a horse-hoe. Well, I suppose it will have to be "My little finger shall be thicker than my father's loins". Nothing like a bit of comparative anatomy for the first before Septuagesima'. He turned, beaming, to Lestrade, 'I am aware that I have been of inestimable help to you already, but if there is yet more you wish to know, do not hesitate to call back after luncheon. I shall be in the Vestry, Harry.'

'Very well, Papa,' the curate helped him up. 'Have a care crossing the road.'

And they all watched the old man teeter away, humming something canonical.

'Perhaps you can explain, Mr Bull, how old Amos's body came to be here.'

The curate sat down and stood up again quickly as he realized he was sitting on George. 'Sorry, sir,' said the sergeant, 'just checking the woodwork.' There were dark brown smears on the panels behind the seat and long sienna runs down to the floor. George shook his head. 'It didn't happen here, guv,' he said. 'Not enough blood.'

'Tsk,' muttered Bull, 'I thought I told Hettie to clean all this up. It's not very pleasant for the children, you see.'

'Your children, Mr Bull?'

'Good Lord, no. My siblings. There are fourteen of us, Inspector. I am the eldest.'

'Fourteen?' Lestrade's eyebrow rose. No wonder the old man was rather vague. 'Do they all live here?'

'Oh yes, of course.'

'And Amos?'

'He was the gardener. Aptly named Flower.'

'For how long?'

'Since he was born, I suppose. Oh, I see. Oh dear, let me see. Eight, no, nine years.'

'He lived in the village?'

'No, in a cottage over at Puttock End. It's about three miles away.'

'And how often did he work for you?'

'Once a week, rain or shine, he'd be over here, snipping and pruning.'

'Really?' Lestrade surveyed the long grass. 'Was he efficient?'

'Well, oddly enough, no,' said Bull. 'For all he wore a smock and carried a scythe everywhere, he really wasn't very good. I asked him once what he thought about marl and he said he didn't like German composers. Didn't seem to have much of an action with the scythe either. Curiously intellectual I thought for a son of the soil.'

'Did he have references when he arrived nine years ago?'

'I suppose so. I really don't know. You'd have to ask Papa.'

'Yes,' sighed Lestrade, 'I feared I might. So, old Amos came to work on a Wednesday?'

'No, Saturday.'

'But his body was found on a Wednesday - or is your father a little confused?'

'A little confused what? Oh, I see, well, yes, he is, but in this particular instance, no; he's right.'

'Did anyone else see Amos this week? Alive, I mean. Your mother?'

'Oh, good Lord, no. Mother hardly ever ventures out these days. She's of a rather nervous disposition.'

Lestrade was not surprised, what with having had fourteen children and all. 'What about your sister ... er ... Marie?'

Bull looked confused. 'I don't have a sister Marie.'

'I'm sorry, your father said he'd seen Marie. I assumed that was your sister.'

'A sister, certainly,' Bull explained. 'Obviously Sunex isn't on the right plane this week.'

'The right ... er ... ?'

'Look, Inspector, I know you'll think us strange, but ... do you believe in spirits?'

Lestrade blinked. 'Ghosts, you mean?'

'Yes.'

He looked at George. 'Well, there was that peculiar figure on the balcony at the Lyceum a few years ago.'

'Henry Irving?' George asked.

Lestrade ignored him. 'I like to think I keep an open mind,' he said. As minds go, few came more open than Lestrade's. As if to prove it, he swept off his bowler and placed it on the seat beside him.

'Well,' Harry Bull squirmed uneasily on the bench. 'The thing of it is, Mr Lestrade, some rather odd goings on go on at Borley Rectory, especially after dark.'

'Oh?' Lestrade was all ears. 'What sort of goings on?'

'Well, look, I think it would be best if you spent the night. Could you do that?'

'We have a body to examine,' Lestrade said. 'I understand they've got him at Sudbury; haven't they, George?'

'Yes, the back room of the International Tea Company's premises in Market Hill. Odd place for a post mortem.'

'That'll be Doctor Trefussis,' Bull said. 'I'm afraid he's rather peculiar. He's a constant visitor.'

'Very well, then,' Lestrade stood up and fetched himself a nasty one on the summerhouse's lintel. 'Sergeant George and I will be back this evening.'

'I shall wait up,' the curate assured them.

The rather peculiar Dr Trefussis was poring over the body when the Yard men arrived. He had a scalpel in one hand and a cup of the International Tea Company's bevy in the other.

'Now,' he barked, 'are you local or Metropolitan?'

'Scotland Yard,' Lestrade said. 'Are you the police surgeon?'

Trefussis shuddered. 'I'd rather vote Liberal,' he said. 'You're the senior man, I suppose?'

'Yes,' said Lestrade. 'But I'd like my sergeant to examine the corpse. If he intends to acquaint himself with the Detective Department, he'll need more acquaintance with mortality.'

'Quite right,' Trefussis approved. 'Help yourself.'

Lestrade took a seat around the wall of the dark opposite the good doctor, who rolled down his sleeves, balanced his cup on old Amos's chest.

'I hear you chappies have a new Commissioner,' he said

'Yes, sir,' Lestrade told him. 'Sir Charles Warren.'

'Hm. Intelligence Quotient vaguely synonymous with a parsnip.'

'I wouldn't believe all that you hear, sir,' Lestrade said.

'Dammit, man, *The Lancet* is never wrong. Warren features prominently in an article on village idiocy. There's another example there.'

George was about to protest about the doctor's pointing finger when he realized that he meant Amos and not his good sergeant self.

'Well, George,' Lestrade said, 'what have we got?'

'Reasonably nourished male, sir,' the sergeant said. 'Five foot ten. Aged about sixty or so. Good deal of scarring to the arms and upper body.'

'Recent?'

George looked at the white weals in the grey flesh. 'Old,' he shook his head.

'Cause of death?'

'Can I turn him over?' George asked the doctor.

Indeed you can, sergeant,' Trefussis said. 'When I've retrieved my tea.' And he did so.

George sucked in his breath. 'Blow or blows to the skull, sir. Fractured all over the shop.'

'Anything to add, doctor?' Lestrade asked.

'Not really. The cranium is completely shattered. I understand the police were picking up bits of bone for hours afterwards. This happened in the garden of Borley Rectory, didn't it?'

'That's right,' Lestrade said. 'I gather you know the Bull family.'

'For my sins, yes. They're all rather peculiar, you know. Hallucinations.'

'Halli ...'

'They see things.'

'Oh?' Lestrade raised an eyebrow. 'For example?'

'Old Fanny, that's the vicar's wife, saw a huge bat in the back passage once. Well, it takes one to know one. She's as stable as quicksilver, that one. The old man of course is narcoleptic.'

George shook his head. 'Terrible thing, tobacco,' he said. 'I never touch the stuff.'

Lestrade had just lit up. 'Did you know old Amos?' he asked Trefussis.

'Only by sight. He used to flit between the conifers of a summer's evening. I was going to employ him at the Ramblings, but

I realized his fingers were anything but green.'

'The Ramblings?'

'My home,' Trefussis said. 'I do a little surgery in the front room and a little tea-planting in the back. That's what comes of a lifetime of medical service in India, of course.'

Lestrade crossed to his number two and glanced down. it was the hands that caught his eye first. He lifted the fingers. 'Anything but green indeed,' he murmured. 'These aren't the hands of a tiller of the soil.'

'I did say he wasn't very good,' Trefussis reminded him.

'Yes,' Lestrade nodded. 'So did Harry Bull. My God.'

'What is it, guv?'

Lestrade was staring into the dark, dead face of the corpse. The eyes bulged with livid bruising and a mark of brown blood was caked on the forehead.

'Yeah,' muttered George. 'Not pretty, is it?'

'Funny you should say that, George,' Lestrade said. 'You see, if this man is Amos Flower, I'm a Chinaman. This is - or was, if my memory serves me aright - Pretty Boy Partridge, otherwise known as Sir Algernon Pilsbury, Rear-Admiral Ponsonby and the Maharajah of Gwalior.'

'Good God.'

'Indeed,' mused Lestrade. 'I've heard him described in amateur detective circles as the Napoleon of Crime.'

'But I thought he was dead.'

'Full marks, George,' Lestrade patted the man's shoulder. 'He is.'

'Suppertime,' murmured the Reverend Bull. 'And the living is easy,' he collapsed back to his slumbers again.

'You do realize,' Sergeant George whispered to his guv'nor, 'that this is the second time we've been in a creepy old Rectory after dark?'

'I do indeed,' Lestrade muttered. 'But if you were afraid of the dark, George, you shouldn't have joined the Force. The colour of the uniform alone . . .'

They sat in the Blue Room. 'And this is the second Blue Room we've come across an'all.' George was fidgeting. 'I'm beginning to get what the Frogs call Day Ja View - and it's not a view I'm particularly fond of.'

The short March day had dwindled to dusk after a magnificent sunset and the last glow still lingered on the appalling wallpaper that spoke volumes for the taste of Mrs Bull. A tiny fire smouldered in the corner, but everywhere there was a chill, a coldness that seeped through jackets and souls. George's teeth were on edge, like the rest of him, as they watched the old vicar's waistcoat rise and fall in time with his snoring.

Lestrade wandered to the window. 'Good view of the summerhouse from here,' he said and glanced back to the bed on which the Reverend had sprawled.

'Is this his bedroom?' George asked.

'No, the curate's.'

'What do you make of him, guv?'

'I don't know, George, yet. But there's something not quite right about this place. Who haven't we seen?'

'Er...' George tried to read his notebook in the gloom, 'Haven't they got any lamps up here?' he tutted. 'Candles?'

'Come on, George. This is the Styx. Ask old Bull who the Prime Minister is and he'll probably say Robert Peel. Who are we waiting for?'

'The daughters ... er ... Millie and Ethel.'

There was a tap on the door.

'Jesus Christ!' George visibly jumped in his nursing chair.

'Come in,' Lestrade said. The Reverend Bull snorted in his sleep.

Two girls, one big and buxom, the other like a willow, peered round the door, giggling.

'Millie?' Lestrade said.

'No,' said the big one, 'I'm Ethel.'

'I'm Millie,' the skinny one piped and squeezed into the room beside her sister.

'Right,' Lestrade said. 'I am a policeman.'

'We know,' they chorused.

'Good. Now, I'd like to ask you some questions. Except ... I rather thought your mother would be present.'

'Oh, Mama doesn't see anyone,' Millie said, flouncing on to the bed. She vaguely noticed the figure lying there. 'Good Heavens, Papa looks quite dead, doesn't he? What do you want to know, Inspector?'

'Oh, she doesn't know anything,' Millie said, bounding across to sit on the other side from her sister. She crossed her father's legs at the ankle. 'There,' she giggled, 'he looks like a crusader now.'

'Er ... how old are you, Ethel?'

'Seventeen,' she said.

'Oh no, she isn't,' Millie snapped.

'Oh, yes I am.'

'Oh ...'

'Ladies, ladies,' Lestrade held up his hand, 'it really doesn't matter. I'm just trying to break the ice.'

'I suppose it is quite cold in here,' Ethel looked around her. 'Old Hettie is useless at fires.'

'It's not the fire, silly,' Millie said. 'It's the Presence.'

'The ... er ... ?'

'The spirit,' she looked at him with wide eyes. 'Hasn't Harry told you?'

'Well, he did mention .

'Well, he's silly,' Ethel said. 'He hasn't seen it as often as we have, has he, Mill?'

'No, he hasn't,' the thin one concurred.

'Um ... how well did you know old Amos?' Lestrade asked.

'The gardener? Hardly at all, really. I didn't like him.'

'Oh?' said Lestrade. 'Why was that?'

'Well,' Millie pondered. 'He was silly.'

'Silly?'

'He was always talking about poetry and music.'

Lestrade could quite see why that was silly.

'No, he wasn't,' Ethel said. 'He was always talking about London.'

'No, he wasn't,' Millie contradicted.

'He was to me,' Ethel said. 'I quite liked him, actually.'

'He was nice to you?' Lestrade asked.

'What do you mean, 'nice'?' the girl frowned.

'Well, er ... pleasant, friendly.'

'Mrs Shubunkin says you shouldn't say "nice".'

'Mrs Shubunkin?'

'Our governess. She's dead now, of course.'

'Really?'

The girls nodded. 'Last year,' Millie said. 'Went of the influenza. just as well. I hated her.'

'I quite liked her,' Ethel said.

'Er ... to get back to old Amos...'

'No, Mrs Shubunkin always said "Don't use the adjective 'nice' dears. There are far better words".'

'She also said', Ethel wobbled and her eyes twinkled, 'there are other words with four letters that we mustn't use.'

She and Millie collapsed across their father's legs, shrieking with hilarity.

'Er ... yes,' said Lestrade, glancing in desperation at George.

'Quite.'

'Of course, Harry uses those words.'

'Really?'

'Yes,' said Millie. 'Especially when he dropped that hammer on his foot. Do you remember, Eth?'

'It was a pick,' Eth remembered.

'No,' Millie was certain. 'It was definitely his foot.'

'Er ... George,' Lestrade felt his knuckles whiten on the window-sill, 'I've got to see a man about a dog. Perhaps you could carry on?'

The sergeant's jaw fell slack, but the guv'nor's word was law.

In any case, before he could re-lick his pencil, the guv'nor had gone.

'What man?' Ethel asked. 'We haven't got a dog.'

'What's he really going to do, sergeant?' Millie sidled over to him. 'Are you married, by the way?'

The sergeant felt his collar tighten. 'Er ... no,' he said.

'No,' Millie looked earnestly into his face. 'I expect that's because you're so very old.'

Lestrade found the downstairs privy after several false turns the near darkness. Old Hettie had put the shutters up now all the younger children were in bed. He was just buttoning up when he felt a blast of cold air. He spun round, but saw nothing. It was as though the door had opened, but the door was shut fast. He turned to the washstand, poured the icy water over his hands and fumbled for the soap. As his fingers neared it, the bar leapt through the air of its own volition and imbedded itself on the rim of the basin. There was a gurgling noise, though the privy had no flush system. He poured the water into the pan and unlocked the door.

In the hall stood a grey, wizened woman, the light, such as it was from the single oil lamp, at her back. Her hair appeared as so many snakes writhing in the twilight. Lestrade felt his own hair crawl.

'Mrs Bull?' he said, since this was the only member of the household he had not met.

The figure slid noiselessly past him and as it did, a sense of deep cold hit him like a wall. He felt his chest gripped like a vice and he bounced back against the dado. When he looked again, the figure had gone beyond the velvet curtain that hung at the end of the hall. He shook himself free and followed it, plucking up his courage to whisk aside the curtain. The brass rings rattled on the pole and he found himself staring at a blank wall. Except that it wasn't quite blank. There, just above his eye level in a childish scrawl, was a pattern he'd come to know quite well - a maze, like a square spider's web, studded with dewdrops. His throat was iron-hard and his skin frozen. How he got back up to the Blue Room he could never afterwards remember.

It wasn't the prettiest of pictures he'd ever seen. It may of course have been a trick of the light, but he could have sworn that just before George George leapt to his feet and came rushing over to his guv'nor, he appeared to have a teenaged girl on each knee. The daughters of the vicar were still giggling, this time even more hysterically and Lestrade sensed that George had never been so pleased to see reinforcements in his life.

'Anything untoward, George?' Lestrade raised an eyebrow.

'No, guv,' the sergeant gasped, 'thanks to you. Blimey, you look like you've seen a ghost.'

'Come with me' the Inspector ordered and the two of them padded through the house to where the figure had vanished into thick brick.

'Recognize that?' Lestrade whispered.

'The maze,' said George. 'How did you find it?'

Lestrade looked at his sergeant. The man was already as windy as the Thames Estuary. No point in disturbing him still further. 'You know my methods, George,' he said. 'No stone unturned, no curtain not pulled aside. Got a lucifer?'

George did the honours. Resourceful for a man who did not smoke.

'What, in your opinion, made that?'

'What?' George frowned. 'Don't you mean "who", guv?'

'Hmm?' Lestrade feigned absentmindedness. 'Yes. Yes of course. What did I say?'

'You said "what".'

'Haha,' the laugh was short and brittle. 'Silly.' And he checked himself. Five minutes in the company of the Misses Bull could have changed his vocabulary for ever.

'Ah, there you are.'

The Yard men spun round at the voice and their heads cracked together painfully.

'Oh, I'm terribly sorry,' it was the curate, padding towards them with oil lamp in hand. 'Didn't mean to startle you. Good Heavens, that's a new one.'

'What is?' Lestrade asked.

'The wall writing.'

'You've seen these before?'

'Oh, Lord, yes, dozens of times. All over the place. In the Blue Room, the dining-room, Millie and Ethel's room. Incidentally, are those girls in bed yet?'

'Not quite,' George muttered gratefully. 'But it was touch and go there for a minute.'

'Must bed the old man down too. He will doze off all over the place. Seems to prefer any bed in the house to his own. Still, bearing in mind Mama, it's not surprising.'

'Er ... yes,' Lestrade walked a little way with him. 'Your mother. Is she a short woman? About five foot? Grey hair, rather unkempt?'

'No,' the younger Bull said. 'Why do you ask?'

'Oh, no reason,' Lestrade said. 'It's a little game we have at the Yard. It helps with observation, criminal identification, that sort of thing.'

'Yes, well,' chuckled the curate, 'I'm not sure Mama counts as an identifiable criminal. Besides, she's been asleep for a couple of hours. I just looked in on her. Snoring like a train.'

'This wall picture,' Lestrade shook himself free of the unpleasantness that lay over him like a shroud. 'You said "That's a new one".'

'That's right. It's usually messages. Look, let me get Papa to his own room and I'll meet you in the library. That's just below the Blue Room and has the best view of the garden.'

'A little late for views, isn't it, Mr Bull?' George asked. 'Must be nearly eleven by now.'

'Nearly eleven?' Bull repeated. 'Ah, no, Mr George. It's actually too early. The best views of all tend to be witnessed around midnight.'

Around midnight, three men sat bolt upright in the firelight of the library. The dying embers threw a soft, red glow on to the dancing figures of monks that gambolled around the fireplace, their enamel eyes strangely manic in the gloom.

'Of course,' said Harry Bull, 'I've grown up with this. All my life odd things have happened in this house. Papa sees Marie often in the garden, just behind the summerhouse, where the stream runs underground.'

'Who is this Marie, exactly? You said she was a sister.'

'Well, she certainly appears in a habit. She looks ... sad, lonely, wringing her hands and glancing anxiously up and down. I've never seen Sunex, but I've spoken to him.'

'Sunex?' Lestrade repeated. 'Ah, yes, the one on the other plane, I think you said. You'll have to forgive us, Mr Bull, I don't believe we have a file marked 'Things That Go Bump In The Night" at the Yard.'

'No,' chuckled the curate. 'I don't suppose you have. Well, Papa and I have a theory - and Sunex confirms this at seances.'

'Seances?' It was too dark for George to take notes and in any case, he couldn't trust his hand on a wobbly pencil against a trembling pad.

'Discussions with the dead, sergeant,' Bull said matter-of-factly. 'We've often held them. Sunex is quite talkative.'

'Who is he?' Lestrade asked again.

'Well, Papa has seen his entirety,' the curate explained. 'Millie and Ethel have both seen his legs - I'm not sure what to make of that.'

'I am,' muttered George, but it went unnoticed.

'We've all seen the coach and four, except old Hettie, but then she won't stay in the house after dark. Funnily enough, we've never had a servant who will.'

'Get away,' Lestrade mused. 'So this Presence your sisters referred to ... ?'

'Well, Papa and I think that long, long ago, perhaps in the thirteenth century, there was once a monastery on this site. When Papa had the house built back in '63 he seems to have found bits of tile and so on indicating a fair-sized House. Dominican, probably.'

'And?'

'And Papa has, or had before he got a bit dopey, quite an affinity with the Spirit World. From the time I was a boy, we've held seances and eventually got through to a monk called Sunex Amures. Now, via a series of raps and knocks, old Sunex told us a rather tragic story. He met and fell in love with a nun from the nearby convent at Bures, about eight miles away. Well, as you know in the Catholic Church, and especially then, such things are frowned upon.'

'Quite,' Lestrade had met this situation in the Confirmation Case, years before.

'So Sunex and Marie Lairre - that was the nun's name - eloped.'

'Don't tell me,' said Lestrade. 'In a coach and four.'

'Precisely,' said the curate. 'But unfortunately, they were discovered and brought back. Poor old Sunex was beheaded and even poorer old Marie was walled up alive.'

George shuddered.

'The curious thing is', Bull went on, 'that we think she was walled up here, in the monastery, not in her own convent at Bures. Nasty beggars, of course, the Dominicans. Rather a vicious twist of irony, don't you think? Putting the poor girl within feet, perhaps inches of the place where her lover had walked and talked only days before? You must remember, these were essentially the same chappies who organized the Inquisition later on. I always think they'd have made jolly fine policemen, don't you?'

Lestrade ignored him. 'So the nun ...'

'Usually walks just out there,' the curate pointed to a stand of elm trees through which a little stream slid blacker still in the surrounding pitch. 'She's still searching, you see. Still peering anxiously up and down the road, watching for her lover's coach. All terribly, terribly sad.'

'And the wall-writing?'

'Ah, yes, well that's what convinced us that Marie was walled up here rather than there. She's crying out to us, you see, a genuine *cri de coeur*. The writing is usually words. Something to the effect of "Help. Light. Mass." That sort of thing.'

'Which means?' Lestrade asked.

'Well, obviously, if you were walled up somewhere, wouldn't you need help? The poor, frightened girl is in total darkness, without food or water and her air is running out. She wants help and she longs for the light - to see the sun again, the sky. But most of all, she wants God's help, a Mass to be said for her, to cleanse away her sins. Pretty rotten, I think we can say, being a promiscuous nun in the thirteenth century.'

'Hmm,' nodded Lestrade. 'A bitch. But the maze design you hadn't seen before?'

'No, no,' Bull admitted. 'But I've been thinking about that. It's probably a map of the monastery. She's drawing us a map to tell us where she is.'

'Is?' George felt his throat bricky-dry. 'You mean her body is still there ... behind one of these walls?' he glanced wildly around him.

'Don't be stupid, George,' Lestrade scolded. 'This house is ... what ... twenty years old? Dammit, man, you've seen as many cadavers as I have. Show me a body that's survived for six hundred years and

I'll show you the contents of my wallet. Get a grip, man.'

'There are more things in Heaven and earth, Horatio.' Bull wagged a finger at Lestrade.

'Sholto, sir,' the Inspector corrected him. 'Unfortunately, I can't arrest a ghost for loitering in the garden and it doesn't get us any nearer to who killed old Amos.'

'Maybe it was old Sunex, guv,' George whispered, his eyes bulging.

'George,' Lestrade gripped the man's sleeve, 'this is 1886, the forty-seventh year of Her Majesty, God Bless Her. The British Empire is the biggest in the world and there's a bloke in Canada who can talk to another bloke miles away through a series of wires connected to a lump of celluloid. That's the real world.'

'Well, there you are,' George remained unconvinced. 'That can't be natural, for a start.'

'Oh dear,' they heard the curate say, 'that's odd.'

The Yard men followed his gaze. Out across the garden, beyond the summerhouse, where the elms stood gaunt and naked and the black stream ran underground, vague shapes were moving through the night.

'Jesus Christ!' George had leapt backwards, sending the chair sprawling.

'What's that, Mr Bull?' Lestrade whispered, standing his ground.

'Er ... damned if I know,' the curate said and began to back along with George.

'Late visitors?' Lestrade prayed that his voice wasn't betraying the tightness in his chest.

'Surely not,' Bull attempted to remain rational. 'They'd come to the front door.'

'Bloody hell!' George hissed.

'Shut up, George!' Lestrade ordered, but he was glad the sergeant was wearing his regulation brown trousers. 'Is that the nun?' he asked Bull.

George had covered his head with his arms by this time but Bull and Lestrade still looked on, their backs to the far wall.

'Possibly. I see two figures.'

'It is them!' George muffled through his fingers. 'It's that bloody monk and that bloody nun.'

The monk and the nun slid noiselessly over the spring grass, pausing now and then as if to check the house for lights or sound. One billowed white in the eerie light, the other dark as death with

a pale face, tall and thin.

'He's a big bugger,' Lestrade heard himself whisper, but the voice was not his own. It was from somewhere else, outside himself. His hand had already found the brass knuckles in his pocket by the time the sash of the window flew up. The scraping wood elicited a scream from George and a similar one from the nun, who fell forward into the room with a heavy thud.

It was Lestrade who had the presence of mind to fumble for a lucifer first and he found himself staring into the pale face of a constable of the Essex Force, the match flame twinkling on his helmet plate.

"Evenin' all,' he saluted when his heart had descended a bit. 'We was under the impression that the house was empty. The family 'ad gorn away for a while.'

'Who told you that?' Bull asked.

'Well, initially', said a voice from the floor, 'I did. It was passed to me by my superiors.' The nun got up, the pale duster coat falling open to reveal what passed on the Suffolk-Essex border for a detective. 'Flannel, CID.'

'Lestrade, Scotland Yard,' said Lestrade. 'This is Sergeant George. Er ... George?'

But the sergeant of that name lay in a dead faint against the skirting board.

'He hasn't been well,' Lestrade explained.

'Who has?' Flannel blew his nose vociferously. 'Three bloody hours I've spent in that perishing garden. Oh, begging your pardon, Mr Bull.'

'Why wasn't I told you were surveilling the house?' the curate asked now that his heart had descended.

'I don't know, sir,' the Essex Inspector told him. 'I only follow orders. "Check the Rectory" they said. Check the Rectory I have.'

'Can I come in now, Inspector?' the tall constable still had one foot in and one foot out of the window.

'Oh, yes, right you are, Topsy. This is Constable Turvey, gentlemen, what for want of a better word I will call my right hand man.'

'Thanks,' Lestrade helped him in. 'Only it's brass monkeys out there, which is why me an' Mr Flannel come in 'ere. Mind you,' he grunted at the dismal grate, 'not much better in 'ere, is it?'

'Look, Mr Bull,' Flannel said. 'you haven't got a poultice, have you? I feel a shocking cold coming on.'

'Walk this way, Inspector. I'm sure old Hettie has something putrefying in the kitchen. Will he be all right, Mr Lestrade?'

Lestrade knelt and slapped George around the head a few times. The sergeant groaned. 'As rain,' the Inspector said. 'So, Turvey, did you know we'd been called in?'

'Yessir,' said the constable, re-closing the window. 'We 'ad 'ad a note to that effect.'

'What can you tell me about the late Amos Flower?'

'Not a lot really,' the lofty law-enforcer shrugged before diving his numb hands into the fire. 'Blimey, stingy lot these churchmen, ain't they? He lived over at Puttock End. I turned the cottage over myself. Nothin' there, of course.'

'You're sure you know who he was?' Lestrade helped the disoriented George to his knees.

'Eh?'

'I mean, you do accept that he was simply Amos Flower, part-time gardener?'

'Well, of course,' said Turvey. 'Who else would he be?'

'No one,' smiled Lestrade. 'No one at all. George? George? Can you hear me, George?'

'I think so, guv'nor,' the sergeant felt the lump on the back of his head where he'd gone down. 'That is, if you just said "Can you hear me?" I did, yes.'

'That's the ticket. No, keep your head down between your knees for a minute. No, not my knees, Sergeant. The constable here will talk.'

'Not me, sir,' Turvey assured him. 'I know when to keep silent. You won't learn anything from the likes of me.'

As soon as Lestrade had struck a match in the man's face he had been sure of that. 'Tell me,' the Inspector said, 'are there any more of your lads out there?'

'No, sir,' Turvey said. 'Just me and the Inspector. Why?'

'Oh,' Lestrade felt the hairs on his neck moving. 'It's just that there are two figures out there on the lawn' and he heard the thud and the groan as Sergeant George slid gracefully to the floor again.

The two figures floated out beyond the trees, one of them peering into the stream bed before swinging wide to approach the house.

'They must be your blokes,' Turvey said, his fist tightening on his truncheon.

Lestrade shook his head. 'Me and George,' he whispered. 'That's all there is.'

'You don't believe this 'aunted 'ouse story, do you sir?' Turvey asked.

Lestrade remembered the wizened thing he had seen in the hall, the ghostly maze chalked up on the wall. The wall through which the thing had vanished.

'No,' he said firmly. 'Unless...' and he said no more before the sash crashed upwards and a tall figure in a tweed Ulster put his right leg to the floor.

There were screams all round and Constable Turvey hooked his truncheon under the throat of the sprawling figure. A shot rang out, illuminating the library in a sudden flash of light. Lestrade leapt for the gun and grappled with its owner, half in, half out of the window. When he'd hauled him in far enough, he dropped the window to bounce with a sickening crunch and the figure stopped struggling. Turvey was sitting on the other one, pinning him to the floorboards.

'Well, well, well,' Lestrade was making good use of his match-striking technique tonight, 'if it isn't Ianto and Dewi,' he let his adversary go and loosened the window frame from his neck.

'Damn you, Lestrade, you nearly broke my occipital.'

'Sorry, doctor,' the Inspector said. 'I'd have offered to buy you a new one. I suspect, however, that when we can get some light into this room, we'll find that you will be buying Mr Bull a new bit for his ceiling. Do you have a licence for that pistol?'

'Of course I do. My God, Holmes, are you all right?' he hastened to the prone figure of his friend, pushing the constable off him.

'Do I detect the fact that you know these gentlemen, sir?' Turvey pocketed his truncheon.

'Sadly, yes,' sighed Lestrade. 'After a fashion. When I saw them last, they were rather badly disguised as Welsh miners.'

'What are they disguised as now?' Turvey wanted to know.

'Private detectives, unless I miss my guess.'

'Golly, how exciting,' Curate Bull was back. 'I thought I heard something go bang in the night.'

'You did,' said Lestrade. 'It was the sound of whatever credence Sherlock Holmes once had, shattering. What are you doing here?'

'Your job for you, Lestrade,' Holmes allowed the good doctor to massage his neck. 'You know who old Amos is, don't you?'

'Yes, well,' said Lestrade loudly, 'I think this is more than enough excitement for one night Where are you staying, gentlemen?'

'The Barley Arms,' Watson told him. 'They do a capital Colchester clam.'

'Excellent, we'll join you,' Lestrade said.

'But ...'

'Please, Mr Holmes,' Lestrade interrupted, 'it's late. Sergeant George can stay here, with your permission, Mr Bull.'

'Oh, yes, absolutely. Of course. He can share old Hettie's poultice.'

'Constable, give my regards to Inspector Flannel. I had intended to visit him tomorrow. Perhaps he'll join me at the pub for breakfast?'

'Very good, sir.'

Lestrade checked his number two one last time while the curate saw Holmes and Watson out. 'I must apologize, sir,'

Holmes was saying. 'My assistant and I were merely trying to find somewhere to shelter.'

'Oh, quite all right,' Bull understood. 'Dashed inclement, March.'

'Poor old George,' Lestrade placed the man's bowler on his chest. 'Quite out of spirits.'

7

They rattled south, courtesy of the London and North Eastern Railway - Detective-Inspector Lestrade, Detective-Sergeant George and a little old lady intent on her copy of the Railway Library.

'I'm sorry, guv,' George was mumbling about last night. 'I don't know what came over me.'

'Terror, George,' Lestrade said.

The little old lady glanced over her pince-nez.

'But don't worry about it. We all have our off days.'

'So the second pair were Holmes and Watson again.'

'Like bad pennies,' Lestrade nodded. He reached for a cigar but the disapproving inrush of breath from the little old lady made him put it away again.

'What were they doing there?'

'You know Holmes's methods,' said Lestrade. 'He's one of those irritating b ...'

The old lady's eyes widened.

'... bachelors who have time and money to wander the country in search of other people's business.'

'But he's dogging our every step.'

'Holmes is the least of our worries, George. It's time you and I recopulated on these crimes.'

The lady's left eyebrow flickered a little.

'Do you ... er ... think we should, sir?' the sergeant asked, jerking his head in her direction.

Lestrade waved aside his objection. 'Murder One,' he said.

'Hereward Rodney,' said George, 'but .

'Yes, I know,' said Lestrade. 'No maze. Even so, I'm prepared to bet my pension he's the first of many. Go on.'

'Rector of Mevagissey, found bludgeoned to death, slumped on his own brass eagle in the church of St Peter.'

'Found by?'

'The oldest curate in the world.'

'Who also saw ... ?'

'Probably the murderer. Tall bloke, posing as a Bishop.'

'Who had the agility to leap nine foot walls. Motive?'

'Something to do with the Rector's unhealthy interest in the young ladies of the parish. My money's on one of the parents.'

'All right,' Lestrade watched the riveting Essex countryside flash by. 'Murder Two.'

'Osbaldeston Ralston, found floating in his duck-pond in the early hours.'

'By?'

'A copper. Er ... Constable Spatchcock.'

'Cause of death?'

'Blows to the head.'

'Clues?'

A maze this time. Fussock the butler had it on him. Did we ever find out why?'

'Still waiting to hear from old Fussock himself. I know the telegraph isn't what it was, but two weeks ... Motive?'

'He was heavily in debt but seemed to have made a huge amount of money recently by rooking people. Universally detested. Either of the sons could have done it - or that cracker who was the daughter of Admiral Ratcliffe.'

'Or Squire Cotterell or Mr Hands, both of whom were Ralston's guests on the night he died. Murder Three.'

'Byngham Batchelor, writer of sorts. Found on the steps of a terrace in Lisson Grove, his head stove in.'

'Clues?'

'Same method of attack as all the others. Screwed up bit of paper with the maze stuffed into his false teeth.'

'Motive?'

'Seemed he was in the habit of pinching other people's work

when he doubled as a publisher's editor. Making a small fortune out of somebody else's talent does get some people a bit miffed.'

'Indeed, Murder Four.'

'John Guest, coal owner. Found at the foot of a quarry in somewhere unpronounceable in South Wales. Same method of murder. Same maze design scrawled on the rock above him.'

'Though not at first. Other clues?'

'A piece of blue serge material on barbed wire nearby, which could of course have nothing whatsoever to do with the crime.'

'Quite. It's my guess it came from a copper at the scene and is therefore a blue herring. Sighting?'

'Not clear. Some bloke seen running away by a Peeping Tom. Not the most reliable of witnesses.'

'Motive?'

'A nasty bastard who let people die every day in his mine, just for profit. If he was anything like his old man, he was totally deranged.'

'Murder Five,' Lestrade said.

'Ah, yes,' George leaned forward. 'Now this, if I may venture the opinion, sir, is the lynchgate of the whole thing.'

'It is? Why?'

'Because, as you so brilliantly observed...'

'You've already got the job, George. Boot-licking I can do without.'

'As you observed, the deceased in the garden at Borley was not who he claimed to be, but an underworld character ...'

'Oh, how thrilling!' the Yard men jerked up as the old lady slammed shut her book. 'I cannot contain myself any longer.'

'Madam, please,' Lestrade adjusted his tie. 'You're old enough to be our mother.'

'Forgive me', she sat down next to him, all shawl and mothballs, 'but I could not help but overhear your conversation. Are you really detectives?'

'Er ... yes, madam.'

'From Scotland Yard itself, perhaps?'

'Yes, madam.'

'Oh, how exciting. I've just been reading ***Murder Most Foul***. It's set in a chicken farm in Neasden.'

'Fascinating,' winced Lestrade.

'So you see, I am something of an amateur sleuth myself. Oh', she gushed, 'not in your league of course. But even if I say so

myself, I guessed the murderer in *Death Sneaks Up Behind One* by page sixty-eight.'

'Remarkable,' sighed Lestrade. 'How many pages in the book?'

'Sixty-nine,' she said. 'But in *The Big Snooze* I'd worked it out by ...'

'Madam', Lestrade interrupted, 'I'm sure your detective powers are legendary, but we were wrong to have discussed delicate and confidential matters in your hearing. I'm sure you appreciate that we cannot discuss them further.'

'Oh, quite, quite,' she raised her hand. 'It's just this mention of a maze. What does that signify?'

'I really don't know, madam,' Lestrade confessed. 'Now, please...'

'No harm in showing her, guv,' George suggested.

The Inspector looked at his number two with something approaching horror. The man was breaking every rule in the book. 'All right,' he said, 'but if this ever comes out, you and I will be back to the horsetroughs for ever.'

He showed her the rough sketch of the maze that George had made after the third murder.

She chuckled softly. 'My dear detectives, this isn't a maze.'

'It isn't?' frowned Lestrade.

'Dear me, no, it's a game board, popular since the Middle Ages, I believe. It's known as Nine Men's Morris.'

'Morris!' Lestrade and George chorused.

'Madam,' Lestrade kissed the little old lady's hand, 'you've made a comparatively young man very happy. Tell me,' he whipped a novel out of his Donegal pocket, 'have you read this one?'

She took the volume. 'Ah... *Slaughter on Shaftesbury Avenue*, sadly, yes. The murderer is ...'

'No, no,' beamed Lestrade. 'Really. You've already told us who the murderer is, madam.'

Where the river bends at Chiswick Ait, within a spittoon-shot of the distillery, stands Upper Mall at Hammersmith and it was here that Lestrade stood the next morning. Yes, it was April Fool's day. Yes, his leg was still playing him up. Yes, Sergeant George was having a Rest Day, the first in a long time, to recover his composure after the unnerving incidents at Borley. But all that was a mere bagatelle, for Lestrade sensed the case was in the bag.

The door of the picturesque house, garlanded with ivy and peacock's feathers, was opened by a still-attractive woman in her middle years. With his decade of experience in these matters, Lestrade divined at once that she was not the downstairs maid.

'Mr Morris's housekeeper?' he asked.

She smiled' 'Housekeeper, confidante, letter-writer and, I hope, his inspiration. I am Jane Morris.'

'Oh, I do beg your pardon,' Lestrade tipped his bowler. 'Inspector Lestrade, Scotland Yard.'

'Oh, what a pity,' she let him in. 'William was expecting a tapestry expert from the Gobelin Works. You don't know anything about vegetable dyes, do you?'

'Sadly, no, madam.' Lestrade was too ashamed to admit he'd missed that lecture and he couldn't remember it appearing on the curriculum at Mr Poulson's Academy for the Sons of Nearly Respectable Gentlefolk all those years ago.

If the hall was unusual, the drawing-room was an experience. Entwined flowers covered the wallpaper, pomegranates and grapes swelled out of the woodwork, the hinges on the doors were ornate beyond belief and knights and dragons did battle up and down the curtains. She squeezed him into an appallingly uncomfortable Medieval chair whose slats pinched Lestrade's bum even through the Donegal. Obviously, people's bums were of a different shape in the Olden Times.

A short man with wild hair and a barbed-wire tangle of beard arrived a little later. 'Mr Lestrade?' he said, extending a hand, 'I'm William Morris. How may I help you?'

Lestrade was grateful to stand up. 'I'll come straight to the point, Mr Morris,' he said. 'This is not a social call. I am conducting a murder enquiry.'

'Good Heavens,' Morris sat down heavily in a chair opposite Lestrade's. It looked a damned sight more comfortable, but the Inspector was left with the painful one.

'Do you know one Isaac Lewis, known as "Happy"?,

"Happy' Lewis, yes, by correspondence.'

'In what capacity?'

'In my capacity as a Socialist.'

Lestrade raised an Establishment eyebrow. 'A what, sir?' he said with a voice like gravel.

'A Socialist, Mr Lestrade. Oh, I know it finds little favour in Gladstone's England, but let me assure you, a time is coming - such a time.'

'It's later than you think, Mr Morris,' Lestrade observed. 'Have you kept Mr Lewis's letters to you?'

'I believe so, but there is only one.'

'One letter?'

'Yes. You must understand, Inspector, that many people write to me, mostly on artistic matters, but also to do with politics.'

'Does the name John Guest mean anything to you?'

Morris frowned, stroking the tangle beneath his chin. 'Wasn't he the owner of the colliery where "Happy" works?'

'"Wasn't he?" You use the past tense.'

'Well, of course. I read the newspapers like everyone else, Inspector. John Guest was done to death, wasn't he? I assume that is the murder enquiry to which you refer.'

'That and others,' said Lestrade, cryptically. 'Does the name Amos Flower mean anything to you?'

'It is true that mosses flower in their season,' the nature lover told him. 'But I much prefer sunflowers. Would you like to see my designs?'

'Another time, sir,' Lestrade said. 'Amos Flower wasn't a work of art, at least not when I saw him he wasn't. The back of his head had been destroyed. Which is precisely what happened to John Guest and three other gentlemen it has not been my pleasure to meet recently. Tell me, are you familiar with the East End?'

'Sadly, yes.'

'Were you familiar with it last September?'

'September?'

Lestrade was grateful to find a moment in the conversation when to lean forward would be appropriate. 'Come now, Mr Morris, it can come as no surprise to either of us when I remind you that you were arrested last September in connection with a Socialist meeting in the East End.'

'Indeed I was,' Morris admitted. 'And I think you'll find I was discharged without trial.'

Lestrade felt constrained to lean back. 'You won't find the English judicial system as lenient in a capital case, sir,' he said.

'Mr Lestrade,' Morris sighed, 'I am an artist, architect, designer, lover of nature, poet, even a dilettante if you will . . .'

Lestrade was surprised to hear that, bearing in mind the attractiveness of Mrs Morris. 'And murderer,' he added quietly.

'That is a slander, sir,' Morris sat on his dignity. 'There are those who say I murder art, which is unkind; that I murder poetry, which is unfair; but that I murder people is a gross calumny.'

'What is this, Mr Morris?' Lestrade played his trump card, the design of the board game.

The artist-turned-Socialist looked at it. 'Looks like ... a rather uniform spider's web,' he said.

'It could be,' said Lestrade. 'What else?'

The architect-turned-poet reconsidered. 'A plan, perhaps, of a barracks or villa.'

'Or else?'

The artisan-turned-interior-designer was stumped. 'I am stumped,' he confessed.

'I am reliably informed,' Lestrade told him, 'that it is a board game called "Nine Men's Morris".'

'Of course!' Morris chuckled. 'I haven't seen one of these since I was a boy.'

'Then you're very fortunate, sir,' Lestrade said. 'I've seen four of them recently, all at or near the scenes of vicious murders.'

Realization dawned in the great man's gentle eyes. 'I see,' he said. 'So are you interviewing everyone called Morris?'

'No, sir,' Lestrade assured him, 'only you. You see, in my experience, if one name occurs more than once in a murder enquiry, that name should be investigated, scrutinized, held up to the light.'

'Ah, I see,' Morris said soberly. 'The connection with Lewis and John Guest.'

'Precisely. Tell me, sir, what particular brand of Socialism do you use?'

'My own,' said Morris. 'I was born with a silver spoon in my mouth, Inspector.'

Lestrade could not conceive how that appalling accident came about, but Morris swept on. 'Marlborough, Oxford, I had all the advantages. Look around you, at this house, the beautiful things in it. Yet yards from here, in darkest Chiswick, is unimaginable drabness. And further to the east, in hell holes like Whitechapel and Bethnal Green, poverty beyond belief. Turn out your pockets.'

'I beg your pardon?'

'Your pockets. Turn them out. Put their contents on that table.'

So thunderstruck was Lestrade by the suggestion that he found himself complying. An omnibus ticket, his battered half hunter, three cigars, money to the tune of four and elevenpence ha'penny and his brass knuckles.

'Take this, for example,' Morris swept up the bus ticket.

'Mass production at its very worst. Cheap, horrible. How much nicer if these were lovingly hand-crafted. And this, a shoddy watch for the mass market ...'

'My father's,' said Lestrade. 'Of great sentimental value.'

'I do not doubt it, Mr Lestrade, but how much nicer if it had been chiselled cold rather than dye stamped. And this ... what's this?'

Lestrade slipped the brass knuckles over his own. 'A companion of a mile,' he said.

'Quaint,' nodded Morris. 'Oriental design, isn't it? Not perhaps what I would expect to be carried by an officer of the Metropolitan Police; however, how preferable if these rings were ornamented with vines and traceries.'

'And how much more painful,' Lestrade nodded. 'Perhaps I'll commission you sometime. What is the point of all this?'

'The point, Mr Lestrade, is that we live in a machine age, an age of hooters and whistles and what may be termed mass-production. We move to the pace of machines, we have lost the ability to make by hand. I want to bring that back, to recreate Merrie England where the artisan was a craftsman and made beautiful things. But I want to add to that a society in which there are no Jacks and no Masters, no hierarchy at all, where we live in one grand Utopia without Poverty and without Want.'

'Bravely spoken,' said Lestrade. 'Unfortunately, some of us have to live in the real world, not one that might be.'

'Yes, yes, of course,' Morris agreed. 'But that does not mean we should not try.'

'We?'

'The S. D. F.'

'The ... er...?'

'Social Democratic Federation.'

'A large organization?'

Morris shook his head. 'Sadly, no,' he said. 'Our numbers are growing, it is true, but there are too many contending schools of thought. Henry Hyndman formed the Federation ... what ... five years ago now. Then there are the Trade Unions of course. And as for the Fabians ... I myself am toying with creating a Socialist League, somewhat apart from the rest.'

'The Fabians?' Lestrade was lost.

'Named after the Roman General Maximus Fabius whose delaying tactics apparently wore down the Carthaginians in whichever Punic War was going on at the time.'

'Wore them down?'

'Yes. They probably died of boredom. Typical of Annie Besant and the Webbs, though, to name themselves after a ditherer. My Utopia will only be achieved by a revolution, Inspector. As dear old Karl said "Working men of all nations, unite. You have nothing to lose but your chains. You have a world to win".'

'Tell me, Mr Morris,' Lestrade said, 'do you by any chance have a list of these people, these Fabians and Federalists?'

'I believe so,' Morris told him. 'But Mr Lestrade, I must ask you why you need it.'

The Inspector stood up. 'Mr Morris,' he said, 'when I arrived a few minutes ago, I must confess I intended to arrest you for the murder of John Guest, possibly others. Now that I've met you,' he scooped up his belongings, 'I'll withhold that pleasure. Withhold, mind you, not forego. It occurred to me that one way to hasten your revolution of the riff-raff is to knock off pillars of the Establishment - a Rector, a prominent businessman, a publisher and a coal-owner.' He looked at Morris's deep chest, the powerful arms under the artisan's smock. 'And you're strong enough, I'd hazard a guess. Then it occurred to me that the Nine Men's Morris is a little obvious. That's when it also occurred to me what a marvellous opportunity it would give to someone who didn't like you, didn't go along with your ideas.'

'No, no,' Morris shook his head. 'Burne Jones and I are one in the Arts and Crafts Movement.'

'I was not referring to art, sir,' Lestrade said. 'I was referring to politics. This Hyndham, these Webbs. Any of them could have the motive to put you in the frame, so to speak.'

'Oh, no, Inspector,' Morris was horrified. 'We may have Socialist differences of opinion, but nothing more. I assure you. they are incapable of such a thing.'

'Well,' said Lestrade, 'we shall see, Mr Morris. The list, if you please, and ... you won't be leaving the country for a while, will you?'

'No, no,' Morris assured him. 'I've done Iceland, I've done Italy. There's nowhere else to go, really.'

Donald Sutherland Swanson, 'Gloria' to his friends, had made Inspector after only fifteen years on the Force. The least obnoxious of the vast army of Scotsmen at the aptly named Scotland Yard, he had been known to put his hand into his deep pocket and buy somebody a chop in a chop house. That occasion was 2nd April 1886, a little after one thirty and the lucky recipient was fellow

Inspector, Sholto Lestrade.

'You got your man, then, Gloria?' Lestrade was making free with the apple chutney.

The heavily mustachioed Scot scowled under his beetling brows. 'No doubt you're referring to Percy Lefroy,' he muttered. 'And no doubt you realize that was four years ago.'

'Good God,' Lestrade chuckled, 'was it really? Well, well, well. You must admit, it was a little foolhardy to let him pop back home to change after you'd arrested him. It's still the talk of C corridor.'

'I know that, laddie,' Swanson refused to be ruffled. 'I can only put it down to ma trusting Presbyterian nature. Anyway, we did recapture him.'

'Four months later, yes,' Lestrade said, readjusting the napkin under his chin. 'Nice bit of lamb, this.'

'It's pork,' Swanson told him.

'Yes, well,' Lestrade explained, 'I've been travelling around the country for a while. What are you working on now?'

'The missing Gainsborough,' Swanson sampled the tea.

'Kidnapping,' Lestrade was impressed. 'Who's got him, d'you think?'

'Not him, Lestrade, it. It. Gainsborough's been dead for donkey's years. It's one of his paintings that's gone missing.'

'Ah, well,' Lestrade dunked his bread and butter in the gravy. 'That's what comes of a classical education. Why did you leave teaching, Gloria?'

'Because it was a dead end job. Look at W. E. Forster.'

'Who?'

'He of the first ever Education Act. I read in the paper only this morning, he's about to meet that Great Examiner in the Sky.'

'Yes,' nodded Lestrade grimly, 'it comes to us all.'

Swanson looked at him. 'Look, Lestrade, you're a decent enough sort of fellow in your own way .

'Oh, thanks.'

'And I don't mind in the slightest buying you this not inexpensive lunch, but I can't believe you sought me out to discuss ancient cases.'

'Ah,' sighed Lestrade. 'Never could pull the wool over your eyes, Gloria. But in fact, it's precisely ancient cases I want to talk to you about; well, one, anyway.'

'Not the Countess of Dysart's jewels,' Swanson beamed. 'Ma pride and joy. Well, the countess said it to me, 'Donald", she said, just like that, "Donald..."'

'No, not that one,' Lestrade used his tie pin as a toothpick. 'Pretty Boy Partridge.'

'Ah,' Swanson's eyes lit up. 'Now there's an interesting tale.'

'So I believe,' Lestrade said. 'Any pudding?'

Swanson reluctantly clicked his fingers and the rather greasy dago waiter hobbled over. 'What's the cheapest thing on your pudding menu?' he asked.

'Cheese ada biscuits.'

'Right. We'll have one of those.'

'You wanta Cheddar or Gruyère?'

'Lestrade?'

'Yes,' the Inspector leaned back, content. 'That's fine.'

The waiter hobbled off, mystified.

'The point is', Lestrade leaned forward confidentially, 'I missed out on Pretty Boy's early career by being an errand boy at the time. I ran into a few of his lads of course in the City Force. Then I gather he perspired to higher things.'

'Higher indeed,' said Swanson. 'Well, if my encyclopaedic knowledge of East End roughs serves me aright, he was born back in the 'twenties in the Ratcliffe Highway. His old man was a suspect, briefly, I understand, in the Pear Tree murders in 1811.'

'Runs in the family, then?'

'Och aye. Yon Pretty Boy would have killed his granny for three ha'pence. Matter of fact, that was his first known crime.'

'Killing his granny?'

'Stealing three ha'pence. He was four.'

'Lucky he wasn't hanged in those days.'

'Aye,' Swanson reminisced, though he didn't go back that far. 'The good old days. Pretty Boy went on through the usual street crime, picking pockets, garotting. Became a gang leader at the age of nineteen. Led a group of social deviants called The Blind Beggars, mostly racecourse thieves, bit of burglary on the side.'

'That's right - and they were still there in 'seventy-three when I joined the City mob. He was a bit long in the tooth by then, wasn't he, for a gang leader?'

'Aye, but at some point during Mr Gladstone's first ministry, Pretty Boy must have realized that he had a brain.'

'Aha.'

'He got involved in some nifty West End burglaries.'

'That's right - Hanover Square, Buckingham Palace.'

'To name but two,' Swanson said, lighting his pipe. 'Specialized in diamonds, then bullion. Must have been a millionaire by the time he disappeared.'

'Which was when?'

'Er...'eighty-one. No, I tell a lie. Tail end of 'eighty.'

'What's your theory on that?'

'Aye, well that's what makes it all so fascinating. Somewhere along the line, Pretty Boy acquired quite an education - even more staggering because he'd been nowhere near Scotland. He wrote articles on music for various learned journals and poetry which he got published.'

'He did?'

'Aye, but we think he had something on the publisher.'

'And the disappearance?'

'He'd booked into the Metropole under the alias of Sir Algernon Pilsbury, a soubriquet he'd used since at least 1869. We'd got an eye-witness to the Abercorn Diamond lift and at last a watertight case.'

'And?'

'I sent my best lads to the hotel .

Lestrade saw by Swanson's face that all had not been well.

'You didn't give him time to change?'

'Dammit, of course not, Lestrade!' Swanson was ruffled.

'What we didn't know until too late was that he was a master of disguise. Walked straight past my lads in full clobber as the Maharajah of Gwalior, burnt cork and the lot.'

'Didn't they challenge him?'

'Of course,' Swanson said. 'But this was C Division. Speakers of fluent Hindoostani were a mite thin on the ground. I kicked myself afterwards of course - and them. A minor miracle had however been achieved and there is now a course of Ethnic Dialects for Metropolitan Policemen. Been on one yet?'

'Not being often in Dorset, I don't really feel the need,' Lestrade shrugged. 'Good God, what's that?'

The Yard men peered simultaneously at the mysterious dish the waiter had just left. Lestrade poked the Gruyère.

'It's off. I'll take it back,' offered Swanson.

'No, don't worry. And after the Metropole?'

'Nothing,' Swanson shrugged. 'As they say in the Penny Dreadfuls, "He had vanished without trace". There was an article that turned up last year in *The Cripple* on the value of prosthetic pinkies written by a P. B. Partridge, but I checked it. Pure coincidence.'

'Really?'

'Aye. Petronella Beatrice Partridge was a bedridden spinster of Stow-on-the-Wold who had lost an arm in a bicycling accident. Oh, I know what you're thinking, but not even Pretty Boy had that much of a mastery of disguise.'

'You're sure?'

'Let's put it this way. I deliberately tipped half a cup of tea over the old lady's front and while her maid was sponging her down, I behaved like an absolute cad and leapt back into the room, having vacated it earlier so that said sponging could take place.'

'And?'

'And I narrowly escaped a damned good smacking from the Assistant Commissioner. At least I proved one thing - Miss Partridge's appendages were most definitely her own. Not, at seventy-three, anything to get excited about, but native to her chest, certainly. Surgical cosmetics have not yet attained the miraculous.'

'So that's it,' Lestrade said.

'Aye, I'm afraid so.'

'Or is it?'

Swanson looked at Lestrade over his tea cup. 'You know something,' he said.

'Does the name Amos Flower mean anything to you, Gloria?'

'Don't think so,' Swanson said. 'Should it?'

'Add it to the list of Algernon Pilsbury, the Maharajah of Gwalior and one you missed I think, Rear-Admiral Ponsonby.'

'Ah yes, neat con that, selling that warship to the Russians. Especially as it was one of theirs. Wait a minute, are you saying you've found him?'

Lestrade nodded, rather as the cat with the cream.

'Well, you wee bastard,' Swanson slapped his back. 'Fancy you getting the collar after all this time. That's Chief Inspector for you, laddie. Not that I'm green at all, y'ken. Just don't turn your back on me when you try to leave this café!'

Lestrade laughed. 'No, it's nobody's collar, Gloria,' he said. 'You see, somebody found Pretty Boy before I did. Bent something blunt and heavy over his head a few times. What I want to know is why.'

"Well, he must have made more than a few enemies in his time.'

'For instance?' Lestrade asked.

Swanson guffawed. 'Half the Metropolitan Police for a start, not excluding my good gentleman self. Then there's anybody he's stolen from or swindled.'

'Not to mention, presumably, the Maharajah of Gwalior?'

'Indeed" Swanson concurred. 'Still, head bashing isn't their style. For that I'd try Chiv Eagle in the Nichol.'

'The Nichol?' Lestrade repeated.

'Och, it's a teaparty in comparison with the Gorbals on a Saturday neet.'

'Why this Eagle?'

'He's still the big pancake among the High Rips, though he's fifty if he's a day. He's held a grudge against Pretty Boy ever since they fell out over a girl back in the old days. Vowed to cave in his head if he ever saw him again.'

'All right,' said Lestrade. 'It's a start. Thanks, Gloria. And thanks for the lunch. Shame about the cheese.'

'Aye. I shan't be frequenting this emporium again, I can tell you. By the by, what are you doing on April the eighteenth?'

'I've no idea,' said Lestrade. 'Why?'

'Well, Assistant Commissioner (Traffic) Rodney's put me in charge of the Police Revue this year. I'm doing "My Heart's in the Heelands" with the Glee Club and PC Corbutt of F Division is doing his gymnastics again, but I'm short of comic turns. I thought perhaps your Sarah Bernhardt ... ?'

'Oh no,' Lestrade held up his hands in horror. 'Once was enough. I still haven't got the rouge off.'

'One good turn deserves another,' Swanson said, waving the bill at Lestrade. 'And if that High Rips tip pays dividends ...'

Lestrade twisted his lip in scorn. 'All right,' he moaned. 'Pencil me in. But the moustache stays, understand? And you get the usual slander clearance.'

'Consider it done, Sholto, m'boy, consider it done.'

'Where, Holmes?' Watson dabbed a little more boot polish on to his cheeks.

'The Nichol, Watson, a knife's throw from Bishopsgate.'

'Isn't that the most dangerous quarter of a mile in the country?'

'No, my dear fellow,' Holmes assured him. 'You're thinking of the Palace of Westminster.'

'I wish I knew what we were about,' Watson complained.

Holmes glared at him. Why was it, he wondered, and not for the first time, that he had the bad luck to be saddled with a congenital idiot for friend and foil.

'Sit down, my dear fellow,' he sighed. 'Let me take you through it one more time. You remember you purchased a copy of that most atrocious rubbish the *Sudbury Recorder?*'

'Yes.'

'Well, it's rather like that other dreadful rag the *Kincardine Intelligence* - a contradiction in terms. just as there clearly is no intelligence in Kincardine, neither does the *Sudbury Recorder* record anything of note, except one small item.'

'Ah,' Watson raised an aware finger, 'that fascinating little piece on thrombosis in the over seventies.'

'No, Watson. The sketch of the late Amos Flower.'

'Oh.'

'It was poor, I'll grant you, but enough of a likeness to stir something in this stupendous differencing machine I call a brain.'

'Oh, that's right, I remember now. The "Napoleon of Crime", I think you called him.'

'Precisely. Grandiose, perhaps, and I'm not sure von Clausewitz would agree.'

'Well, those Jews don't know everything.'

'Funny you should mention Jews, Watson, because that's precisely what our Napoleon was.'

'Really?'

'Levi Partridge, known as Pretty Boy. From underworld rough to brilliant cracksman and confidence trickster. If the man had had any moral fibre at all, he'd be in the House of Lords by now. Come to think of it', he arched a demonic eyebrow, 'since when has moral fibre anything to do with the House of Lords? Got your service revolver?'

'Yes,' Watson patted his threadbare pocket, 'no thanks to Lestrade. I really took umbrage his laying about me like that.'

'The man's a vegetable, Watson. You have to make allowances. He won't have made the connection yet between Flower and Partridge. It isn't likely he ever will.'

'But if Partridge was clubbed to death in a garden in Suffolk, why are we going to the East End?'

'There are those who sought his blood, Watson, back on his own turf. If there's a clue to the death of Pretty Boy Amos, we'll find it in the Nichol.'

A horrified Mrs Hudson arrived back from shopping at that moment, her hair awry in the gusts of April. She stared in disbelief at the ragged pair before her. 'Look at this,' she handled Holmes's collar with some distaste, 'and clean on this morning.'

Fournier Street. Midnight. That time on the shift that every copper dreads. The old day not dead and the new day as yet unborn. The People of the Abyss lurched from pub to pub, chatting drunkenly at street corners, nipping up back passages to make the beast with two backs. Or, because the night was chill and the ground dank, the beast with one back. The world of the Abyss looked halfway bearable with your head down and your skirts up over your arse.

'Are you feeling good natured, dearie?' a creature of the night accosted the youngest of four men.

'I'm not feeling anybody,' he admitted.

'Run along, there's a good girl,' grunted the older man and batted her aside.

'Oh yeah,' she wagged her backside after them. 'After a bit o' brown, are we?'

'Are you sure you want to do this, Tyrrell?' Lestrade asked. He noticed the boy looked pale in the pawnshop window's reflection.

'I'll be all right, sir.'

'Well,' Lestrade said, 'first time in the Nichol can be unnerving. Green?'

'Here, sir.'

Lestrade looked along the line of men. 'Yes, I am aware of that. Put that bloody life-preserver away and stop looking so much like a copper. Fancy a pint at the Britannia? I seem to have left my wallet at the Yard. George?'

The sergeant patted his pocket and sighed. 'I've got the wherewithal, guv,' he said.

It was Lestrade who saw them first, as they turned into Nichol Street, their boots clattering on the cobbles. The gaiety from the Horn of Plenty around the corner died away. There was no light here at all, only a fitful moon appearing and vanishing in a huge puddle at their feet. He brought the strolling squad to a halt and tucked his fist into his brass knuckles.

'Well, well, well,' a Cockney-Jewish voice called from the darkness. 'Toffs, Ezra. Slummin' it. Come to gloat at the poor people.'

There was a snigger and scrape of steel. Tyrrell tensed.

'Easy boy,' Lestrade muttered out of the corner of his mouth. 'Remember what I told you on the 'bus coming over here. Scare tactics. How many, George?'

'Three I see.'

'That's at least six, then,' Lestrade said softly. 'We're going to walk a few paces forwards. If we can just reach that fire-escape ...'

'That's far enough,' another voice called. It came from behind them.

'All right,' Lestrade kept up his whisper. 'George, you and Green turn, slowly, now. No sudden moves. Tyrrell, you and I will keep looking ahead. At all times, I want to feel serge at my back. Understand, Green?'

'Got it, sir,' the constable swallowed. 'But there's eight, nine of 'em.'

'"Yea, though I walk through the valley of the shadow of death, I will fear no evil,"' murmured George.

Now it was Lestrade's turn to worry. His number two had got religion.

'The hands,' said the first voice. 'I want to see all the hands.'

Eight of them appeared from pockets and climbed slowly for the air.

'Right. Ezra. Hymie. Feel some linings.'

'Pretty Boy Partridge,' shouted Lestrade.

There was a silence; then scuffles at the far end of the alley and muttered voices. Lestrade lowered his hands as he heard boots scrape on the cobbles towards them. A middle-aged Jew with a black wideawake on his head emerged into the gleam, his reflection black in the moonpuddle, his coat, nearly to the ground.

'"Chiv" Eagle?' Lestrade did as the Jew did, placed his hands in his pockets again.

'Who wants to know, already?' Eagle asked.

'I smell Miltonian,' Hymie whispered at his elbow.

'I got a nose,' Eagle stated the obvious.

'Not local though,' Ezra peered through the gloom. 'I'd remember a mug like that.'

'Not local,' Chiv mused. 'But a Miltonian, nonetheless. That can only mean one thing.' He called to Lestrade, 'you from the Yard?'

'Second floor,' Lestrade nodded.

Chiv spat in the moonpuddle, sending little rippling moonlets out to its edge. 'Not even top brass they send me. What do you want, copper? Out collectin' for widows and orphans? 'Cos there'll be a few more come mornin'.'

'They say you own this patch,' Lestrade said.

'They say quite right,' Chiv grinned, his teeth flashing silver.

'From here to the Chosen People's Cemetery.' He walked forward, his hand-tooled shoes splashing through the puddle, Ezra and Hymie close by him. 'An' I don't like it when coppers, Miltonians even, come saunterin' across my turf. An' what's all this about Pretty Boy Partridge? He's long dead.'

Lestrade walked forward too. The serge of Green's jacket had gone from his back, but he cradled the knuckles in a fold of the Donegal and he felt the catch that would release the blade in an instant. 'He's been dead about six days,' he said.

He saw the Jew's composure crack. A rubbery tongue lashed his thick lips in the gloom. 'Six days? What you givin' me, six days?'

'All I want is the man who caved in the back of his skull,' Lestrade said.

'So do I,' said Chiv. 'I'd give 'im a medal. A gong, already. The Freedom of the City. 'Cos you know, copper, me 'n' the Mayor, we're like that,' he held up entwined fingers.

'Come off it, Chiv,' Lestrade said. 'It's common knowledge you wanted Pretty Boy dead.'

'I may 'ave said so,' Chiv lisped. 'But that was a long time ago.'

'What was it about?' Lestrade asked.

Chiv tapped the side of his nose. 'That's your trouble, copper. Typical Commissioner's Office. You've poked it in too far tonight.' He stepped back. 'Ezra. Hymie,' and he snapped his fingers.

A blade flashed in the darkness and Lestrade had leapt over the puddle, the four inches of steel glinting wickedly under the Jew's ear. 'One more step from anyone', Lestrade shouted, 'and the High Rips will be electing a new leader.'

'He's bluffin',' the Jew rasped, but his head was thrown back at a painful angle and his wideawake had rolled in the dirt.

'Four inches,' Lestrade said.

'Is he boasting again?' George asked Green, their life-preservers ready for the attack.

'Four inches of steel,' Lestrade shouted. 'If I push, just a teensy-weensy bit harder, the point of my blade will be tickling old Chiv here right between the eyes. But it'll be from the inside.'

The scream of a police whistle shattered the moment. At both ends of the alley, the High Rips broke and ran, their boots dying away on the cobbles. Chiv tore himself free and stood in the darkness, the long, slim-bladed knife from which he took his nickname gleaming in his hand.

Lestrade had never taken the fencing option at school, but he came to the on guard position and waited. Three burly Miltonians clattering to his rescue gave Lestrade an edge all his own.

'Another time, copper,' Chiv spat. 'You and me. Another time. I'll wear your guts to keep my socks up, believe me.'

'Quick, Chiv,' Lestrade slid the blade home into the knuckles. 'Shabbas soon. The Rabbi won't like you being out.'

'Mind how you go!' George called after him.

'Brilliant, George,' Lestrade slapped his arm. 'The whistle. Inspired. I didn't know you carried one.'

'I don't, guv,' George said. 'It wasn't me.'

'Oh, well, never mind,' Lestrade led them back to the relative light of Fournier Street. 'Don't be ashamed of being upstaged by a rookie. You, Tyrrell?'

'No, sir.'

'No, I thought not. Well done, Green. Stout fellow.'

'It wasn't me, sir.'

The police whistle shrilled again, urgent, frantic.

'Over there,' Lestrade shouted. 'Someone's in trouble.'

There were as many people running away as were running towards the sounds of chaos. A bullseye lantern flashed in a dismal court off jacob Street and the detectives hurtled to it, Lestrade's leg playing him up with the exertion of it all.

'Who's there?' he called.

'Constable 319, Chingford, J Division. Who are you?' An overweight, over-aged copper crouched in the darkness.

'Inspector Lestrade, Scotland Yard. What's up?'

'Murder, sir. I saw the blokes who done it running that way.'

'Which way?'

'In a north-easterly direction.'

'Tyrrell. Green. At the double. What are they looking for, Chingford?'

'Two men, sir. One tall wiv a 'awk-like nose, the uvver short, little moustache. Workin' men, but wiv posh accents.'

'How posh?'

'Er ... Baker Street, I'd say.'

'Oh God ...'

'What is it, sir?'

'Nothing, Green. Pray that I'm wrong and get after those men.'

The constables dashed away.

'Constable,' Lestrade squatted beside the body. 'Your bullseye if you please.'

The shaft of light fell on the glistening head of a middle-aged man. Dark blood trickled over his astrakhan collar and was forming a growing pool under his face. His eyes stared sightless, his face creased in a frown, as though something lying in the courtyard didn't please him at all. It didn't please Lestrade either. He swivelled the lantern to the right and the flickering beam fell on a symbol crudely daubed in blood on the nearby wall. It was the board of Nine Men's Morris.

'Blimey, guv,' George muttered. 'Do you recognize this bloke?'

Lestrade looked at the face again. 'No,' he said, 'should I?'

'Maybe yes, maybe no,' said the sergeant. 'It's Sir Anthony Rivers, Advocate. He won't be getting anybody else off.'

8

Lestrade was no stranger to the Temple. It was through the vanished Bar that he had walked those years ago as he swapped his City helmet for one of the Metropolitans. Springtime gilded the blossom of the little trees among the cobbles and the Inspector limped up the steps to the Chambers at King's Bench Walk.

A clerk in uncompromising grey with a wing collar he appeared to have borrowed from Mr Gladstone showed him into an oak-panelled office lined with dusty tomes labelled 'Regina versus'. Roger Derringham QC sat with his feet on his desk, poring over an enormous brief.

'Inspector Lestrade to see you, sir,' the clerk bowed and made his exit.

'Thank you, Foskett. When the Russian Ambassador arrives, give him a small vodka, will you, and check his antecedents? After all, the crime of which he has been accused has never been brought before an English court before. And it's certainly never been perpetrated in St James's Palace. Tea, Lestrade?'

'Thank you, sir.'

'Foskett. The *thé ordinaire, s'il vous plait. Il n'est qu'un simple agent.*'

'Very good, sir,' bowed the old clerk, used to cryptic messages from his gentlemen.

'Sir Anthony Rivers,' said Lestrade.

'Hmm. Poor old Tony,' the QC closed his brief, waving Lestrade to a chair.

'He was your boss, I understand?'

Derringham smiled darkly. 'He was Head of Chambers, yes. Not quite the same thing, old boy.'

'How long had you known him?'

'Tony? Ooh, six, no, seven years. He was in some ways my mentor.'

'We have spoken to his wife,' Lestrade told him.

'Ah, Calpurnia, yes. She's above suspicion, of course.'

Lestrade sensed a chink in the advocate's armour. 'Why would you think we'd suspect her, sir?'

'Why? My dear fellow, don't you read the Court columns? She was filing for divorce. Tony had some rather nasty habits.'

'Indeed?'

'Mr Lestrade,' Derringham swung his feet down from the desk, 'I am breaking no confidences when I tell you that in common with a high percentage of public men, Tony had a certain penchant.'

Funny, thought Lestrade; the post mortem hadn't revealed that.

'He had?'

'Ladies of the Night,' Derringham said. 'Ah, Foskett, the tea. It's all right, I'll be mother,' and he waved the old boy out. 'One lump or two, Lestrade?'

'Two, please.'

'Good, I like a man who's fastidious.'

'Ladies of the Night?' Lestrade reminded him.

'Ah yes. Not just any ladies, mind you. Not for him the demi-mondaines of Duke and Jermyn Street, oh dear no. The wretches of the Abyss were more his cup of tea. How's the ***thé superieur***? To your taste?'

'Oh affluently, thank you,' Lestrade said.

'I have it shipped in from the Carnatic,' Derringham said. 'Mysore.'

'Lovely. So Sir Anthony enjoyed slumming?'

'I'm afraid so. Clap of course was the least of his worries.'

'What was the most of them?'

'Well,' Derringham paused, his little finger jutting from the porcelain, 'it's not for me to speak ill of the dead, but I did detect a certain falling off, shall we say, in his advocacy of late. I was his junior in Regina versus Bickerstaff.'

'The mass murderer of Chipping Ongar?'

'The same.'

'But he did it, didn't he?'

'Of course he did it, Lestrade; what's that got to do with it? Bickerstaff Senior owned half of Essex. Tony and I cleaned up as they say.'

'You knew he was guilty?'

'Lestrade,' Derringham was amazed, 'I am quite amazed. How long have you been a policeman?'

'Er ... thirteen years, sir.'

'At the Yard?'

'Ten.'

'And you still ask a question like that? A man's guilt or innocence is an irrelevance in this day and age. A chap can have blood all over his fingers, but a good advocate will get him off. Alternatively, he can have been out of the country on the Night in Question and he'll swing. It all depends on his counsel.'

'And Sir Anthony was the best?'

'Formerly, yes. Latterly ... Personally, I think he'd lost it.'

'It?'

'That essential dash and fire. That ability to look straight into the eyes of a jury and tell them a load of bilge. That ruthless attack that reduces police officers to mindless wrecks ... although to be fair, that last isn't usually too difficult.'

'And to what do you attribute this loss?'

'Syphilis,' Derringham chirped. 'Softening of the brain. Henry VIII, Beethoven, he's in jolly good company.'

'Was there anywhere specific he ... frequented?'

'God knows,' said the QC. 'Essentially it's a solitary vice, Inspector. At least, before he meets his Unfortunate it is. Not the sort of thing he'd want a colleague tagging along for. Especially a colleague who has taken silk.'

'And Lady Rivers knew?'

'Put a pair of detectives on to it, I understand.,

'A pair of detectives? Not ... ?'

'Yes, I believe so. Grand and Batchelor.'

'Who?'

'They have an office off Chancery Lane. I've used them myself before now.'

'Er ... this is rather by the way, Mr Derringham, but you've never been tempted to use a pair called Holmes and Watson?'

'No,' the lawyer shrugged. 'Never heard of them.'

Lestrade breathed a sigh of relief.

'Anyway,' Derringham poured himself another cup, 'I don't wish to be uncharitable. You're doing your job, I know, but I am a very busy man as, you can see. Why all these enquiries into poor Tony's death? You can't be surprised at a street crime in the Nichol, surely? The man's astrakhan coat alone would have been incentive enough to any of our unwaged brethren east of the Bar.'

'Quite likely,' nodded Lestrade, wrestling with a recalcitrant tea leaf wedged somewhere on his tongue. 'But this was no ordinary street crime. To begin with, nothing has been stolen. And then, there was this,' he passed the advocate a piece of paper.

'What's this?'

'It's a board game plan,' said Lestrade. 'A game called Nine Men's Morris.'

'What has it to do with Tony?'

'That's the question I am trying to answer, sir,' Lestrade said. 'It's a copy of what was daubed in blood just feet away from the body. And we've seen it before.'

'Really?'

The Inspector nodded. 'In a variety of forms, it's turned up near four other bodies since February.'

'Has it now?'

'All over the country. All bludgeoned to death in the same way.'

'My, my. What's the link?'

Lestrade sighed. 'When I've established that', he said, 'I'll have my murderer.'

'One moment,' a thought had occurred to Derringham. 'Foskett!'

The ancient clerk of that name appeared at the door.

'What was Sir Anthony working on when he died?'

'The llchester Impersonation, sir.'

'Oh yes. That's right. Nothing gripping there, Lestrade, I shouldn't have thought. Alöis llchester stands accused of impersonating a Greenwich pensioner. Mind you, they'd have hanged him for that in the good old days. Foskett, I seem to remember some chap calling for Sir Anthony on Monday.'

'The day before he died,' Lestrade observed.

'That is correct, sir,' the old man said.

'Did he see Sir Anthony?' Lestrade asked.

'No sir. Sir Anthony was at his club, at luncheon.'

'And this visitor was in connection with the impersonation case?'

'I don't know, sir. He wouldn't state his business.'

Lestrade grunted. 'Or leave his name, I suppose?'

'Oh, yes sir. He left a name. It was Merrill.'

Lestrade and Derringham looked at each other. 'Was it now?' said Lestrade. 'No address, though?'

'Why yes. Er ... let me see,' the old clerk shuffled away and returned in a trice with a ledger. 'The Home Office, Whitehall. Opening hours 11-6.'

It was not to the Home Office that Lestrade went first. After all, this Merrill might have no connection with Rivers's death at all. It was not unusual for a Home Office boffin to contact a leading advocate and no doubt Mr Merrill would turn out to be somebody's private under-under secretary and no harm done. And there was more pressing business. For three days, two East End roughs had been held in custody in Leman Street Police Station, charged, in the first instance, with resisting arrest and one with the carrying of a firearm for no really good purpose. The taller of the two had attacked young Tyrrell with what appeared to be a violin bow as the constable had brought him down in a rugby tackle to the south of Fournier Street. It was little things like that that disturbed Lestrade. Orders had been issued by the Superintendent of H Division into whose territory the felons had run, that no one but Inspector Lestrade was to interview the men. That no one of course, did not include Sergeant George.

'Watch my lips, George,' the taller rough was saying. 'You know me perfectly well. I am Sherlock Holmes of 221B Baker Street.'

George was not convinced. 'Every time I see you, Mr Holmes,' he said, 'you're in a different disguise. You were keeping a welcome in the hillside when I saw you last. More recently, I understand, you were being a ghost.'

'Ah, so you admit it's me.'

'I admit nothing of the sort, sir. I am merely pointing out that as Mr Sherlock Holmes is constantly purporting to be someone else, I cannot be sure he really exists. Is he purely a figment of someone's fevered imagination?'

Holmes lolled back in the chair in the dank little cell, without a light. 'You're curiously quiet, Lestrade,' he said. 'It's not like you.'

'What were you doing in the Nichol on Thursday night?'

'We ...'

'Shut up, Watson,' Holmes hissed. 'The grown ups are talking. We were merely pursuing our enquiries.'

'That's my line,' Lestrade said, clasping his fingers over his waistcoat.

'We are, in an odd sort of way, on the same side, Lestrade,' Holmes thought he'd never have to admit it. 'It's merely that our methods differ. Public sector, private sector. Right hand, left hand.'

'Either could have killed Sir Anthony Rivers. Why did you resist arrest?'

'Resist arrest?' Holmes shrieked. 'When two burly idiots come running out of the darkness at you, you don't stop to examine their credentials. In any case, they both behaved improperly. As soon as I am allowed my one telegram, I shall be suing the lot of you for wrongful arrest.'

'Quite. I ...'

'Do shut up, Watson,' Holmes snarled. 'I feel one of my heads coming on.'

'It's just that I shudder to think how many tea and toasts poor Mrs Hudson will have made over the last three days.You've no right to keep us here, Lestrade. Or haven't you heard of Habeas Corpus?'

'One case at a time, please, Doctor,' the Inspector said.

'Aha,' chortled Holmes. 'An own goal, I think, Lestrade. Well done, Watson, old fellow. And do forgive my petulance earlier.'

'Well, I'm not sure I want to,' Watson bridled.

'Why, I repeat,' said Lestrade, 'were you in the Nichol?'

'You knew perfectly well why, Lestrade,' Holmes said. 'You know I recognized the sketch of Pretty Boy Partridge, the Napoleon of Crime. The Nichol was his old stamping ground. That was where we'd learn something about his death.'

'And did you?'

'No. Because we'd only just set foot in the place when a police whistle blew and we were being chased.'

'You were seen running away from the scene of the crime,' Lestrade said.

'We were running away from two very large men intent on doing us harm,' Holmes persisted. 'It's a natural enough reaction, God knows. We had no idea that a prominent advocate lay dying streets away.'

'Do you know what this is, Mr Holmes?' Lestrade showed him the same piece of paper he had shown to Roger Derringham.

'Of course,' said the World's Greatest Detective. 'It's the game plan of Nine Men's Morris.'

Lestrade nearly fell off his chair. Then he looked closely at Holmes. Could he, in one of his interminable disguises, have been the old lady on the train? Unless he had shoes strapped to his knees at the time, unlikely. He turned to Watson. 'May I have a second opinion, Doctor?'

Watson screwed up his baggy eyes to focus. 'Well, er ... it's not

for me to contradict Holmes, but it looks like a maze to me. Or a spider's web.'

'Of all the people I have discussed this with, Mr Holmes, you and one other are the only two who have correctly identified it. Tell me, Doctor, was there a time when you and Mr Holmes were apart during your sojourney to the Nichol?'

'No,' remembered Watson.

'Not even a moment?'

'Not even a moment. Why do you ask?'

'Because, Watson,' Holmes said darkly, 'my recognition of this piece of paper has somehow put me squarely in the frame. Your failure to recognize it has got you out of it. It follows therefore, that in Lestrade's warped sense of logic, I killed Sir Anthony Rivers and you were merely my alibi, my stooge.'

'I say, Holmes,' Watson protested. 'Steady on.'

'Am I correct, Lestrade?'

'After a fashion,' the Inspector nodded.

'Well, I take it back,' Holmes told them, 'I always said you were the best of a bad bunch. Now I'd like to reserve judgement. What is the significance of the Morris game?'

'One of those little snippets we kept back from the newspapers,' Lestrade said. 'This, or something like it, was found near the bodies of Osbaldeston Ralston, Byngham Batchelor, John Guest and Amos Flower, also known as Pretty Boy Partridge. It was also found in his own blood near the body of Anthony Rivers.'

'Why?'

Lestrade leaned forward. 'You're the Great Detective, Mr Holmes. You tell us.'

'Holmes?' Watson said, but the great brain was already working, the forehead furrowed, the brows knitted.

'We should start with the game,' Holmes said. 'Nine Men's Morris. There are also versions played with six or three men, but nine is the most popular. A form of it has been played since the fourteenth century at least and it is also known as Nine Men's Mill or Merrill ...'

'What?' Lestrade leapt to his feet, overturning the chair.

'What did you say?'

'Er ... we should start with the game...'

'No, no. The last bit. The last bit.'

'Er ... it is also known as .

'Merrill. You said Merrill.'

'Yes.'

'George. Take a photograph of Mr Holmes. Usual thing. Side. Front. Back. Get PC Bailey over from the yard. Or Snowdon if it's Bailey's Rest Day. He's to process it double quick and you're to take it over to a bloke named Foskett at 24 King's Bench Walk. Got it?'

'Got it, guv. What about these two?'

'After the photos, let 'em go. And, Mr Holmes...'

'Yes, Lestrade.

'Let us get on with our job, please, in the future.'

'If I thought you could do your job, Lestrade,' sighed the Great Detective, 'it would give me the greatest of pleasure.'

'Where will you be, guv?' George asked.

'The Home Office,' Lestrade said.

Now Lestrade had met bureaucracy before. Many times. He was part of it in his own singular way. But in the corridors of power at the Home Office he was shunted from private secretary to under secretary to doorman and back again. The magic hour of six had arrived and the cleaners were in, trailing those same corridors with buckets and mops. A world-weary Inspector of Scotland Yard was just about to leave before he was thrown out when a man rather of his stamp, but clean shaven and infinitely better dressed - come to think of it, scarcely like him at all, really - hailed him in the back passage.

'Inspector Lestrade?'

'Yes.'

'I'm Evelyn Ruggles-Brise, private secretary to the Home Secretary. May I have a word?'

'Of course.'

The civil servant led the way through a part of the building which Lestrade had not found in the last two hours. The photographs of former Home Secretaries grew fewer and the paint-work patchier. At a door without a label, Ruggles-Brise stopped.

'Beyond this door, Lestrade, is your Lord and Master and mine, the Right Honourable Hugh Childers, Her Majesty's Secretary of State for the Home Office. He is not a man to be trifled with, Lestrade, and he is deeply worried. He wants a word. I shall be outside should either of you need me.'

He opened the door to reveal a cosy little office lit by oil lamps. A large bearded man the wrong side of fifty-eight sat behind a scarred desk covered in worn leather. A fire crackled in the grate.

'You sent for me, sir?'

'Did I?' the Home Secretary looked up. 'No, Evelyn, don't go. You're Lestrade, aren't you?'

'Yes, sir. You're the Home Secretary.'

'Hugh Culling Eardley Childers,' nodded the Home Secretary. 'But for how much longer I don't know. What are your views on the Home Rule issue, Lestrade? Oh, of course, you're a policeman. You don't have any views. How's Charlie Warren settling in?'

'Er ... the new Commissioner and I aren't exactly on chatting terms, sir.'

'No, no, quite. Well, to business. You know, Lestrade, I thought I'd seen all sorts in my time. I've sculled at Wadham, punted at Trinity, farted around in the Antipodes for years before settling back here at home. You don't get any thank yous for representing Pontefract for five years either, I can tell you. Nor do you win accolades at the Treasury, the Admiralty, the War Office or the Exchequer. That little saunter through my life thus far, that condensed curriculum vitae, will give you some idea that I'm no stranger to problems. But I've got one now, haven't we, Evelyn?'

'We have, Home Secretary.'

'Lestrade, I'd ask you to sit down, but I don't want to embarrass you, with your lowly rank and so on. You'd only feel uncomfortable. What can you tell me about the death of Sir Anthony Rivers?'

'Very little at the moment, sir. Except that it's one of a series.'

'A series? Is it, by Jove? Evelyn, why wasn't I informed?'

Evelyn was clearly a little nonplussed. 'Er ... I had no idea, Sir Hugh. No idea at all. Would you like me to see that heads roll?'

'Yes, just a few. Anyone without an Oxbridge degree, that sort of thing. But not just yet. I want you to hear this. I understand you've been asking questions today, Lestrade, here at the Home Office?'

'That is correct, sir.'

'Why, in heaven's name?'

'My information is that Sir Anthony was visited on the day before his death by a Mr Merrill from this office.'

'This office? Do we have a Merrill in this office, Evelyn?'

'No, Sir Hugh. No one at all.'

'Well, then, Lestrade. Are you answered?'

'No, sir, I'm afraid not. I was quite prepared for Merrill not to be his real name.'

'Aha, a soubriquet, eh?'

'I've no idea what his nationality is, sir. But why should a man give his address as this office if it is not?'

'Is it usual', Ruggles-Brise broke in, 'for murderers to leave correct addresses?'

'Invariably, no.'

'Then why should this one be so?' Childers asked.

'It may not be, but next to Buckingham Palace or Scotland Yard, this is the most ludicrous address for anyone to give. So ludicrous that it just might be the right one.'

'It's ... oh, this is difficult ... it's not so much the manner of Sir Anthony's death that concerns us here, Lestrade,' the Home Secretary fidgeted. 'Shocking of course though that is. No, it's more his lifestyle that concerns us. You know, of course, that he was a personal friend of the GOM?'

'The ... er ... ?' Lestrade was confused.

'Should I pop out, Sir Hugh?' Ruggles-Brise asked.

'No, no, Evelyn my boy. Good God, man, we have no secrets here. You do realize, Lestrade, how vital it is that this should not get out? I've had a word in the collective ear of Fleet Street already.'

'Get out? You mean Sir Anthony's night time wanderings?'

'Precisely,' Childers shuddered. 'If it becomes known that the GOM and Sir Anthony went trawling the streets for a bit of rough, well, we wouldn't need Home Rule to finish us. William Gladstone's third premiership is up the Limpopo and the Liberal Party might as well change its name and vanish without trace. Now tell me, Lestrade, honestly and truly, have you in your enquiries found any link between Sir Anthony's perambulations and the Prime Minister?'

'None sir. Mr Gladstone's rather shocking secret is safe with me.'

'I wonder, Lestrade, I wonder,' and the Home Secretary mopped his sweating brow. 'You'll keep it under wraps then, old chap?'

'Oh buried, sir, buried,' Lestrade assured him.

'And no more snooping around here? Mud has a tendency to fly, you know.'

'I have completed my enquiries here, sir, thank you.'

'Good man. Good man. Remind me to have a word with Charlie Warren. See if we can't get you promotion or a servant or something. Good day to you.'

'Sir Hugh,' and Ruggles-Brise saw Lestrade out.

'What was all that about, Mr Ruggles-Brise?' the Inspector asked.

'Parliamentary paranoia,' the private secretary said. 'Think nothing of it.'

'Very well. Could you show me the way out?'

'Of course, but let's go the pretty way, shall we?'

He led Lestrade through a labyrinth of corridors, every bit as dark and tangled as those at the Yard and down into the basement. At another unlabelled door, he stopped. 'Beyond this door, Lestrade, is the man I fancy...'

'I beg your pardon?'

'...the man I fancy will be our Lord and Master come the next election.'

'Election?'

Ruggles-Brise nodded. 'My money's on July.'

'But Mr Gladstone ...'

'Only took over the reins of power in January. Yes, I know, but seven months can seem an awfully long time in politics.'

'Er ... should he have an office in this building?'

'Who?'

'Whoever it is who's beyond this door?'

'Let's not be too naïve, Lestrade,' Ruggles-Brise smirked. 'Secretaries of State may come and Secretaries of State may go but I and the Civil Service go on for ever. Whichever way the cat jumps, I've got a job for life.'

'A servant of two masters?'

'I'm not proud, Lestrade. And it could be worse. I could be working for "Lulu" Harcourt. As for this office, on the plans it's merely marked "Stores". As for the man, it's the Right Honourable Henry Matthews. A fine legal brain, but not much of a cross-examiner. Rather lightweight for a statesman, really. We call him the French dancing master. Oh, by the way, he's of the papist persuasion. If Salisbury does get back in next time, Matthews will go down in history as the first Catholic in the Cabinet. So if he suddenly genuflects, I should leave the room if I were you.'

'Oh, yes,' Lestrade assured him. 'I always do.'

Ruggles-Brise tapped out a rather curious code on the door and a sonorous voice invited him in.

'Ah, Evelyn.'

'Ecce homo,' said Ruggles-Brise, indicating Lestrade.

The Inspector was about to deny it vehemently when Henry Matthews crossed the floor to him. The wrong side of fifty-nine, he was as smooth as Childers was hirsute. Wisps of lacy hair curled over his ears and the mouth was tight and small.

'What have you got on Sir Anthony Rivers, Inspector?' he asked.

'Er ... got?'

'Come, come, man. I am the Home Secretary-in-waiting. Don't be coy with me.'

'I rather think these are matters for the current Home Secretary, sir.'

'Evelyn,' Matthews motioned the man aside. 'A word?'

They whispered together in the corner of the Stores, the scruffiest part of which was palatial by Lestrade's standards. Assuming he had any standards.

'Evelyn, I thought you said this man was sound.'

'I've checked his file, sir. I assumed he was.'

'Well, what did it say in the "loyalty' section?'

"Unpredictable".'

'Well, there you are. You've sold me a pup, Evelyn.'

'Not intentionally, Home Secretary-to-be.'

'No, no, dear boy,' Matthews patted his shoulder. 'I don't doubt your loyalty. Er ... Lestrade,' he turned to the Yard man.

'You know of course that the late Anthony Rivers was a confidante of the GOM?'

'So I believe, sir.'

'Sir Anthony was in the habit, I understand, of frequenting low spots in the East End in search of the low life.'

'So it would appear, sir.'

'We are men of the world, Lestrade. We know that the GOM has similar predilections, but he's such a damned snob he frequents the West End. Affairs of state are involved here.'

'I don't believe the Prime Minister is in any danger, sir.'

'Damn the Prime Minister, Lestrade. What about the rest of us? The public has a right to know, on a need-to-know basis, of course.'

'What are you saying, Mr Matthews?'

'Come July, Lestrade, you'll be taking your orders indirectly from me. How much more sensible to start now. I want you to have the Prime Minister followed. I want his name linked with the life and death of Sir Anthony Rivers. In short, I want him smeared. You can leave the newspapers to me.'

'With respect, Mr Matthews, that is not my job.'

'Talking of jobs, Superintendent ...' Matthews's smile was oily.

'Sir,' Lestrade stepped backwards. 'If I find, in the course of my enquiries, that the Prime Minister is involved somehow in this case, then you may rest assured that I will interview him. If I believe him to be guilty of some crime, then you may rest assured that I will arrest him. Good afternoon.'

Ruggles-Brise saw him out. At an unlabelled door that led to the street, somewhere behind Whitehall, he turned to Lestrade. 'I take it you know what you're doing,' he said.

'Let's put it this way,' the Inspector told him, 'when I do, either of those gentlemen will be the last to know.'

Lestrade stood in what was left of his office a little after dawn the next morning. His first thought was a Fenian bomb, but there was no brickdust, no shattered glass. His cup, it is true, lay on the floor minus its handle, but that was where it usually was and it had never, as far as he knew, had a handle in the first place.

Beside him stood Sergeant George and Constables Tyrrell and Green, looking as astonished as their guv'nor.

'I don't believe it,' George kept saying, 'I just don't believe it.'

'Shut up, George,' Lestrade snapped. It was a bitch of a day already and the sun wasn't up over Southwark abattoir yet. 'We've just got to face facts. The office of an Inspector of Scotland Yard has been turned over. Your job, today, gentlemen, whether you decide to accept it or not, is to find out what's missing. Who was on the desk last night?'

'George Dixon, sir,' George told him.

'Still there? I came in the back way.'

'He was a minute ago.'

'Right. Green, find the kettle. Tyrrell, I want all these bits of Bath Olivers swept up and collected on a plate, wherever the plate is. We've got to establish some sort of priority.'

George Dixon had the sort of face that looked as if it had been lived in by a colony of rats, scrabbling through the granite of his pores. As a copper, he was so-so. As a desk man he was second to none. Two years earlier when a Fenian terrorist had lobbed a bomb at the front door, Dixon had caught it like a rugby full back and drop-kicked it into the bloke's cart. It had made a terrible mess of the Embankment but it brought Dixon a citation, checked the Fenian dynamite campaign and ensured him an annual season ticket at every game the Harlequins played. But today he was stumped.

'No, Inspector,' he was adamant, 'I come on duty at eleven forty-five. No one has passed through without a pass since then.'

'You're sure, Dixon? If this ever gets out, that someone's burgled Scotland Yard, we'll never live it down.'

'On my ol' mum's life, guv,' the sergeant said. 'And you know I always look after dear ol' mum.'

'Yes, yes,' Lestrade sighed. 'All right, Dixon. Run along and get your bacon and eggs, I think I can find my way back to C corridor.'

'Nothing, guv,' George said, stirring his guv'nor's tea.

'What do you mean, "Nothing"?'

'There's nothing missing.'

'But there must be.'

'Tyrrell. Cases A-L?'

'All present and correct, sarge.

'Green, Cases M-Z?'

'All there, sarge.

'Well, bugger me,' muttered Lestrade, but no one took him up on it. 'What about this present case?'

'Turned over, sir,' Green said. 'Along with everything else. At very least, it's given the place a good dusting.'

'Yes,' said George, 'saved you and Tyrrell putting your pinnies on for the annual spring clean. That's what I like about rookies, guv, don't you? The positive thinking.'

'I'd settle for any sort of thinking from a rookie,' Lestrade said. 'Tyrrell, I did rather hope when you swept up the Bath Olivers, you'd remove the grit before putting them back on the plate.'

'Sorry, sir.'

'Never mind. Do your penance by standing by that door. If anybody tries to open it, you are to die to prevent it. Understand?'

'Er ... yessir.'

'Right. Gentlemen, we have a dilemma here. George, you know Dixon. If he says no one without a pass passed him, do you believe him?'

'Illicitly, sir.'

'Me too. Which means what?'

'My God,' the colour drained from George's cheeks. 'This is an inside job.'

'Precisely.'

'What?' Green was perplexed. 'You mean somebody from the Yard ransacked this office? Who? Why?'

'In answer to your four questions, constable,' Lestrade leaned back in his chair, 'I said "Precisely"; yes; I don't know; I don't know. But this might just tell us.' He flicked a page from a ledger onto the desk.

'What's this, sir?' Green asked.

'While dear old George Dixon was making his way to the

canteen for his usual bacon and eggs, I was helping myself to a vital piece of evidence from his ledger. It's a list of all those who came on duty last night. One of these is our ransacker.'

'But, with respect, guv,' said George, though he had little enough of that when the chips were down, 'you came in the back way. So could anybody else.'

'No, they couldn't, George,' Lestrade insisted. 'I am unique in that respect. Ranks of Superintendent and above aren't here at night time anyway. I happen to know that no other person of my level or below has a key. That only leaves the Chief Inspectors.'

'Well, there you are, guv,' George had made his point. 'I wouldn't turn my back on any of them for a start.'

'Yes, all right, George. You may have something, which is why I'm not sitting too close to you. But let's start with what we know, shall we? These lads haven't been here long enough, so the character assassination that is about to follow is down to you and me. Inspector Brownlow. Came on at one thirty.'

'Good bloke, Bernard. Honest as the day is long.'

'I'd agree with that. Chief-Inspector Swanson. Ditto.'

'What about Sergeant Routledge, guv, you missed him out.'

'With respect,' Lestrade raised an eyebrow, 'sergeants and below wouldn't have the brass neck for anything like this. Inspector Arbalest.'

George wobbled his fingers. 'Dipsomaniac, isn't he?'

'Possible,' nodded Lestrade. 'But he certainly drinks. Whoever did this did it swiftly and silently. Arbalest would have fallen over. Inspector Andrews.'

'Walter Andrews. Don't really know him, guv.'

'Idiot of the first water. Promoted out of harm's way to Lost Property. He only comes in at night to get a bit of overtime. They say Mrs Andrews has expensive tastes. Which leaves Chief Inspector Littlechild. Came on duty at three o'clock. What's this?'

'What's what, guv?' George craned his neck.

'I just asked that,' Lestrade said. Things were not going well.

'This, look. After Littlechild's name. "Section D'. What's Section D? I've been at the Yard now for a decade and I've never heard of that? What time is it?'

Tyrrell checked his half hunter. 'It's nearly ten, sir.'

'Right, so he's still on duty. You boys have pinned all the paperwork back to the board, so get your thinking caps on. When I come back, I want a suspect.'

'John Littlechild.' Lestrade said, extending a hand, 'Sholto Lestrade.'

'Ah, yes. 'Morning, Lestrade. Bath Oliver?'

'No thanks. I just have. So this is Section D.'

'What?'

'Section D. I always thought this was F Corridor.'

'Oh, you know the new Commissioner.'

'No, I don't. Have you met him?'

'No, but they say he's a Tartar.'

Lestrade would have thought an Englishman better suited to the job but it wasn't perhaps his place to say so. 'Do you know, I was only saying to my sergeant this morning, "I've been at the Yard now for a decade and I've never heard of Section D.' Something new?'

'Yes ... er ... Administration. Ha, bloody paperwork. I don't know, I joined the Force to see the streets and what did I see? I saw bloody paperwork. It's the mandarins at the Home Office, Lestrade. Paper mad, they are.'

Mandarins, Tartars, mused Lestrade. Was the yellow peril getting nearer?

'Somebody turned over my office in the wee small hours,' he said, nonchalantly.

'Never!' Littlechild exploded. 'Who?'

'Well,' Lestrade lit up a cigar, 'not to put too fine a point on it, you.'

'Me?' Littlechild exploded more forcefully this time. 'How bloody dare you?'

'Calm yourself, Chief Inspector,' Lestrade waved the man back into his chair. 'Just fishing. I'm seeing everybody who was in the building last night. Just routine.'

'Routine, Lestrade? Routine? I'll have you on a charge for this.'

Lestrade stood up. 'That's your purgative,' he shrugged. 'But next time you want to know anything about the cases I'm working on, ask me rather than turn over my office, there's a good chap.'

By the time Lestrade had returned to C corridor, he was face to face with a face he'd never expected to see at the Yard.

'Inspector Towgrass, as I live and breathe,' he said.

'Morning, Lestrade. I've got a numb bum from the London, Midland and Scottish and I lost twenty nicker on a horse last week.'

'Ah, so this isn't a social call, then?'

'Good God!' Towgrass stopped abruptly at the door to Lestrade's office and the Yard man caught himself a nasty one on the man's hat-brim.

'What's the matter?' Lestrade mumbled as the room swam before his eyes.

'This place looks as if it's been turned over.'

Lestrade looked at him rather oddly. 'No,' he said, 'this is my office after it's been put to rights.'

'Bloody hell,' thundered Towgrass, 'I'd hate to see it when it's just been done. Bloody hell, Lestrade, things must be worse than I thought. I knew I'd done right, not to join the Metropolitans, extra allowance or no extra allowance. Your security's shot to buggery, man.'

'Yes, well, thank you for your fair and independent assessment, Towgrass, but I don't expect you put your hem ... hemmm ... piles on the line just to tell me that.'

'Listen, you,' Towgrass snarled, 'I happen to be the most conscientious detective south of Potters Bar. I leave no stone unturned in my quest to catch the criminal. Know how many collars I've made since turning Chief Inspector?'

Lestrade shook his head.

'Three hundred and fourteen. Convictions two hundred and seventy-eight. Executions eighty-nine. And that's only because of namby pamby judges, devious lawyers and nice policemen who let too many of the bastards off.'

'Perhaps we should all hang up our truncheons and let the amateurs take over.'

Towgrass looked him up and down. 'It looks as though they already have,' he grunted.

'I was thinking more of people like Sherlock Holmes.'

'Oh, yes,' Towgrass threw himself uninvited into a chair.

Luckily it had recently been vacated by George George. 'The giant prat of Sumatra. Waste of space. This', he held up a piece of paper, 'is why I'm here.'

'Ah, the Morris board.'

'Ah, so you know about it?' Towgrass frowned.

'Of course. Where did this one come from?'

'That silly old duffer, Fussock, Squire Ralston's butler. The senile old git had found it on the Squire's person when they fished him out of the drink. It was only yesterday he thought to tell me about it. I gather you sent him a telegram about it?'

'That's right,' smiled Lestrade.

'Well, it was only yesterday he remembered that too. You can't get the staff any more. How come you know about it already?'

'Fussock showed me,' Lestrade said. 'Oh, he didn't mean to. And at the time I wasn't aware of its significance. Of course,' he passed it to the standing George who proceeded to pin it to the green board behind him, 'it'll be nice to have the set.'

'The set! Well, lance my boils,' Towgrass tilted back his homburg. 'More of the buggers.'

'One near nearly every body we've found on this case. The Case of the Nine Men's Morris. The only one that's missing is the first. The Reverend Rodney. I suspect some Verger swept it up along with the humbug wrappings after a service. Well, I should think you'd have to while away the time during old Austin's sermons somehow.'

'How close are you?' Towgrass asked.

'Huh!' Lestrade grunted. 'How close is Christmas? I'd offer you some tea, Towgrass, but we're completely out. Aren't we, Tyrrell?'

'Like the tide at Weston-super-Mare, sir,' the constable confirmed.

'Look, Lestrade,' Towgrass edged forward. 'I've got a stake in this too, you know. Fill me in ...'

Lestrade was about to when the door crashed back.

'Don't you knock, Dixon?' he snapped.

'Sorry, Mr Lestrade, sir, but I was just goin' off duty and the news came in. 'Orrible murder, sir. Bludgeonin's.'

'Bludgeon*in's*?' Lestrade thought he'd heard the plural.

'Yessir, there's two of 'em.'

With Towgrass in tow and George paying the cab fare, Lestrade followed instructions to the little hotel on the edge of Hounslow Heath. Here it was in the Olden Times that James II camped his vast army of cut-throats and Irishmen to overawe the parliament in London; and where more recently such upright citizens as 'Swift Nick' Nevison had plied their bloody trade on the roads.

By the time the policemen got there (it would, as Towgrass kept saying, have been quicker by train) dusk was descending and an eerie stillness fell over the Last Post. A knot of policemen were stripped to their shirtsleeves even in the evening dews and damps and beside their bullseyes they were doing an impressive job on the hotel garden.

'Got another one, Inspector,' a sweating sergeant waved an arm through the trailing fronds of a weeping willow. It was not his own.

The Inspector jumped down from the top of his station wagon, only to collide with Lestrade.

'Aaggh,' he screamed, 'Lestrade, isn't it?'

"Yes, who are you?' since Lestrade was seeing double, identification was difficult.

'Pentridge, T Division. My lads have got six bodies back there and they've only dug the cabbage patch so far.'

'Six?' Lestrade repeated. 'I was told two.'

'Ah, two bludgeonings, yes. You'd better go inside. Constables Head and Bolger are in there. They'll give you the details. There should be a doctor there as well. Found the head yet, sergeant? Dr Willie says that last find was the jawbone of an ass.'

'Well, he ought to know,' Lestrade heard somebody grunt as the Yard men and their Hertfordshire visitor swept indoors.

The hall was gloomy enough, as befitted a tiny hotel that carried a sign saying 'No Vacancies. Gone Away'.

There were introductions all round. A squat little man in a white coat was perched at the top of the cellar steps.

'They found the first one here, Lestrade,' he called, his voice echoing. 'Can you get past me? Only I'm trying to take a rectal temperature, and it's n-never easy.'

'He might as well stick it up his arse,' Towgrass heard a voice behind him.

'Who are you?' he whirled round.

'Constables Head and Bolger, sir. T Division.'

'Right. This isn't my patch and I'm not one to step on toes. That man over there is Inspector Lestrade of Scotland Yard. Mark him well and should you ever meet him again after tonight, you will snap to attention, understand?'

'Very good, sir,' the constables chorused.

'And in the meantime, straighten those tunics, you slovenly sentinels of society's safety.'

'Well, Dr Willie. Time of departure from this vale of tears? How's the wife?'

'N-n-no better. Been at death's door n-n-now for three months. I've got to get out sometimes - I was grateful when I got this call. Difficult to say.'

'Can you guess?'

'N-no, I kn-know what time it was,' he removed the thermometer with a slurp. 'It's just that I've always had problems pronouncing n ... see, there I go again. N ... n ...'

'Nine?'

'Thirty, yes. N-not a pretty sight, I'm afraid.'

'The corpse?'

'N-no, the wife. Still, she n-never was. Seemed a good idea at the time, to marry the boss of the practice's daughter. N-ow, I'm n-not so sure. How's the Yard?'

'Same as ever,' Lestrade angled the bullseye. 'Over-crowded, overworked, over that way somewhere.'

'You want my theories?'

'No,' Lestrade said, 'but I suppose I'm going to get them.'

'This one died second. Your blokes just put their feet in the blood. It's my guess the first one died down there, at the bottom of the stairs and the other one put his head round the door at the wrong moment. He got about halfway across the hall when the first blow landed. That dented his cranium and he went down. Lost a tooth on the tiles. I haven't found that yet. He got up from that and got the second one facing his attacker. See the bruises on the arms?'

Lestrade did.

'Instinctive defence reflex, but he was pretty groggy from the first blow. Wouldn't have had much fight in him.'

'Who was he?'

'Mine host, I understand. I wouldn't kn-now. I'd n-never stay in a hotel without at least eighty rooms. The people one has to share a breakfast table with .

'Can we see the other one?'

The doctor flashed the bullseye down the stairs. 'N-not from here, n-no. We'll have to go down. And watch it, there's blood ...'

But the doctor's words were a trifle late. As Lestrade negotiated the body of the first party, he somersaulted neatly down the stone steps to plummet into the body of the second.

'I just did that,' Constable Head called down. 'Fetched myself a nasty one.'

'Yes,' groaned Lestrade, 'I of course did it to prove a theory.'

He rolled over, feeling decidedly tender behind, to come eyeball to eyeball with a corpse. 'God, it's a woman!' He hoped his shriek hadn't been too falsetto.

'That's what I always remember about you from the old days, Lestrade,' Doctor Willie said. 'Such thrusting observation, such critical faculties. Sholto Lestrade, meet Mrs Mine Host.'

The bullseye's beams flickered on the dead face of a woman in her middle years. One eye was closed completely, the other a mere slit in a purple mass. A rather cheap wig lay on her chest and dark brown blood had congealed over her bald head.

'Alopecia,' Willie said.

'Bless you,' muttered Lestrade. 'She died first, you say?'

'By about half an hour, I'd say. Of course, it's bloody cold down here. Plays the devil with my instruments. I wouldn't give any of this in a court of law.'

'All right,' Lestrade had lain with the dead long enough.

'Help me up, doctor, would you? And if you have any liniment, I'll be forever in your debt.'

9

Lestrade wasn't in the habit of drinking on duty, especially when George George was out in the garden, leaving no distance at all between Lestrade and his own wallet. Even so, tonight was an exception. The stench of death lay over the cold hotel and the bar was surprisingly free at that time of the year, with ghostly druggets over the furniture and shutters at the sad windows.

'Head, is it?' Lestrade waited until the men had lit a fire in the freezing snug.

'Yessir, Constable T391.'

'That's a nasty bump you've got.'

The constable bridled. 'The police surgeon said it wouldn't show through my clothes, sir.'

'I meant the one on your head,' Lestrade told him.

'Oh, oh, that one. Yessir. Them bloody ... beggin' your pardon, sir, uneven steps.'

'So you're Bolger?'

'That's correct, sir. T413.'

'Long with the Force?'

'Seventeen years, sir, come June.'

'Right,' Lestrade swilled Their Hosts' brandy around his moustache. 'That's the niceties over. Who were these people? Head?'

'Mr and Mrs Kelly, sir. Kept the Last Post for the best part of four years.'

'Children?'

'None.'

'Dependants?'

'None known.'

'How old were they?'

'Ooh, you've got me there. Kept to themselves quite a bit. Ben?'

Bolger scratched his head where the helmet rim had worn a

permanent groove, 'I dunno. He was sixty, maybe. She was a few years younger.'

'Nice people?'

'Oh, charming. Charming,' said Head.

'You'd better ask the Inspector,' said Bolger.

'Ask me what?' A tired, cold and grimy Inspector Pentridge arrived in the snug at that moment. 'Ah, thank you, Head, mine's a Scotch.'

'About the charmingness of the late Mr and Mrs Kelly,' Lestrade told him.

'Well', Pentridge threw himself down in the chair, hauling off his boots and wringing out his socks, 'I didn't know them all that well, although we'd talked often enough.'

'You had?'

'Lestrade, it might have escaped your attention, but we've found a total of nine bodies out there. The doctor's working his way through them as we speak.'

'Nine?' Lestrade repeated.

'All men we think. Can't be any women - the mouths aren't open!' he guffawed loudly, then caught the glum faces around him and swallowed hard. 'Sorry. Bit tasteless, that, under the circumstances. Look, I'll be frank with you, Lestrade, this is my first murder.'

'You'll get into the Police Book of Records at this rate,' Lestrade assured him. 'Eleven bodies your first time out. Some coppers don't get that in a lifetime. Cigar?'

'No, thanks. The bits get under my plate. What do you make of it all?'

'You say you'd talked to the dead couple before?'

'Yes. Three times, I think. Always in connection with missing persons, last known at their hotel.'

'Really?'

'Yes. Various witnesses saw them arrive - cabbies, postmen and so on. But no one remembers them leaving.'

'What about the hotel registers?'

'Burnt.'

'What?'

'They had a small fire here about three months ago. Somebody careless with a cigar, I suppose.'

Lestrade didn't intend to be careless with his. He carefully tapped the ash into Head's upturned helmet before the constable arrived with his master's scotch.

'Here's lead in your pencil,' he raised the glass and downed it in one.

'And the Kellys denied seeing these men?'

'Totally.'

'Didn't that surprise you a little?' Lestrade asked. 'How many people went missing?'

'Two. Both travelling salesmen. Well, you know how it is, Lestrade, these blokes. Half of them are on the road to escape the wife and half of them are in ladies' underwear. You show me a straight travelling salesman and I'll show you a clean pair of heels. Talking of which, just look at these socks,' he held the grisly items up for police inspection. 'I don't know what Mrs Inspector Pentridge is going to say.'

'Depends on her olfactory sensibilities,' Bolger muttered.

Everyone looked at him.

'You'll 'ave to excuse old Ben, sir,' Head said. ''Is dad was a hactuary. Used long words like you and me use privies.'

'Anything known on these Kellys?' Towgrass asked. 'Any previous?'

'They kept the Rolling Gate at Itchen Abbas,' Head said.

'Anyone go missing from there?' Lestrade asked.

'I don't know really,' Pentridge scratched his head. 'S'pose I should have asked them.'

'Well', sighed Lestrade, 'it's a little late now. Who found the body?'

'Trumpeter Armstrong.'

'Who?'

'Bugle Master at Kneller 'All,' Head told him.

'Kneller 'All?' Lestrade repeated.

'Army Music School, sir,' Bolger said. 'It's over the fields.'

'What was he doing here?' Towgrass asked.

'Look here', Pentridge felt he ought to say, 'this is my enquiry, you know.'

The Inspectors from the Yard and Hertfordshire both glared at him and he turned to squeezing more water out of his socks.

''E was cyclin' past, sir,' Bolger said, 'Exercisin' an enflamed epiphysis.'

'Is that all right in T Division?' Lestrade asked the local Inspector.

'Er ... I don't know of any bye-laws.'

'Yes,' Dr Willie clumped in. The garden mud on his boots made him several inches taller. 'Nine bodies,' he confirmed.

'Cause of death?' Lestrade asked.

'Garotting.'

'Garotting,' Lestrade mused. 'Haven't seen much of that in many a long year.'

'You're familiar with it?' Pentridge asked.

Lestrade scowled at him. 'How long have you been an Inspector, Inspector?' he felt bound to ask.

Pentridge looked at his half hunter. 'Twenty-one hours,' he confessed.

'Right,' sighed Lestrade. 'Garotting was all the rage when I was a young copper. Time was you couldn't move in Spitalfields for trassenoes with wire loops. A quick wrap around the throat and while the victim's hands are up there trying to avoid a damned good choking, his pockets are fleeced and the trasseno's away. Neat.'

'The difference here, Lestrade,' Willie poured himself a brandy, 'is that the "trassenoes' as you put it, didn't get away.'

'No,' muttered Towgrass. 'They're lying in their own cellar.'

'You're very sure of that,' Lestrade said.

'When do you reckon these nine blokes died, doctor?' Towgrass asked.

'Difficult to say,' Willie shrugged. 'I tried rectal temperatures, but there just weren't enough rectums to go round. Or is it recta? I failed my Latin viva first time, you know.'

'Don't worry,' Lestrade patted his arm reassuringly. 'We won't tell your patients.'

'No, they've been gone a long time.'

'Your patients? Pentridge asked.

'The deceased in the grounds,' Willie explained. 'Several months at least. Some of them a couple of years or more. The soil is quite peaty. They're preserved quite well. When I get a couple of stomachs back to my laboratory, I may be able to tell you what they last had to eat before they died. I say, Pentridge, you've gone a little green.'

'Must be the Scotch,' the Inspector said. 'I'll be all right in a minute.'

'So', Lestrade thought it best that somebody got on with the investigation, 'this Trumpeter Armstrong came upon the bodies ... how? Did he knock at the door?'

'The door was open, sir,' Head told him. 'Me and Ben was on patrol, cyclin' 'cross the 'Eath when we seen 'im runnin' out of the 'otel. shriekin'.'

'Shriekin?'

'Like he'd seen a critter out of 'ell,' Head assured him.

Lestrade knew how he felt. He'd just rubbed noses with the late Mrs Kelly. 'As I may have asked before, what was Armstrong doing here?'

''E said 'e was just passin',' Head said. 'Saw the door open an' thought to 'imself, '''Ello, Caedmon ... ''cos that's 'is name, see, Caedmon. 'E said to 'isself, ''I think as 'ow I'll 'ave a drop or two at the Post.' Wet 'is whistle, so to speak. So in 'e goes an' he finds old Pa Kelly there on the step.'

'Already dead?' Lestrade checked.

'As a dum-dum,' Head assured him. ''E saw summat else too.'

'Oh?' the three inspectors chorused.

'Two blokes wasn't it, Ben?'

'It was, Dick. Two bipeds of the human species, masculinely inclined.'

'Actin' suspicious,' Head leaned forward, as though to underline the fact.

'I don't suppose we have a description?' Lestrade raised an ever-optimistic eyebrow.

'Dick?' Bolger could handle long words, but not the long sight.

'One was tall,' Head said. 'Big 'ooter. Wore a deerstalker. The other was shorter. Daft moustache.'

'Any sign of a vehicle?' Lestrade asked.

'Armstrong didn't say,' Head shrugged.

Lestrade rose unsteadily, 'Gentlemen,' he said, 'I think Constable Head has just solved the case for us. Doctor, I look forward to your report. Inspector, to yours. Towgrass...'

'Sir, sir,' a bedraggled Sergeant George flapped his way through the snug, 'I've found it, guv. The Morris board.'

'Where?'

The sergeant took his guv'nor outside. 'There,' he said,

'Staring down at us all the time.'

Lestrade looked up. Over their heads, in the driving rain and the pitch black of the Hounslow night, the sign of the Last Post creaked and whined and on one side of it, dribbling in white runs down the painting of a bugler, somebody had daubed the design of death.

The old flower seller tapped her way blindly along Baker Street, her white-painted stick beating an erratic tattoo against the kerb. Once or twice she placed her ungainly size elevens into the horse droppings before the crossing sweeper could reach them. By and large though, she coped very well for a thirty-one year old detective with perfect vision.

'Buy my lucky 'eather, dearie.' Lestrade felt a fistful of the stuff thump into his chest.

'Not just now,' he brushed it aside. 'I bought the other day.'

'Guv,' the flower-seller hissed around the pipe stem, 'It's me. George.'

'Wha ... Good God, man, isn't this a bit over the top?' He flicked her eyeshade and kicked her gammy leg, with his good one, naturally.

'You said "Keep an eye on the place". I thought you meant literally. Have you got it?'

'Thank you, my good woman,' he called for the benefit of passers-by, then quieter, 'got any change? I seem to have inadvertently ...'

George hauled up his grimy unmentionables, revealing a very sturdy thigh as limbs of flower sellers went and passed his guv'nor a threepenny bit.

'Blimey,' Lestrade sucked in his breath, 'Haven't you got anything smaller? Oh, well, in for a penny ...'

'There, dearie,' George drove a pin through Lestrade's lapel into his chest so that the guv'nor winced and his eyes watered.

'Now you'll be lucky all the live-long day. Have you got it?' he whispered.

'No, I haven't got it,' Lestrade hissed. 'Just my luck it was old Bagster on duty - not for nothing known as the Most Awkward Magistrate in London.'

'He wouldn't play ball?'

'Play ball?' Lestrade made great pretence of finding the threepenny bit in his inside pocket. 'I know I have it in here somewhere,' he bellowed. 'He wouldn't even come out to inspect the pitch. Which means plan B.'

'Monro?' George clicked his fingers in delight. '"Insufficient probable cause, laddie," and I quote.'

Lestrade nodded.

'Guv,' George closed to his guv'nor, 'I'm not sure I can manage Plan C in this frock.'

'You should have thought of that before you ransacked the Yard Lost Property Department.'

'But you said...'

Lestrade rammed the threepenny bit into his sergeant's hand. 'I said 'Keep your eye on 221B". I didn't say commit an act of gross indecency with a bunch of lucky heather.'

'Oh, sorry, guv,' and George removed the offending article from the Inspector's person.

'Right,' said Lestrade without looking up. 'The front is hopeless, even now it's dusk. You used to patrol this beat. Does Baker Street ever get quiet?'

'Not quiet enough for a full frontal assault up the brickwork, guv, no.'

'Back passage job, then?'

'There'll be a fire escape, but I can't guarantee it'll be working.'

'Thank you, my good woman,' Lestrade said and nipped into the blackness of the nearest alleyway.

George was tapping his way back along the kerb when he collided with a toff hurrying home. 'Ah,' said the man. 'A bunch of lucky heather, please.'

George scowled at him and tore off the eyeshade. 'Why don't you bugger off?' he asked and followed his leader.

There was a rustling of borrowed clothes as George George removed such fol-de-rols as were likely to impede his progress.

'After you, then, guv,' he said.

'Yes,' muttered Lestrade, 'you usually are. Get ready to catch me should I stumble up there. And you're not bringing that stick, are you?'

'No, no.'

Lestrade paused. 'Wait a minute. Are you sure there's no one in?'

'Holmes and Watson left this morning, early. Caught a growler down the road and went west. Their housekeeper went out later, came back and now she's gone again. Come to think of it, a search warrant wouldn't have been a lot of use with no one to serve it on.'

'We'll just have to be a little un-Greek Orthodox, that's all. Are you game?'

'That's afoot, isn't it? At least according to the conversation I overheard between Holmes and Watson this morning it is. Mind how you go.'

Lestrade was doing just that. The fire escape behind 221B extended about halfway up. At this level, Lestrade paused, his Donegaled silhouette black against the purpling clouds of the city. The street sounds were curiously muffled here and the policemen were at pains not to scrape their boots on the metal rungs. A sash window shot up and a bucket of uncertain contents appeared, gripped by ancient hands, to splatter on the raffia wig of an old flower seller perched halfway up. The window slammed shut again.

'Who'd be the neighbours of Sherlock Holmes?' Lestrade whispered, peering in through the grimy glass.

'That's the last question going through my mind at the moment, guv.' George parted his grey hair to see where he was going, spitting things into the night.

'Right,' hissed Lestrade. 'There's a parapet up here, but it's pretty ... ouch ... crumbly.'

A piece of cement whistled past George's shawl to shatter in the courtyard below. A cat mewed from the darkness.

'Guv,' George called up as sotto voce as he could with his chin against brickwork, 'when we get in, what are we looking for?'

'Anything, George,' Lestrade said. 'Anything at all. Eek!'

'What?'

'It's all right. There's a ... loose ... ah, that's it,' and George saw the window above him slide up and his guv'nor disappear inside. He hauled up his skirts and followed suit, hand over hand, heaving himself up by the parapet and scraping his knuckles on a carefully placed piece of barbed wire. Suddenly his guv'nor's 'eek' fell into place, but he was bleeding by then and past caring. His feet found the windowsill and he was in.

'Lucifers, George?' Lestrade whispered.

The sergeant obliged. They stood in what was clearly a man's bedroom. A range of pipes rested on a rack in one corner among a debris of paperwork on a gnarled old desk. A violin lay at a rakish angle against the headboard and a dressing gown of a particularly tweedy appearance was draped across the coverlet. Lestrade lit a lamp with the extended lucifer and another one for his sergeant.

'Right, George,' he said, 'this must be Holmes's room. It's my guess there's a study somewhere.'

'Guv... '

'I'll take the wardrobe.'

'Guv ...'

'What's this?' at the back of a drawer, the Inspector's expert fingers had located a small packet of white powder. He opened it, dipped in a finger. It tasted revolting. 'Talc,' he said.

'Guv ...'

'What is it, George?' Lestrade stood, hands on hips.

'Well, I'm sorry, sir, but I'm still not clear why...'

Lestrade crossed to him. 'Look, George,' he held the man by his ample shoulders, teasing back the wet raffia from his face. 'Not that I want you to worry your pretty little head unduly about this, but what happened in South Mimms?'

'Squire Ralston died.'

'And which pair of private detectives were there within hours?'

'Er ... Holmes and Watson.'

'Exactly. And while we were playing Murder in the Dark at Blaenwhatsit? Who should turn up in heavy disguise as coal miners from those parts?'

'Holmes and Watson.'

'And at Borley - the spooks who came in from the cold?'

'The very same!' George was clicking his fingers in all directions. 'Guv, you've cracked it.'

'Even down to the description of the two men seen on Hounslow Heath by Trumpeter Armstrong and relayed to us by Constables Head and Bolger.'

'So Holmes and Watson did it ... er ... them?'

'Returning to the scenes of the crimes,' Lestrade returned to his rummaging. 'Sycologically unable to stay away.'

'But Guv ...'

'Yes, George,' Lestrade sighed.

'Well, even if we find anything here, without a search warrant, it's inadmissible isn't it? In a court of law, it'd be thrown out, along, I suspect, with us.'

Lestrade slammed the drawer shut and crossed again to his man. 'You know what it is about you, George? What in three years I have found so infuriating?'

'Er ... no, guv.'

Lestrade's moustache twisted in the half light. 'It's that when the chips are down, when it really matters, you're always so bloody right.'

There was a pause, both men, tired, aching, looking at each other. 'The simple point is', Lestrade whispered, 'that eight people are dead. And we're no further forward than when you and I first arrived in Mevagissey.'

'Who's there?' a querulous voice called from the stairs. 'What are you doing in my room?'

Both detectives leapt to the funnels of their respective lamps and blasted themselves into blackness.

'I know you're there,' the voice called again. 'I have a 54-bore

Swiss percussion bench rest target rifle by Vannod of Lausanne. It has an octagonal twist barrel, screw adjustable hair triggers and I'm not afraid to use it.'

'Who is that?' George whispered to his guv'nor from his hiding place behind the wardrobe.

'Unless Holmes or Watson is rather stranger than even I considered', Lestrade said, 'it's the housekeeper. It's Mrs Hudson.'

George straightened. 'Then she's bluffing,' he said confidently.

There was a blast that blew lamplight from the landing into the room and beyond the hole in the central panel stood a little lady of lowland Scots descent, eyes blazing, wreathed in smoke.

'Bluffing be buggered,' Lestrade hissed, fighting George to get to the window. 'Christ, she's reloading.'

It was no more than the truth. The Inspector somersaulted over the windowsill, scrabbling on the parapet before plunging like a flying squirrel, Donegal afloat, for the fire escape. George was half a second behind him and he rolled into the darkness just as Mrs Hudson's second volley illuminated the courtyard. The sash window of 221 flew up and an exasperated neighbour called out, 'Do you mind? This is a residential neighbourhood', prior to emptying the contents of an ornate privy on to the running head of Sergeant George.

'But you said it was Holmes and Watson, guv,' George was lying on his front across Lestrade's desk.

'No, I didn't,' the Inspector was adamant. 'I'll be the first to admit, I'm clutching at straws.'

'Damn!' George jumped.

'Sorry, sarge.' It was Tyrrell at work with the tweezers. 'What I can't understand, is how did she hit you in the arse when she was firing from above?'

'Yours not to reason why,' George hissed through clenched teeth, beads of sweat standing out on his forehead. 'Yours just to get rid of all that bloody buckshot.'

'Shut up, George,' Lestrade pushed the wedge back in the sergeant's mouth. 'And keep chewing on that. I can't think of a better use for the *Police Manual*. Come!' he bellowed in response to a knock, kicking himself metaphorically for sounding more like an Assistant Commissioner every time he opened his mouth.

A constable peered around the door, saw George's backside blue with buckshot and ducked back again.

'Yes?' Lestrade called.

'Constable Huxtable, sir, with a message from Chief Inspector Swanson.'

Lestrade tried to see the man behind the door. 'Are you embarrassed, by any chance, Constable?'

'Er ... yessir. A little.'

'It's all right, lad. I'm sure Sergeant George hasn't anything you haven't got. And probably not in such profusion either.'

He ignored the scowl from his number two.

'Even so, sir,' Huxtable said, 'I'd prefer to give you the message from here, if I may.'

'Very well,' Lestrade sighed.

'The Chief Inspector's compliments, sir. He's got a last minute addition to the Police Revue - a multi-force entry rejoicing in the name of Culpepper And His Crooning Chocolate Coloured Coons.'

'Marvellous,' Lestrade dropped some blood stained cotton wool into his 'Out' tray. 'So he doesn't need me?'

'Oh, yessir. Sergeant Berryman and his performing seal have had to pull out on account of the death of said performing seal.'

'Well, we should be grateful for small mercies, I suppose,' Lestrade said. 'Huxtable, do you know who's reviewing the Revue?'

'Constable Tinker, sir, L Division.'

Lestrade sat bolt upright with an inrush of air just as Tyrrell's probing tweezers elicited an excruciated roar from George.

'Well might you scream, sergeant,' Lestrade nodded. 'Joe Tinker is the most ferocious reviewer in the West End today. I've seen grown bass-baritones crying like babies after reading one of his critiques. Tinker the Stinker they call him. So I'm filling in for Berryman's seal, am I? Well, I can't guarantee to handle the ball so well, but at least my diction will be a damned sight clearer.'

'So Chief Inspector Swanson can ink you in then?' Huxtable checked.

'Ink and be damned,' Lestrade rolled his knuckles around in his eyes.

'Eight o'clock start, sir,' Huxtable reminded him, 'Tomorrow night, Nestling Hall, Conduit Street.'

'I can't wait,' the Inspector said and Huxtable exited before he'd even come in.

'Who was that?' George looked up, his eyes brimming with tears.

'Constable Huxtable,' Green said, without looking up from the report he was reading.

'What division?' George asked.

'He came from Swanson,' Lestrade said, staring again, as he had countless times over the last weeks, at the pictures on the wallboard ahead of him - the artists' impressions of 'men seen loitering' and that damned Nine Men's maze. 'Must be here at Headquarters.'

'I don't know anyone by that name,' George grunted. His eyes met Lestrade's.

'Did you see him, Tyrrell?' the Inspector asked.

'No, sir. I was busy with Mr George's bottom.'

'Yes, I wouldn't noise that abroad too far if I were you. Green?'

'I was reading this report, sir,' the constable said.

'George?'

'Vision's a bit swimmy at the moment, sir. You're not thinking what I am, are you?'

'A Headquarters constable that no one's ever heard of, who's embarrassed by colleagues' backsides or afraid of blood and buckshot, whose face nobody's seen? Yes, George, I am thinking exactly what you are.'

He wasn't in the corridor. He wasn't on that floor at all. Chief Inspector Swanson was out on a case. No one knew when he'd be back. Huxtable? Must be from a Division somewhere. No one had heard of a Huxtable. But yes, there was a list of turns for the Police Revue. Yes, Culpepper's Coons were on seventh, before Prestidge the Prestidigitator from J Division and shortly before Lestrade himself. 'Lookin' forward to it, sir,' his informant had called after him. 'Last time the lads and I couldn't stop laughin' for a week.'

Not bad for one of the great Bernhardt's most tragic pieces.

Lestrade reached the first floor in double-quick time. He rapped on the frosted glass of the office of the Assistant Commissioner (Crime).

'Come,' he heard the Scots growl from within.

'Mr Monro.'

'Lestrade,' the Assistant Commissioner paused in the middle of lighting his pipe, 'I was about to send for you.'

'Really?'

'Came this morning,' he tapped a telegram on his desk. 'From a Mrs Hudson of Baker Street. Familiar?'

'I am reasonably acquainted with Baker Street, sir, yes.'

'Don't come the old copper wi' me, laddie,' Monro scowled at him, stabbing the air with his pipe stem. 'You don't have the experience for it. This lady was burgled last night by a man and a woman. The woman was a flower seller. The man was you.'

'I?'

'Aye. We'll have to employ this woman Hudson here at the Yard. I've never known a clearer description.'

'I emphatically deny it, sir,' Lestrade said.

Monro laughed. 'I bet ye do,' he said. 'Quite a coincidence, that the very day you ask me for a search warrant to nose around the premises of 221B Baker Street, said premises, said search warrant request having been denied, are turned over by a man answering your description.'

'Incredible, sir,' Lestrade shook his head, astonished anew by the wonder of life.

'Admittedly, the female accomplice was inspired,' Munro said, sending out clouds of smoke to wreath the panelled ceiling. 'But I fear it was not inspired enough. It's the horse-troughs for you, Sergeant Lestrade.'

'Sergeant?' Lestrade was almost speechless. 'I can assure you, sir.'

'I am sure you can, Constable,' Munro went on, 'but I wouldn't protest your innocence any longer, laddie. I can't break you any lower.'

'All right,' Lestrade raised a hand. 'Let's talk, before I get my helmet back on, about turning over.'

'Eh?'

Lestrade threw himself, with as much bonhomie as a man with buckshot lodged in his leg who had recently leapt off a fire escape could, into a chair specifically specified for Chief Inspectors and Above by Commissioner Warren.

'The turning over of my office.'

'Your former office?' Monro frowned, refusing to be brow-beaten by Lestrade's insubordination. The man could not hope to rise again beyond the level of Lost Property.

'As you say,' Lestrade said.

'What do you mean, turned over?' Monro asked.

'Rifled, ransacked, burgled, broken into. A mere constable of H Division has no more words for it than that, sir.'

'When was this?' Monro asked.

'Six days ago,' Lestrade told him.

'Why wasn't I informed?'

Lestrade leaned forward in the way he'd seen the great founder of the CID, Howard Vincent do, in this very chair not nine years since, while stroking his pet iguana. 'Because you ordered it, sir,' he said.

'I?'

'You. And your minion was John Littlechild, Head of Section D.'

Monro stood up, his pipe tobacco smouldering all over the papers on his desk. His face was as white as his collar and he crossed the room in three strides to snick the key in the lock. A sickly smile creased his immobile face and he patted Lestrade's shoulder. 'Sergeant, I've been too hasty,' he said. 'After all, the constant arrival of this Holmes and his assistant is a little curious, isn't it? Let's just put it down to a little over-zealousness on your part, shall we?'

'Section D,' repeated Lestrade.

Monro reached his desk and flicked open the silver case. 'Havana, Inspector? Come to think of it, you're probably right. Holmes and Watson are obviously guilty as hell. I'll just file this telegram,' and he tossed it on to the fire. 'Go and pick 'em up. How many men would you like? Thirty? Forty?'

'Section D,' said Lestrade quietly.

Monro sat back in his own chair, flicking a desperate tongue over his thin, desperate lips. 'Chief Inspector Lestrade...'

Lestrade stood up and made for the door.

'Where are you going?' Monro was on his feet too.

'Fleet Street,' said Lestrade. 'That's where I've been told they keep the newspaper offices.'

'All right!' Monro bellowed, then quieter. 'All right. You'd better sit down, Lestrade. What I'm about to tell you is so hush-hush it scares even me. Understand?'

Lestrade shrugged. 'Not yet,' he said, 'but I hope I'm about to.'

'You've got a little list,' Monro said.

'Yes, I fell off a ... pavement,' Lestrade said.

'No, not your deformity,' Monro explained. 'A list of names.'

'Have I?'

'Well, let's put it this way. It wasn't in your office. It wasn't in your home.'

'My home?' Lestrade was on the edge of his seat.

'I'm sorry, Lestrade,' the Assistant Commissioner blustered.

'But you must admit the lads did an excellent job there. You didn't even know it had happened, did you?'

Lestrade had to admit he didn't, but his inscrutable face gave nothing away. 'You mean this list?' he said, producing from his inside pocket a piece of paper. 'The one given to me by Mr William Morris.'

'Um ... yes,' Monro said casually. 'I believe that may be the one.'

'All you had to do was ask,' Lestrade said. 'I thought we were all on the same side.'

Monro looked at his man. 'Ach, laddie, so did I. Och, I've never walked those mean streets. I've never worn that stupid helmet. Never reported of a freezing night to the fixed point station. But I'm a copper nonetheless. Through and through. But the times, Lestrade, are a-changing. Out there, for all I know streets away from us as we speak, are a whole bloody race of bastard Irishmen.'

'The Fenians?'

'Aye,' Monro growled, 'the Fenians. The dynamite campaign.'

'I have heard of these things, sir,' Lestrade said.

'Aye, laddie,' Monro leaned back. 'Ye've also heard, I ken, of Section D.'

'Ah yes,' Lestrade smiled grimly. 'Section D.'

'It's also known, rather fatuously, as my secret department. Well, it is a department, it is secret and I suppose it's mine after a fashion. It's still bloody fatuous that it has to exist at all. And doubly bloody fatuous that it's got to be secret. It's the Special Irish Branch of the Yard, Lestrade. I created it eighteen months ago out of sheer necessity. Section D is up in the attic with a growing list of Irish malcontents, dynamite users, known sympathizers and the like. It's headed up by Littlechild. Recently, we've widened the net to include political ne'er-do-wells and layabouts like this William Morris laddie. You can see how vital that little list is.'

'As I said,' Lestrade said, 'all you had to do was ask. That's all I did to get the list in the first place.'

'Really?' Munro chuckled. 'Well, don't tell Littlechild it's as easy as that. He'll have your throat out. Er ... the list?'

'Er ... Mrs Hudson?' Lestrade withheld the paper for a second.

'Never heard of her', Monro shrugged, 'Superintendent.'

Lestrade smiled and passed the paper over. 'No thank you, sir. When I get to Superintendent, I'd like it to be for what I've done rather than what I know.'

Monro crossed to him again. 'Well spoken, Lestrade,' he said, 'I knew you had some Scots blood in there somewhere. Oh, by the by,' he whispered in his ear, 'not a word to anybody, mind, about Section D. It is, if you'll excuse the pun, dynamite.'

'Your secret department's safe with me, sir,' Lestrade said.

'Good!' Munro slapped him on the back. 'Looking forward to tomorrow night, by the by. Mrs Munro will be there, the Commissioner and Lady Warren. Mrs Munro told me to tell you that last time she saw your Sarah Bernhardt, she laughed for a week.'

The lights burned late at the Yard that night. Down the Embankment, in the echoing halls of the Mother of Parliaments, the cry went up 'Who Goes Home?'

Not Sholto Lestrade at any rate. He sat with his head in his hands, chewing over as he had so many times in the past weeks the murders of the Nine Men's Morris. Eight victims, all save the last two unrelated. All dead by the same means, a crushing blow to the head, delivered by person or persons unknown. And the clues? A piece of blue serge cloth plucked from the barbed wire on a lonely hillside. And even that may have had no bearing on the case at all. And as for the eye-witness descriptions, the murderer was clearly a chameleon, able to change not only colour but height and weight and girth at will. Hereward Rodney, despoiler of young girls; Osbaldeston Ralston, swindler; Byngham Batchelor, pincher of other people's literary ideas; John Guest, exploiter of workers; Amos Flower gang leader turned Napoleon of Crime; Anthony Rivers, frequenter of fallen women; and Mr and Mrs Kelly, genial host and hostess with a menu of murder on the side; all in all, not a very prepossessing lot.

And over it all that damned silly game. Lestrade was idly playing with it now as he pondered the imponderable, moving the nine pieces mechanically around the maze on his desk, meeting, like them, the brick wall of the next piece. Just like a maze, this case; every corner an obstacle, every twist a blind alley; every ray of hope blocked by an impenetrable hedge. Then it came to him, as he sat in the lamplight with only the mice for company and somewhere away in the building the erratic knock of a broom on the stairs. *Eight* murders. Only eight. And yet the name of the game was the Nine Men's Morris. Nine. One of the pieces slipped from his grasp to bounce on the wooden floor and lose itself behind some shoeboxes. He got up and crossed to the window, saw himself reflected in the half light; the parchment skin, the hollow eyes, the face of the ferret. Out there, he thought to himself; somewhere out there, alone, perhaps. Perhaps like him staring into a glass darkly. Out there was murder victim number nine.

And all Lestrade had to do was find him.

Eight o'clock. Nestling Hall. Conduit Street. It was Commissioner Warren's first Police Revue and he was late. Behind the curtain, a nervous Sholto Lestrade chewed the end of his cigar. He flung it into the nearest sand bucket as he suddenly realized he had been champing on the wrong end. He thanked his God it hadn't been alight at the time.

'Ah, Lestrade,' a top hatted gent wearing too much rouge swept past him with doves fluttering out of every orifice, 'I'd check that lipstick if I were you. People will talk.'

Instinctively, Lestrade's hand came up to his lips. No. The moustache was still there. Was it the crown of the Lower Satrap that had slipped? The blue-gold eyeshadow from Abu Simbel? Damn the stage for a lark. He hauled up his skirts and skipped on gossamer sandals past a chorus line of scantily clad lovelies he vaguely recognized as G Division's Tug-'o'-War team. His dressing room was up a flight of stone steps and left a bit. True, he shared it with the Amazing Armbrusters and Mr Memory Maurice, alias Sergeant Spettigue of Lost Property, but as the ranking officer it was his name over the door. He felt the power of the myriad sulphur bulbs around the mirror scorch his face again. Damn, that idiot with the doves was right. He remembered now. When the Armbrusters had been rehearsing something truly amazing, his hand had jumped in surprise and drawn a crimson track across his cheek. How did women manage this stuff, he wondered. Let alone Queens of Egypt.

A sweating Sergeant George appeared at his elbow. 'Sorry, guv,' he wheezed, 'seems there's a bit of a run on ostrich-feather fans. World shortage.'

'World shortage?' Lestrade snorted. 'What happened to your face?'

A purple bruise had developed across the sergeant's left temple.

'Delegation from the Plumage League; you know, those old biddies who are opposed to using feathers for trimmings. I sort of ... bumped into them.'

'Hmm. Occupational hazard.'

'Sir, sir,' a gasping Constable Green tumbled in through the door. 'No asps, Inspector. Not the season.'

'Dammit, man, I didn't want a live one. Stuffed. I wanted it stuffed. Didn't you try Ottershaw's in Drury Lane?'

'Yessir. They had a python. But I thought a thirty foot reptile might detract from your act.'

Lestrade sighed. And did so again as he saw an exhausted Constable Tyrrell drag himself into the reflection in the mirror.

'Don't tell me,' the Inspector said, adjusting his left breast. 'You couldn't find a little black boy anywhere.'

'You guessed it, sir,' Tyrrell told him. 'Some old Jew offered me a little white girl, but I said the Yard wasn't interested. He turned quite pale at that point and scarpered.'

'Ho-hum, ' said Lestrade.

'Don't suppose he had change for a pound.'

'Never mind,' the Inspector buffed up the eagle-headed god whose wings crossed his forehead, 'the show must go on. Is this wig all right, George?'

'Excellent, guv.'

'Mind my frock, Tyrrell. You ladder these stockings and I'll set the crocodiles on you. You don't think the lads will mind, do you? Sarah Bernhardt with a limp?'

George took the liberty of patting his guv'nor's shoulder. 'If they can handle the moustache, guv, they're not going to baulk at a bit of gamminess down ... there. Break a leg, guv'nor.'

'Thanks, sergeant.' The fixity of Lestrade's grin could have cut glass.

Below in the auditorium, the ripple of white glove on white glove told the artistes that Commissioner and Lady Warren had arrived. The band (B Division Philharmonic) struck up 'for He's a Jolly Good Fellow' and the Lion Comique who was Master of Ceremonies pounded his gavel and introduced the first act. 'Commissioner Warren, Lady Warren, Assistant Commissioners and their ladies, Superintendents, Chief Inspectors, Sergeants, lads. It gives me great pleasure - but that's really none of your business, is it?'

Howls of laughter from all except the Commissioner and his lady who clearly had no intention of being amused. Bemused, possibly. But amused? Never.

Out of courtesy to his exalted rank, Assistant Commissioner Monro led off assuring the audience that his heart was in the Heelands.

'Take it away, Maestro,' he said, extending a gloved hand towards the orchestra pit. It fazed him just a little when a constable walked off carrying a double bass, but he was soon in his stride. It left Constable Tinker of the *Police Gazette* wondering in the notes he was scribbling for his review where, if the Assistant Commissioner's heart was in the Heelands, his voice had gone. A polite applause saw him off.

The Armbrusters then did various Amazing things, at least two of which Lady Warren had never seen before (but then she had led a very sheltered life) and the idiot with the doves followed in swift order, until his shoulders were encrusted with guano and he looked vaguely as though he'd been tarred and feathered.

Constable Elton persisted in telling some rather off-colour jokes relating to various members of the Royal family and ending with what he described as everybody's favourite - 'There's No Shove Like The First Shove'. Lady Warren had to have smelling salts applied smartly to her nostrils and the hard-eyed Commissioner passed a note to Monro, who had apparently relocated his heart and other bits of his anatomy and now sat in the front row on the wrong side of Lady Warren. Elton was to be on the carpet tomorrow at eight a.m. sharp and on the horsetroughs by nine.

Glee Clubs various came and went with ditties appropriate to the occasion and then Culpepper's Crooning Chocolate Coloured Coons, a rag-bag of assorted coppers with wide check trousers, huge bows under their chins and burnt cork and flour on their faces. Lestrade waited impatiently in the wings as the Coons strummed their little banjos for all they were worth and ran through the culinary favourites of Mammy's little baby. The little fat one on the end kept breaking out of the line and with his hands waving frantically, screamed out 'put on de skillet' ' whenever the company seemed to flag. Still, mused Lestrade, they were billed as from different forces. It must have been a bitch to find time to rehearse.

The interval came and went and the raffle was drawn. A jeroboam of champagne was the prize, won, by the most astonishing coincidence, by Commissioner Warren. He accepted graciously. Part Two began with Prestidge the Prestidigitator, who turned out to be the same idiot with the doves who had appeared in Part One. Only now he was producing rabbits from his topper and the stage was quickly sprinkled with currants the Coons were presumably quite partial to.

'Who *is* that?' Lestrade hissed to Mr Memory Maurice beside him.

'Ooh, now you've asked me,' the constable admitted.

'That's Inspector Reid, J Division,' a passing Armbruster told him. 'One of the most remarkable men of our century.'

'Who told you that?' Lestrade asked.

'He did,' he and the Armbruster chorused.

Constable Runciman of P Division followed, singing to a small guitar, which seemed peculiarly unmoved by the experience and Sergeant Whitman gave everybody his Little Nell. Lady Warren felt unhinged at the very idea but the sergeant soldiered on and there wasn't a dry eye in the house.

The act that Lestrade had to follow was a model of wit. Sub-Inspector Catchpole from the Dock Police belting out a dialect they only understood along the Ratcliffe Highway -

'*Now kool my downy kicksies - they're the style for me*

Built on a plan very naughty.'

Lady Warren felt constrained to adjust her opera glasses at that point.

'*The stock around my squeeze is a guiver colour see!*' Catchpole thundered.

'*And the vestat with the bis so rorty!*'

'I don't know,' said the idiot with the doves and rabbits to Lestrade. 'I think I got more sense out of old Berryman's seal. Going to the funeral?'

'You're on, guv,' Lestrade heard George hiss and he staggered on to the stage. A sea of faces met him over the green of the footlights.

'And now,' thundered the Chairman, slamming his gavel down with gusto, 'the Divine Sarah as Queen Cleopatra, Yon Ribaudred Nag of Egypt.'

There was deafening applause, which was gratifying. And a few cries of 'Resign!' which weren't. Lestrade hobbled into position and struck a pose he assumed Sarah Bernhardt would strike were she portraying the consort of Caesar and Antony.

Lady Warren consulted her programme and turned to her husband. 'How very different from the home life of our own dear Inspectors,' she observed.

'I don't know,' Warren scowled, 'the moustache is about right, but what's he think he's playing at with that limp? Monro?'

The Assistant Commissioner took his life in his hands by leaning across the starched frontage of Lady Warren, 'Sir?'

'Who is that?'

'Lestrade, sir. Headquarters.'

'Never heard of him,' Warren grunted.

The Queen of Egypt stood centre stage, his hands on either side of his face as though his crowns were killing him, which they were, 'Give me my robe,' Lestrade commanded, in a Franco-Egyptian way, though in the absence of an Iris or any appropriate little black boy, nobody moved. 'Put on my crown,' but he already had. 'I have immortal longings in me,' he pirouetted to the side of the stage, as far as his gammy leg would allow. 'Now, no more the juice of Egypt's grape shall moist this lip,' and he tapped his moustache, smearing his lipstick again. 'Yare, yare, good Iris; quick,' and he cupped a hand behind his left ear. 'Methinks I hear Antony call,' he shaded his eyes with his right hand. 'I see him rouse himself to praise my noble act; I hear him mock the luck of Caesar, which the gods give men to excuse their after worth.' He hobbled across the stage, brushing his nether garments in the footlights. 'Husband, I come!' he shrieked, clutching the stuffing up his frock. The conductor of the orchestra noticed it first; a certain smouldering, a whiff of wincyette and then Lestrade turned sharply as he had read the Great Bernhardt did and the moment was lost. 'Now', he was in full flight, his eyes closed, his hands clasped together, 'to that name my courage prove my title!' He breathed in for the next line and suddenly smelt smoke. He glanced wildly to left and right, but the wings seemed intact. Only to his left was George George, gesticulating wildly. Idiot, thought Lestrade, I know my lines. 'I am fire and air,' he intoned. 'Oh God, I'm on fire!' and he suddenly buckled at the knees and began rolling around furiously. George hurtled on and threw a blanket over his conflagrating guv'nor.

'Shouldn't that carpet thing happen earlier in the play?' Commissioner Warren asked his wife. He had long served in Africa and hadn't had much time for culture.

'Tsk,' Monro complained. 'Typical of Lestrade to make a complete asp of himself.'

And mercifully, to a mixed reaction, the curtains closed.

It was gone midnight. The bouquets had been given, the speeches made and another Police Revue had closed after only one night. The only similarity it had to a West End run was that some of its participants ran around the West End regularly in pursuit of felons. Lestrade of course had missed the closing acts and the phenomenal finale of the Flying Filberts, inevitably from F Division. He would have liked what he saw. One of the Filberts flew rather high and sailed off the stage to land in the lap of Lady Warren and an awful lot of trouble. It was to be two years before anyone in F Division got a promotion.

Lestrade had been down the road at Charing Cross Hospital having his burns dressed. He had thanked Sergeant George for saving his life, had sent Tyrrell and Green home with instructions to be back at the shoe-boxes by eight and he himself had limped back to his dressing room. Here he pulled off the hired crown and unstuffed his bodice. He was just about to remove the black lines that circled his eyes when he was aware of a dark figure over his shoulder, its white lips outlined in the mirror.

'Just leave the flowers, Mr Culpepper,' Lestrade said. 'Good of you to bother.'

But it wasn't a bouquet the nigger minstrel carried. It was a single Arum lily. The flower of death. He threw it on to Lestrade's dressing table. The Inspector turned as a second Coon strolled into the room, then a third, then a fourth.

'Yes?' he said, realizing that the niggers stood between him and his brass knuckles, hanging with his Donegal behind the door.

'The stage,' said one of them. 'You've got a death scene to rehearse.'

He toyed with staying where he was. He toyed with tackling them. But they were four to his one. And two of them were very big niggers indeed, quite colossal Coons. He'd probably have more room to manoeuvre on stage.

'Very well,' said Lestrade, 'I hope somebody's brought a snake.'

He led the way down the twisting spiral of the stair where the sulphur lights burned dim. Someone had thoughtfully re-lit every other of the footlights and in a row facing him on the opposite side of the stage, stood five other Culpepper Coons, still in their burnt cork, still in their top hats and garish trousers.

But they carried no banjos. Instead they swung regulation truncheons, rosewood, twelve inches long, policemen for the use of. The four crossed to form a line with the five, facing the former Queen of Egypt, still wearing his scorched frock and his rouge.

'Well, well, well,' said Lestrade. 'One thing I learned at Mr Poulson's Academy all those years ago is that four and five make nine. Nine as in Nine Men's Morris. That, I confess, is what threw me. That's why no two eye-witness accounts were alike. I was looking for one murderer, but I should have been looking for nine murderers.' Not one blunt object, but nine of them. And who'd have suspected the good old truncheon? Well, I never.'

The nine took one pace forward, like automata, their eyes bright in the dull brown faces, their lips curled in the white circles, the astrakhan of their wigs shimmering under their pink toppers.

'One moment,' Lestrade held up his hand, thinking desperately. 'Aren't I permitted one last request?'

'Name it!' Culpepper snapped.

'An indulgence,' said Lestrade, wondering if he could leap the orchestra pit in one bound, what with the encumbrance of buckshot, third degree burns and an Egyptian frock. 'Let me discuss your lives and crimes one last time.'

Culpepper glanced along the line. 'Be our guest.'

'Section D,' said Lestrade. 'You ... gentlemen ... are members of it.'

'We are?' asked Culpepper.

'You are,' Lestrade was sure. 'Oh, yes, Assistant Commissioner Monro gave me some guff about the Special Irish Branch, but I wasn't remotely fooled by that.'

'You weren't?' Culpepper checked.

'Not in the slightest. Section D is a department of killers, of trained assassins.'

'And what was our motive?' the head Coon asked.

'You have extended what a police force is supposed to be,' Lestrade said. 'You have become jury - even your number is the same as a coroner's jury; judge - but the sentence is always the same; the executioner - death by blunt instrument. But I was a problem, wasn't I? I knew too much. Isn't that what this little show this evening is all about, Mr Culpepper ... or should I call you Inspector Littlechild?'

'Littlechild?' Culpepper frowned blackly.

'And which of you is Constable Huxtable?' Lestrade scanned the line with his pointing finger.

'Oh, that's me,' the fifth from the left stood forward.

'Know too much?' Culpepper laughed and the line behind him began to rock with mirth too. 'Don't be puerile, Lestrade. Is that what you think this is all about? This "little show" as you put it? Did you think that we thought you were on to us? Lads, I think it's about time we introduced ourselves to Mr Lestrade, don't you? From the left . . .'

The first nigger took a step forward. 'Constable Widger, sir, Cornwall Constabulary.'

Then the second. 'Matthew Spatchcock, sir, Hertfordshire Constabulary.'

And the third. 'Nutty Slack, sir, D Division, Metropolitan Police.'

Then the fourth. 'Myrddin Williams, Mr Lestrade, Glamorgan Constabulary, innit?'

The fifth, Huxtable, already stood forward. 'Topsy Turvey, sir, Essex Force.'

And the sixth. 'Constable Chingford, Inspector, J Division, the Met.'

And the seventh and eighth stood forward together. 'Dick Head, sir, and Ben Bolger, T Division.'

'Also of the police of the Metropolis,' Bolger concluded.

'Which leaves me, Lestrade,' said Culpepper, 'the ninth man of the Morris. I don't know who this Littlechild is, but you know me as Chief Inspector Edward Towgrass, Hertfordshire CID.'

'Towgrass?' Lestrade was almost speechless.

'A motley crew, I'll allow,' Towgrass said. 'And not without our faults. Poor old Widger there collapsed at the sight of the corpse of Hereward Rodney. It was a bit gratuitous, Turvey, thumping the old lecher so hard. I'm not sure propping him up on his eagle was such a good idea, with hindsight.'

Lestrade took half a step sideways. The orchestra pit was still his best bet. If he could make it to the aisle, he had a chance in the darkness to reach the street and call for help.

'But then, I'm afraid old Tom had problems later, didn't you, Widger?'

''Fraid zo, zir,' said the Cornishman, 'I panicked a bit, Mr Lestrade, at the Last Post. I was all right with Mr Kelly. But I couldn't bring mysen to kill a woman.'

'That's where I came in,' Head said, 'Ben and me was on 'and to direct Tom. After all, 'e was a stranger an' there was two of 'em. While Ben was strengthenin' 'is resolve with stirring speeches, sod me if old Pa Kelly didn't get up and land me one on the forehead.'

'And you told me you'd fallen down the steps,' Lestrade reminded him, 'tsk, tsk, what a fib.'

'These men aren't chosen by accident, Lestrade,' Towgrass said, 'they were handpicked, by me. Dick here is one of the fastest thinking uniformed men I've ever met.'

'Who left the bit of uniform on the barbed wire?' Lestrade asked.

'Er ... that was me, sir,' Slack confessed. 'Deeply ironic, really. It wasn't my uniform at all, but the only civvy suit I got - blue serge.'

'So you all did each other's murders?'

'Ar, aye, yus,' they all chorused according to their dialects.

'Of course,' said Towgrass, twirling his truncheon. 'That way there could be no suspicion. Every copper at the scene of the crime had an alibi. Even those first to the body behaved normally, as shook up as the next man because they had no idea exactly when and where the nine targets were to be hit. And even though Bolger and Head got carelessly involved, it didn't matter. One policeman looks just like another under the helmet. Mind you, liaising by telegram wasn't easy. You've no idea of the complexity of arranging Rest Days. But we did it. Not one man went off sick or lost a day's pay to accomplish his killing.'

'Spooky old house, though, Borley, innit?' said Williams.

'You killed Amos Flower?' Lestrade checked.

'No,' chuckled the Welshman, 'I killed Pretty Boy Partridge.'

'Why?' asked Lestrade, his palms outstretched, playing for time.

'Gentlemen,' said Towgrass, 'perhaps you'd like to account for the murder on your own patches? Widger?'

'The Rector,' said the Cornishman, 'Mr Rodney. He were molestin' the young girls of the parish. We knew it by rumour and innuendo; but we couldn't prove it, for all Sergeant Smith tried his best.'

'He didn't tell me that,' Lestrade complained.

'That's what we relied on,' Towgrass said. 'The natural reticence of the provincial force, the reluctance to help any outside enquiry there may be. Especially from Scotland Yard. Go on, Widger.'

'Even the girls' families didn't want to know. The Porthluneys and the Tresilians. clammed up like clams and young Emily Carrick's dad carted 'er off to Lunnon.'

'That's where I came in,' said Towgrass. 'I had a fishing holiday in Mevagissey last year and met Constable Widger on the Harbour wall. We got talking, Constable Widger and I. We came to an understanding, didn't we, Tom?'

'We did, sir. An understandin' that the Reverend Rodney would die.'

'And die he did,' nodded Towgrass. 'Matthew?'

'Osbaldeston Ralston,' the Hertfordshire man said. 'He'd been rooking people right, left and centre for years. He even stole the local police benefit back in '79 but there was no proof. The Chief Inspector says to me one day "Of course, Spatchcock", he says, "we don't really need proof, do we?" and I says

"How'd you mean?" and he slams a truncheon down on his desk. Well, I got his drift straight away. See, I reckon I'll make detective in about twenty years.'

'Indeed you will, Matthew,' Towgrass grinned. 'Indeed you will. Slack?'

'Byngham Batchelor,' said the constable. 'No ordinary thief. 'E stole uvver people's works an' sold 'em like they was 'is own. A harrogant bastard wiv it. So Bolger bashed 'is 'ead in. And stole 'is wallet an' tie-pin.'

'If there's one thing I can't tolerate, it's literary plagiarism,' Bolger told the company. 'Constable Slack conveyed the situation to me at the Inter-Divisional Beetle Drive of November last. I was, quite naturally, appalled.'

'Of course,' said Lestrade. 'That's why, despite immaculate hearing, Slack claimed not to have heard Batchelor scream. He screamed all right, but had you admitted that and got there fast, you'd have seen Bolger making his getaway. That could have raised awkward questions, couldn't it?'

'Williams?' Towgrass said.

'John Bloody Guest,' the Welshman tapped his palm with the truncheon. 'An absolute bugger 'e was, an' no mistake. Been killin' blokes for years down Yns-y-Bwl pit. Authorities couldn't touch 'im for it. But I 'ad 'eard, on the grapevine so to speak, of a group of blokes in the police - and what force I did not then know - 'ad a final solution, you might say, for blokes like John Guest. Retribution. Lovely word, innit? Retribution. Sort of rolls off the tongue. Sounds even better in the Welsh...'

'Yes, thank you, Williams,' Towgrass interrupted. 'So the good constable contacted me. Turvey?'

'Well, the entire Metropolitan Force 'ad been lookin' for Pretty Boy Partridge for years. We knew who 'e was, but not even Inspector Flannel could prove it. I s'pose 'e wanted the collar for 'isself eventually, Mr Lestrade, that's why 'e didn't voice 'is suspicions. 'E 'ad it comin', mind you. Partridge, that is, not Flannel. Although, I don't know though.'

'Don't tell me', Lestrade said, 'Chingford, that Sir Anthony Rivers had to die for visiting fallen women?'

'God bless you, no sir. Half J Division would need topping in that case. No, it was the fact that 'e was such a bloody good lawyer, sir. Got some real bastards orff, 'e did. That made 'im a bastard 'isself. 'Is comeuppance was way overdue if you ask me.'

Lestrade hadn't but that seemed irrelevant. 'And the Kellys?'he asked.

'Murderers both,' said Head. 'We couldn't get a search warrant to dig the garden at the Last Post.'

Lestrade had some experience of that himself when trying to put his nose behind the curtains of 221B Baker Street. 'We knew they'd done for a load of travelling salesmen. Cut their throats for the valuables they carried. You saw what a ninny Inspector Pentridge is, Mr Lestrade. Well he'd been a bloody sight worse before his promotion, I can tell you.'

'I can corroborate everything my colleague has vouchsafed to you,' Bolger added.

'So there you have it, Lestrade,' Towgrass said. 'The complete catalogue of crime. You see, they all needed it, Lestrade. Good God, man, you've been a copper long enough. You've seen all kinds of riff-raff get off because of clever lawyers, bungling coppers, namby-pamby judges...'

'Ah, yes,' Lestrade nodded. 'You said as much to me once.'

'I know I did,' grunted Towgrass. 'Got a bit carried away - Not that you noticed.'

'And am I one of your bungling coppers?'

Towgrass closed to his man, the Chocolate Coloured Coon eyeball to eyeball with the Queen of Egypt. 'I've never liked you, Lestrade, I've never made any secret of that. Even so, I speak as I find. You're a damned good copper. But your problem is, you've got a heart. A conscience. I know and you know, there have been ... shall we say ... irregularities in your conduct? Times when you've given a criminal the benefit of the doubt.'

'Only when I haven't been sure,' Lestrade stood his ground.

'Well, that's once too often,' Towgrass said. 'We're sure. The Nine Men's Morris are always sure. We don't make mistakes. We're the nine points of the law. You're a weak link, Lestrade - a copper with a soft streak. There's no place for you in Gladstone's England.'

'So ...' Lestrade felt the hairs prickle on the back of his neck.

'I am the ninth victim?'

'You are,' said Towgrass. 'And you're all mine,' and he brought the truncheon up above his head. Lestrade was faster, driving his sandalled foot into Towgrass's groin. Both men went down, each clutching bits of himself. It was Lestrade's gammy leg that had done the kicking. He didn't have time to think what it was about Towgrass that was gammy. In an instant the rest were on him, dragging him upright, gripping his arms, wedging him tight between them. Towgrass, his eyes watering, staggered to his feet. Lestrade still had his legs. He lashed out with the good one this time, but Towgrass was ready and he batted it aside with his truncheon, before driving his fist into Lestrade's stomach. The Inspector jack-knifed, but a nigger behind him ripped back his hair, forcing his head to snap painfully on his shoulders.

'That's it, Matthew,' gasped Towgrass. 'Now, move your hand, there's a good lad.'

Lestrade shut his eyes. His whole life flashed before him in the darkness. The bright buttons on his old dad's tunic, the warm sudsy hands of his dear old mum, the ...

'Lestrade, you're under arrest!'

Lestrade's eyes opened. His and all the others' turned to the darkened auditorium when a medium sized man with a Webley Mark Something or Other in his hand walked into the sulphur glow.

'Dr Watson,' shouted Lestrade, never so glad to see an unfriendly face in his life.

'Who are you?' Towgrass snapped.

'Dr John Watson, of 221B Baker Street and I am making a citizen's arrest. You fellows will have to have your rehearsal without the Inspector.'

'No, no,' Towgrass's scowl cracked into a chill smile. 'Inspector Lestrade is breaking no law,' he explained, lowering his truncheon. 'He doesn't usually wear these clothes. It's only an act. Isn't it, Sholto? Sholto?'

'No, it isn't,' Lestrade shouted, struggling to break free. 'I always wear this or something very like it. I have a complete ladies' wardrobe at the Yard.'

'Stop prattling, Lestrade,' Watson commanded, waving the gun around. 'I'm not arresting you for transvestism. I'm arresting you for murder.'

'Whose?' Towgrass demanded.

'Everybody's,' said Watson. 'Who are you, sir?'

'He's Edward Towgrass,' Lestrade shouted. 'And he's...' but a powerful cudgel punctated his sentence and he dropped to his knees.

'I say, steady on,' said Watson. 'That sort of thing can wait 'til he's safely in a police cell.'

'Watson,' Lestrade moaned, arms outstretched. 'Save yourself, man.'

'Myself? Oh no, Lestrade. You're the one who needs to be saved.'

'That's right,' the Inspector groaned, but Watson appeared to have split himself in four and was revolving eerily around the orchestra pit.

'Sholto Lestrade,' Watson cleared his throat, 'I arrest you for the murders of Hereward Rodney, Osbaldeston Ralston, Byngham Batchelor, John Guest ... er ... who are you gentlemen?'

Towgrass dropped down from the stage so that he was on Watson's level. 'We realized that Lestrade was guilty,' he said. 'Only a moment ago we were going to beat a confession out of him.'

'Quite,' Watson said, but the gun was still raised. 'It was obvious, really.'

Two or three of the Coons were dropping silently on to the area below the stage, their truncheons still in their hands.

'Er...' Watson began to draw back. 'As soon as we realized that Lestrade was present at every murder, we realized...'

'We?' Towgrass halted.

'Holmes!' Watson shrieked, not at all liking the look in the niggers' eyes.

'Fire!' came a shout from backstage. 'But not, Watson, until you see the whites of their eyes.'

A lone figure swept across the stage in a death-defying dash more amazing than anything of which the Armbrusters were capable. The Ulster, the deerstalker, the firm jaw, all quite unmistakeable. And with Mrs Hudson, on the end of the same rope, was Sherlock Holmes, the Great Detective. Like a pendulum on a grandfather, the sleuth and his housekeeper swept the remaining niggers off the stage. A single shot rang out in the semi darkness and Chief Inspector Edward Towgrass lost his head. A small red circle punctuated the burnt cork of his forehead and the back of his skull splashed scarlet across the stage.

The niggers still on their feet stood stupidly as Holmes and Mrs Hudson swung to a standstill at the end of their tether and proceeded to round up the Coons, who looked numbed and dazed.

'Are you all right, dear fellow?' Holmes asked.

'I killed a man, Holmes,' Watson muttered mechanically, staring at the smoking Webley. 'I just killed him.'

A shattered Sholto Lestrade staggered off the stage with the aid of a small housekeeper. 'Don't feel too badly about it, Doctor,' he said. 'You've not only saved my life, you've brought nine murderers to book into the bargain.'

'Have I?' Watson frowned. 'By Jove, how capital.'

'Your collar, I believe, Mr Holmes,' Lestrade said.

'I know,' tutted Mrs Hudson, brushing him off and straightening her own deerstalker. 'The number of times I've told him about it.'

'No, Lestrade,' Holmes ignored her. 'There's no satisfaction for me here. I must confess that I had come to the conclusion, wrongly as I now see, that you were the murderer in this case.'

'That's funny,' said Lestrade. 'For a while I thought you were.'

'Well, well,' Holmes nodded. 'Mrs Hudson, be a dear, will you, and summon police assistance. That's quite enough excitement for a woman of your years for one night. I think we'll need a Maria for this lot.' She skipped off up the aisle, having given each of the Coons a cheerful slap around their faces before she went. 'Lestrade, Watson, I'm hanging up my magnifying glass once and for all.'

'What do you mean, Holmes?' Watson asked.

'Giving up the great game, dear fellow'. Stopping sleuthing, dropping detection. How can a man be so wrong?' he shook his head, not once but several times.

'Oh,' said Watson and both he and Lestrade fancied they saw a tear in the Great Detective's eye. 'But my friend, Conan Doyle is sharpening his pencil as we speak, to put your already legendary exploits into print.'

'Er ... Mr Holmes,' said Lestrade, feeling the lump growing on the back of his head, 'I had some correspondence recently concerning a rather bad business at 3, Lauriston Gardens, off the Brixton Road.'

'Really?' said Holmes dully.

'Yes. Something about a murdered American.'

'An American?' Holmes looked up.

'Murdered.'

'A murdered American?' Holmes's eyes blazed.

'A man is dead,' Lestrade confirmed.

Holmes clapped his hands for joy. 'Oh, I'm sorry,' he said, frowning again, 'that was a little callous, perhaps.'

'Frankly, I'll have so much paperwork from this case ... Look, I know it's a little unorthodox, but I wondered if you and Watson ... oh, but of course, you've just retired.'

'No,' said Holmes, a little too quickly to be convincing. 'No, I... er ... I think Watson and I can come out of retirement ... just this once, of course,' he wagged a warning finger. 'Just to help a chum.'

'Thank you, Mr Holmes,' said Lestrade. 'See my man George at the Yard tomorrow. He'll fill you in.'

'Come along, Watson. There isn't a moment to lose. The game's already afoot. I feel it in my water!'

'Er ... Lestrade?'

'I'll be all right, Doctor,' Lestrade said. 'Perhaps if you wouldn't mind leaving me your pistol, just until the Maria arrives? This lot look docile enough now, but a few minutes ago they were ready to dec ... depac ... cut my head off.'

'Be my guest, Lestrade. Er ... about that firearms licence.'

'What licence is that, Doctor?' And Lestrade sat on the edge of the stage, the Chocolate Coloured Coons crooning over their dead leader, glycerine tears trickling down their cheeks.

10

A gentleman with a mournful face and obsolete Dundrearies picked his way through the debris of the half-finished Opera House. With him, on that lovely Spring morning, hobbled an odd-looking cove with a bandage round his head and what appeared to be black makeup under each eye.

'Wot of capital, then, Arfur?' Clarence asked, leaning on his shovel.

'Well, Ricardo tells us, oh Bruvver-in-Chains, that capital is that part of the country's wealf which is employed in production and consists of food, cloving, tools, raw materials and machinery necessary to give effect to labour, does he not?'

'Indeed he does, Arfur,' Clarence concurred. 'Economic capital, by the harnessing in a scientific way of the forces of nature, enables mankind to perform the tasks demanding millions of times the strengf of the human upper limb.'

'True,' said Arfur. 'And such materials to which you so rightly adduce is referred to, is it not, by Karl Marx, as 'constant capital' because of itself ...'

A whistle shattered the morning.

'Statutory elevenses, Clarence?' Arfur asked.

The younger man stood on tiptoe to see the clock. 'Statutory half past tenses, possibly, Arfur. 'Ere it's that mournful bloke with the obsolete Dundrearies again. I thought we'd 'eard the last of 'im.'

'Oh, I don' know, I can always listen to the bootifully rounded vowels of the 'aute bourgeoisie, Clarence. It's one fing they still do well. Blimey. 'ave a butchers at that sketch wiv 'im.'

'This is Inspector Lestrade', shouted Norman Shaw, 'from Scotland Yard. He is investigating the recent finding of a torso in these very foundations.'

''Ere, Clarence,' Arfur nudged his friend, 'wasn't it your very own peepers that made the tragic discovery, wot brought us all to that brush wiv mortality?'

'I blush to say it was, Arfur,' Clarence said.

'Anyone working here four months ago', Lestrade said, 'I shall want to talk to in the next hour or so. No one is to leave the site without my permission.'

'Unfinkin' lackey of a bourgeois Imperialist State,' Arfur nodded, accepting Clarence's wad of tobacco. 'Vis is where I came in.'

Lestrade remembered to duck as he entered the foreman's shed. Somewhere, in the bowels of this very building, he would one day have an office of his own. One that was not merely a converted privy, jammed floor to ceiling with dusty shoeboxes. One day, one day ...

What was it Assistant Commissioner (Crime) Monro had said? 'Well done, laddie. A good job well done. Now get over to Mr Rodney. He wants a word.'

And what was it Assistant Commissioner (Traffic) Rodney had said? 'Thank you, Abberline, for nailing my cousin's er ... but there's still that matter of the torso under the ... er ... foundations of ... you know.'

And so here he was, on his Rest Day. His leg hurt, his head hurt, but he had nevertheless a glow of satisfaction about him. Commissioner Warren was in his Heaven and all was tolerably well with the world. And the case of the Nine Men's Morris was over at last.

'Show me', he said to Shaw's foreman, 'where the body was found.'

'Er ... here, sir,' the man pointed a stubby finger.

'What's this?' Lestrade's eyes widened.

'Er...' the foreman twisted the paper sideways. 'That's the main sewerage trench, sir. Where the body was found.'

'Not that, man,' Lestrade bellowed. 'This.'

'Er ... well, that's it, sir. That's the whole Opera House. The plan for the new Scotland Yard. Is something wrong?'

Lestrade blinked in,disbelief at the squares before him, one inside the other, rather like a maze, or a rather geometric spider's web. He dashed to the door.

'Er ... Mr Shaw,' he called. 'Could I have a little word?'

ANOTHER RIVAL OF SHERLOCK HOLMES

EUGÉNE VALMONT: his triumphs
by Robert Barr

With true Gallic humility, Eugéne Valmont, once Chief of the Paris Police, tells of his dismissal from that post after a jewel theft and a fruitless chase down the Seine. He left France in disgrace but bounced back to here recount some of his subsequent exploits as a private detective in turn-of-the-century London. These include his explanation of an assassination in Greenwich, his investigations into the theft of a hundred pounds at a private dinner party, his discovery of the Chezelrigg fortune and, probably his most celebrated case, that of the Absent-Minded Coterie.

First published in 1906

£9.95

Ian Henry Publications, Ltd.
20 Park Drive, Romford, Essex RM1 4LH
01708 749119